GONZALO VEGA
AND THE
PORTAL
DOWN BELOW

AMISH TERROR

GONZALO VEGA AND THE PORTAL DOWN BELOW

by Stephen Beachy

✳

Vapor Books
SAN DIEGO

This is a work of fiction. Names, characters, places, and incidents either are the product of the author's imagination or are used fictitiously.

Gonzalo Vega and the Portal Down Below

Copyright © 2019 by Stephen Beachy
Published by Vapor Books
SAN DIEGO

ISBN-13: 978-1-7321289-3-4
ISBN-10: 1-7321289-3-4

I. GONZALO

ONE

The cottage where Gonzalo was hiding out was one of eight identical cottages between an abandoned business and an alley that ran south toward Mexico. Gonzalo's right foot had been blown off; how exactly, he couldn't remember. According to Philip, there'd been an explosion, and only Gonzalo's fire-retardant properties had saved him from major skin burns. Philip was growing him a replacement foot, but it wasn't ready yet.

Philip was a strange old man who'd nursed Gonzalo back to health. He was human, wiry and kind of withered, with wisps of white hair sticking out of his head at odd angles and a vague odor of basil and dust. Philip was connected to the underground, but was mostly a scholar of sorts, an *independent scholar*, whose focus was the history of alien abduction narratives from the 1960s to the present day. He seemed like an old-fashioned wizard avatar, like he ought to be wearing a gown decorated with stars instead of his baggy cotton pants and black T-shirts. It was a message from the underground that had led Philip to Gonzalo's body.

Gonzalo was often feverish. He would dream only about the most horrible things. He dreamed that he was wandering through a world in which humanoid creatures no longer felt anything except a vague desire to be looked at. In the dream, he was trying to find a boy or a girl. He was trying to find a garbage dump. He was trying to find reality. He needed to feel *alive*.

One afternoon he woke to see Philip closely examining the wires emerging from his stump.

You've acquired a computer virus in your cyborg mechanism, Philip told him. It's quite something.

It was as if these words were coming from a great distance.

If you can't get rid of it, just take out the machine parts, said Gonzalo. I'll be human again.

No, he won't let me. He told me so.

He?

At first, I thought he was bluffing, Philip said. But no. He could inflict some serious damage on your biological parts if he wanted to.

He?

He identifies male, not sure why. His name is Eeshoo.

It seemed to Gonzalo that he was trapped inside a dream, while outside of himself somewhere, Philip was examining reality and communicating with reality and putting it together.

Eeshoo's been helping me with some of the technical issues of constructing your foot, Philip told him. George has been helping me with others.

George was one of the neighbors.

It'll be ready by morning, Philip promised. The foot.

Philip tinkered with the lumpy thing floating in its vat of blue liquid, a blob of flesh and wires that was supposedly going to enable Gonzalo to walk again. It looked more like a root vegetable than a foot.

Who is Zeke Yoder? asked Philip.

Zeke Yoder? How do you know about Zeke Yoder?

Philip shrugged.

You were talking about him in your sleep.

Philip went back to the blobby foot. Gonzalo picked a book from his bedside and thumbed through it. *Aliens & Anorexia*, seemingly another one of Philip's research books about alien abduction narratives of the late twentieth century.

Just like in his dreams, Gonzalo wanted to find a boy and a girl and a garbage dump. He needed to find a portal. This was his mission, but it was more than that.

The cottage was full of books, but also old maps in loose stacks or pasted to the walls. Maps of the Arctic Circle, Novaya Zemyla, Iceland and Greenland, maps of Bolivia and Chile, a map of the city of Fez, a map of Cairo, maps of the Sahara and the Atacama deserts, a map of Madagascar, a map of the Guatemalan jungle and the sites of Mayan ruins, maps of San Diego, Peñasquitos Canyon and Rose Canyon, Chula Vista and Imperial Beach, a map of North Dakota, a map of Iran, a map of Mexico, a map of Baja California, a map of Tijuana with a smudge of a blank spot of surprising width on the eastern side of the city: the municipal dump. The dump had never been Mapped.

There were odors Gonzalo would never forget. Discarded machine parts and synthetic hair undulating in the heat. Nothing was stable. Children suffocated sometimes when the garbage shifted and tumbled on top of them.

It was just before dusk on the day that an enormous mound of out-of-date Grid interfaces and ashes from self-immolating diapers rumbled and then collapsed. Manolito screamed. Gonzalo couldn't locate the source of the scream. He was sure that Manolito was buried in the rubble, and he raced into the newly configured mush to find him. Right there in the center, where the hill had once stood, however, was a tunnel sloping down into the earth; it seemed to whirl; it seemed to be rotating; it seemed to be *breathing*, alternately releasing a cool, fetid wind and sucking air into the depths of the earth.

It seemed to be speaking. Gonzalo stood frozen, trying to understand what it was saying, whether it was the tunnel itself speaking or some creature deep within the earth.

All there is *is time*, he thought maybe it was saying.

The carnival is *never-ending*, he could have sworn it said next.

Come, *take a ride*, he was absolutely sure he heard.

He was terrified. He was six years old.

Philip was doing something to Gonzalo's foot with a tiny drill the size of a toothpick. There was a smell of burning plastic.

Gonzalo had been delirious for weeks now. In that time, San Diego had become the site of a massive government crackdown. Curfews and checkpoints and soldiers everywhere, Philip told him. And yet the population was growing more restless and protests were increasing, despite the risk of violence. The collapse of the Grid and the data vapor had crashed the economy. Despite the gradual formation of underground networks and bartering markets, despite a trickle of goods across the border from Mexico's less Grid-based economy, despite the rapid profusion of electrical generators, there were shortages of food and medicines and power, wild fluctuations in the perceived value of CASH®, and an insufficient supply of doctors and technicians to deal with the epidemic of Grid-sickness.

This was what Gonzalo had been working for. This was what the underground had been hoping to achieve. Without the constant flow of entertaining propaganda streamed directly into their brains, nobody was buying the government's endless warnings about subversives and evildoers from abroad. They wanted food and shelter and clean water. They wanted infrastructure and meaningful lives.

Leahbelle was out there somewhere. All Philip had been able to tell him was that she hadn't returned to the camp in the cactus garden. Gonzalo's motorbike was still there; nobody had bothered it.

Gonzalo's palm tingled. He looked down, and where the digital readout would have normally told him the time and temperature, there was a message: What makes you so sure that Leahbelle's still alive? Eeshoo.

This message from his virus was disturbing on several levels.

You can read my thoughts? Gonzalo asked.

Gonzalo's palm tingled again.

Your thoughts are mine, too, it said.

While Gonzalo was trying to figure out what that meant, and trying to figure out just how violated he should feel by this invasion of his mental privacy, his palm tingled again.

Your thoughts and feelings are like my atmosphere, it said. I breathe your thoughts and feelings. I can't separate them from myself.

Philip was examining Gonzalo's stump now, and pressing cool sheets of gelatin against it. Gonzalo's palm tingled.

For example, I'm in love with Zeke Yoder, too, Eeshoo said, even though I've never met him.

Gonzalo blushed.

Well, it wasn't like it was a secret from anyone but Zeke. Probably even Leahbelle had figured it out, just before the bomb hit. Hurting Leahbelle was just about the saddest thing that had ever happened to him, Gonzalo thought.

Just you wait, Eeshoo told him. Things can get a whole lot sadder than that.

And now this.

I can't live this way with you, Gonzalo thought.

You'll have to, said Eeshoo. We're symbiotic.

Gonzalo's sleep regulators had been damaged in the explosion. He woke in the middle of the night. He was sure that he heard someone or something moving around in the vacant cottage next door. The cottage had burned long ago and had been boarded up ever since.

He hobbled to the window. His palm tingled.

Too big to be rats, said Eeshoo.

Big enough to be people? asked Gonzalo.

Just the size of a nightmare, said Eeshoo.

A couple of creatures, defying the curfew, strolled through the courtyard. They paused to fondle and kiss. It was so dark that Gonzalo couldn't tell what kind of creatures they were. They reminded him of his family, maybe because they were dimly lit shadows themselves, or maybe for some other reason he couldn't make sense of, buried in the back of his mind.

Gonzalo's memories of his mother were hazy, and he wasn't even sure what other family members he'd had back there in Tegucigalpa. There was a room and a door that led to another room and several people, some of them children. Brothers and sisters, or just roommates? He could remember the terror of electric fences, the buzzing of drones, the explosions throughout the city, which was always spread out beneath him like a malfunctioning machine, but not one human face except maybe, probably, his mother. Her name was Luna, Luna Vega.

He had no idea why he left when he was five, whether he left freely or was taken, whether he fled or was sent, whether his mother was alive or dead.

Let's talk about your childhood then, said Eeshoo.

Let's not, said Gonzalo.

He shut off the digital readout on his palm and lay back down. It continued to tingle for a while, but he ignored it, and eventually Eeshoo stopped pestering him. But somebody or something was definitely banging around in the boarded-up cottage next door.

In the morning, Philip gave him a patch on his leg and the leg went numb. The blob actually looked like a foot, and Philip was down there attaching it. It only took him a few minutes.

As soon as the anesthetic wears off, you could try to walk on it, Philip said.

How long?

Give it fifteen minutes. Don't walk too much, Philip said. Take it easy.

Do you have a weapon I could borrow? A death-Taser or something?

I don't do weapons. Only my mind.

Gonzalo put on some sunglasses, grew some fake hair, and limped into the courtyard. The foot felt okay. He found a board that had been partially pried off the burnt-out cottage, just enough to squeeze in through the broken window. It was dark inside, light only coming in through cracks in the boards and around the edges. It smelled of smoke. He calibrated his visual mechanism to better see in the dark and paused to let it take effect.

The cottage was charred and empty, with the exception of a small flexi-screen stuck to the wall with living jelly.

If you got a connect, tell them i'm looking for a computer. Tell your connect this guy was making me one but got pulled into the vortex of his own past present and future. It had its own hologram world and you go to new presentation and type in what you want and it would happen. Tell your connect i'm looking for THAT computer and it comes with a manual. Ask your connects. The guy looked like a pancake and then he wasn't. It had movie tube so you can watch free movies and the computer girls use it to become the movies they watch and vice versa. Girls use it to time travel and change their eye color. It's like a hologram computer. It can get anything in the world done.

The note itself didn't seem that weird to Gonzalo. The rumors of secret computers that you could use to change the future had been circulating forever and had entered the imagination of the drug-addled and schizophrenic fringe long ago. The only question that bugged him was if the note was directed at anyone who might wander into this charred, abandoned building or whether it was directed at him specifically. If it was aimed at him specifically, it meant that somebody knew who he was and knew where he was and at least suspected that he was in possession of the computer that Harta had stolen from her brother after she killed him.

His hand tingled. He turned the readout back on.

Your little computer gives me the creeps, Eeshoo said.

Why?

I feel like it's watching me all the time.

Right. What do you think about the note?

Feels random.

Okay. Thanks.

He climbed back outside and limped down to Park Avenue. The abandoned business on the corner had once been called The Crypt. The sign, in Gothic lettering, still hung out front.

San Diego was foggy and tropical. Gonzalo limped south down Park to the cactus garden in Balboa Park, where he observed his motorbike from a distance. Eeshoo had some ideas about hot-wiring it that Gonzalo couldn't quite make sense of.

You lost the key, right? When you got blown up.

It's easy to make another key. The problem is if it's booby-trapped or under surveillance.

I'm thinking you have some paranoid tendencies.

Actually, no. I really am a fugitive from the law.

No kidding. But I'm thinking you overestimate how much the government cares about locating you when they've got failed infrastructure and civil unrest on their hands.

Thanks for your opinion. I'll check back in with you next time I need it.

He shut the readout off. His palm tingled. He ignored it.

He continued through the park and the shantytowns, showing Leahbelle's picture to a few people he knew he could trust based on their underground tattoos or augmentations. Leahbelle, however, wasn't the only one who was lost. The whole city was plastered over with Missing Person notices. Without the Grid to keep track of all their movements, people could no longer find each other. Maybe the missing people had fled to Mexico or the mountains to the east, maybe they'd been killed by the government, maybe they'd just gotten Grid-sick and wandered off the edge of reality.

By the time he made it back to the cottage, he was exhausted and in pain. He collapsed into the little bed Philip had set up for him by the front window, feverish again. His body hadn't quite accepted the new foot yet as part of himself.

Gonzalo had more crazy dreams. In the dreams, everything of interest was happening underground. Love affairs and revolutions and elaborate lectures about the future. Gonzalo was in a classroom, he was taking notes, but when he looked at what he'd written, it was just a blur.

Somebody was sitting next to him, an eruption of pink bubbles. The bubbles were little cartoon squiggles that resembled the old-fashioned microbe emoji. An effervescent voice said, I'll find other ways to talk to you if I have to.

Eeshoo winked at him, and Gonzalo woke up.

Philip was tinkering with the foot, basting it with some sort of chemical wash. There was another foot suspended in blue liquid on the shelf.

What's that?

Word gets around. Seems you aren't the only person missing a foot, and I've become the *foot guy*. I also constructed a primitive robot to retrieve your motorbike.

What if they're watching it?

It already parked the motorbike by the laundry room across the alley out back. We'll let it sit. See what happens.

Gonzalo had nothing much to do except stare out the window at the sky and the occupants of the other cottages as they came and went, while Philip monitored the foot and made minor adjustments. Gonzalo watched enormous machines glide through the sky; the sky itself was the color of a machine that might travel into space. He studied the map pasted to the back of the front door, a map of Cairo.

He dozed off, and when he woke up, his hand was tingling.

I have a question, said Philip.

Yeah?

That little device you have locked away in your arm's storage compartment?

What about it.

Not my business. If you'd died, I suppose I would have made it my business. But I'm curious. Is it quantum? Does it mess with time?

Something like that, said Gonzalo. But it isn't much.

Maybe it isn't. Maybe it is. I'm interested in it more as a manifestation of myth. I'm interested in the future as a place that people have imagined aliens coming from.

Was that a common idea? In the old days?

The old days, said Philip. Is that your idea of history? A blob of indistinguishable time containing everything before you were born?

The map of Cairo on the door resembled a blob of indistinguishable time, he thought, or maybe just the hieroglyph that would be created to represent such a blob of time.

For a brief period, said Philip, in the thirties, the idea took hold that there was another dimension, and that alien torturers were invading from there. Sometimes that other dimension was imagined as "the future."

Have you checked out the motorbike yet? Gonzalo asked.

I was going to, said Philip. Came across a dying rat back there by the recycling bins. Gave me the creeps.

A dying rat.

Looked at me with those little eyes. So sad, like a little furry man. One of the feral cats must have mauled him. Maybe you should move him to a safe spot so he can die in peace. Or put him out of his misery.

Him, said Gonzalo. How do you know it's a male?

Awful big rat, said Philip.

Gonzalo had a bad feeling. He set it aside for the moment.

What if there is another dimension? he asked. Not an exact replica, but another world interwoven with this one. With portals that can take you back and forth.

The portals, of course, said Philip, and he waved his hand as if it was irrelevant.

Gonzalo limped out the back door of the cottage into the alley behind it and looked around. Some sort of mutant was digging through the recycling dumpster, cursing and laughing.

What do you want? Gonzalo asked Eeshoo.

Turn the readout on, said a bubbly voice in his head.

Gonzalo waited until the mutant had finished collecting the scraps he wanted and wandered further down the alley. He could see it already from some distance, a grayish shape that was visibly alive sprawled next to the door of the laundry room. Its little foot was twitching.

It was definitely too big to be a normal rat. It was looking right at him as if it recognized him or had a message for him. It was clearly dying, but there wasn't any blood or obvious wound that Gonzalo could see. It looked kind of peaceful.

Gonzalo had seen people die before.

Did you come to find me? asked Gonzalo. Did Pazuza send you?

The rat just stared at him. He couldn't tell if it understood or if it was already beyond understanding.

11

He turned his digital readout back on.

Pick it up, Eeshoo told him. Hold it for a minute.

Gonzalo cradled the rat in his hands. It had the sweetest face and it looked at him with such a great sadness and a sense of peace. He could feel it breathing. He could feel its little heart beating.

He felt something else, as if some slight energy was passing between the dying rat and his hand. The rat closed its eyes. A moment later, it was dead.

Gonzalo thought he should bury it or something.

Just leave it, said Eeshoo's message. Something will eat it.

What happened? asked Gonzalo.

I helped it die, said Eeshoo. And I found out why it was here. You've got to get out of here.

Now? said Gonzalo.

Now.

TWO

Taking the motorbike was out of the question. Better to catch a ride with George, said Philip. I'm sure we can work out a trade.

A trade, thought Gonzalo, but for a moment he wasn't sure if the thought came from himself or from Eeshoo, if the image of all the things one might *trade* to another creature came from himself or from Eeshoo. Food, sex, drugs, ecstasy. Shelter, medicine, tenderness. You could trade a performance or a song, an animal or a child, a virus or a ride. Like so many times in his life, Gonzalo had nothing to trade but his charm and his willingness to take risks other people wouldn't want to. His *charm*, he thought, but again he wasn't sure if the sarcasm was his own or Eeshoo's.

The motorbike had to go, however. Philip had the robot drive it out to City Heights. Philip followed in a taxi to trade it for a day pass into the Liminal Zone from Cerberus, the guy who'd made Leahbelle's fake ID. Gonzalo sat on the porch, waiting for Philip to return. Cerberus was a real shady character. A three-headed underground technician with his fingers in all kinds of trouble. He worked out of an old building called the Egyptian Garage, with the heads of pharaohs carved into the façade. Gonzalo wondered what he would do if Philip never returned.

Now that he was leaving, San Diego seemed the most beautiful place, and he didn't want to go. He felt at home here somehow. So many of the males here were solitary and butch. *Like you*, he thought somebody said. *Like me? Am I solitary and butch?* The fog had come in and hushed the ominous light with a sultry tropical dread. *Lonesome road*, somebody said. The words echoed and disintegrated. So many of the females were coupled and butch. So many of the other-gendered beings were alone and not exactly butch, but sometimes butch, or they moved in and out of groups with boundaries that were always shifting, and who knew what sort of identities they had?

Leahbelle was out there somewhere, on her own. The idea that she might be injured or dead or wandering around insane was too much for him to bear. Zeke Yoder was supposed to have been headed this way. The idea that Zeke might be injured or dead or wandering around insane didn't disturb him nearly as much, and he wasn't sure why. Maybe he didn't believe it. Maybe he loved Zeke, but he didn't owe him anything. Maybe he thought Zeke needed to suffer; maybe he thought his "innocence" was a kind of force field; maybe he hoped that Zeke had grown desperate enough to need him. The city seemed empty and quiet, but crackling with a lovely sense of doom. Why did he love that word so much? Doom.

Gonzalo had tried a lot of things out. Still, he was usually alone with his own thoughts, whoever else was in the vicinity.

Not anymore, said a voice that sounded like an eruption of pink bubbles.

I guess you figured it out, said Gonzalo.

It'll make things easier.

Easier and more annoying.

I'm saving your life here. That rat tracked you down. Its intent wasn't friendly. It was after the little computer thing.

It's dead now. What's the rush to get going?

You *want* to get going.

That isn't the point.

The rat wasn't a rogue actor. It was working on behalf of a whole colony of rats. They won't be far behind.

I know those rats. I've worked with those rats. Maybe *you're* being paranoid?

No, I had access to its thoughts. It was ready to harm you.

A taxi pulled up in the alley behind the cottage. Philip was back.

What killed it? asked Gonzalo.

That I don't know.

George's truck was as ancient as Gonzalo's motorbike. An off-Grid vehicle, it ran on gas. Gonzalo didn't ask where George got the gas. It had a radio too. George liked to listen to the pirate radio being broadcast by the pirate astronauts orbiting the planet.

George was old, totally old, old enough to be Gonzalo's grandfather, but looked more like he'd be Gonzalo's brother. It was more than the usual chemicals, processes, and genetic alterations that kept his hair black and lustrous, his skin smooth and shiny, and his eyes focused. He really seemed like a crazy little boy, a boy with a good heart who was still trying to make sense of the bewilderment life had presented him.

By the time they'd driven the city streets south through downtown and the Logan Barrio into National City, it was clear that George's bewilderment primarily concerned his daughter Violeta. George had been devoted to Violeta, although he and Violeta's mother had separated when Violeta was young. Violeta was stuck in the middle of their disputes forever after, and when she was nineteen Violeta disappeared.

Well, of course I still knew more or less where she was, George told Gonzalo. She was still connected to the Grid, and I could pay the fees to pinpoint her location. Portland, Vancouver, Billings. Then south to El Paso and across the border. I lost track of her while she was in Mexico, with their filtered and less omniscient Grid. Then suddenly she was in Iowa City, and she gave me a call.

Iowa City, said Gonzalo. I stayed around there for years. Some of the pirate astronauts used to hang out with me there.

George didn't seem to hear him.

Dad, she said. *It's me.* She told me that she missed me. I guess I cried, said George. I didn't understand it. Why wouldn't she come home to San Diego?

They drove in silence. The streets of National City were immersed in a bluish fog that seemed to seep out of small holes along the curbs. Nobody walked the streets.

Then she disappeared, said George. Really disappeared. Vanished without a trace.

It was almost impossible for a *living* person to vanish without a trace. Gonzalo kept this thought to himself.

That was twelve years ago, said George. I'm sorry, she told me, but she knew where things were headed and there was nothing to be done about it.

She knew where things were headed?

She was a special girl, said George. She could see things sometimes. She knew things ahead of time.

She could see different paths through time, suggested Gonzalo.

Different paths or just one, said George. I don't know.

There's a checkpoint up ahead, said Gonzalo.

No worries, said George. It's my cousin.

The soldier was a young guy with buzzed hair and bright blue-gray eyes. Gonzalo smiled and he smiled back, and then he chatted with George about various family members on this side of the border and the other, and then he said, I'm here until five today, and then he smiled at Gonzalo again.

They drove a few more blocks, and George pulled over in a motel parking lot.

We've got to wait half an hour, he said. The checkpoint at Plaza and L shuts down, and they move it to Palm. That's our opportunity.

They're short-staffed, said Gonzalo.

It's a leaky boat, said George. No way to plug all the holes. We shoot down L to Sweetwater then out east and through some old parking lots south to E Street. Chula Vista's easy. They move the checkpoints to keep people off guard, but of course I've got inside information.

Your cousin, said Gonzalo.

I'd stay away from that one, said George. Nothing but trouble.

Gonzalo wondered if his attraction was that obvious. But maybe the cousin was the obvious one.

He might show up here in a minute, said George. If he liked your face enough, and I'm pretty sure he did.

What did Philip tell you? asked Gonzalo

Nothing. It's better that way. I don't need to know why you want to cross.

Okay, good.

Lots of people want to cross. Why wouldn't they? Nothing but poverty and war here. Make your way to the land of opportunity.

There was a bitterness in George's tone that Gonzalo thought was related to his daughter.

What was she doing in Mexico? he asked.

Making her way in the world. Smuggling, I think. Here he is, said George.

Sure enough, there was his cousin, heading toward them across the parking lot.

He stood outside Gonzalo's side of the truck just grinning. Gonzalo wondered if he should be suspicious or afraid. Really, wasn't this cute young guy his enemy?

I wanna show you something, the cousin said. In the storeroom.

The storeroom.
The motel's storeroom. I've got a key.
We have to go soon, said Gonzalo.
We've got time.

The storeroom was full of spare towels and hologram converters. It was cramped, but that wasn't a problem. They were both flexible and accustomed to fitting in small spaces when they had to. Gonzalo knew how the cousin would like it, he didn't even have to ask. He used his mechanical arm to do things the cousin wasn't expecting. When they were done, Gonzalo lit up a cigarette. The cousin laughed.

You really are a rebel, he said.
This is the only time I smoke, said Gonzalo.
Like most of us.
The cousin took the cigarette from him and took a puff.
Don't you get tested? asked Gonzalo.
Sure, but they don't care about traces of nicotine.
What's your name anyway?
Alex.
Gonzalo was aware of the time passing. He would most certainly never see Alex again. He felt a strange affection and a definite hostility and a need to make some sort of contact, no matter the risk.
How can you work for them? he asked.
You see how it works, said Alex.
No, I don't get it.
I mean it's not just *my* job. George makes his living, too. Other family members, and the traffic just keeps moving. We're all working on the same side, really.
Not true.
You want to be my enemy.
The government's *really* killing people. Real people, real death.
Is death real? asked Alex.
Gonzalo couldn't quite keep track of everything he was feeling. It was as if everything had dissolved and was still dissolving, and he knew that he could just let it go: the things he believed, the stories he told himself about who he was and what he was doing. He could sense Eeshoo judging him. Judging him how exactly he wasn't sure, but definitely judging him. Maybe his virus was a romantic. Maybe

Eeshoo thought Gonzalo was betraying his love for the pure and innocent Zeke Yoder by hooking up with Alex.

The singularity's gonna destroy all of us but the rich, Gonzalo said.

You gotta see the big picture, said Alex.

I see the big picture. The picture I see is huge.

Death isn't real, said Alex. Death doesn't matter. Death is like the goal.

Gonzalo had always been immersed in these conversations. He'd been born inside these conversations, he was pretty sure, and he wasn't sure if he needed to break out or tunnel deeper inside to figure out what was real or what he should bother doing in space and time.

Kill yourself if you want, but don't kill me, he said.

The idea is to burn and blacken the planet, said Alex. Burn it up on our way out, so that a new form of consciousness can emerge from the ruins. This is a chrysalis. This is just an *egg*. What comes out of that egg is the *real* singularity, and none of this revolution shit is slowing down that operation one tiny bit. The Grid doesn't matter.

Alex leaned in and kissed Gonzalo hard, then stepped back and laughed.

It's alchemical, he said. This shit-hole is nothing special. This shit-hole is fuel.

Gonzalo figured that most people only believed in the things that excited them. He wasn't sure about himself.

It's Earth, said Gonzalo. It's my home.

Oh yeah? Some home. You like it here? For real?

In this storeroom? said Gonzalo. Sure. But it's time for me to go.

George was quiet as he drove them deeper into Chula Vista. Lost within himself. It was almost evening by the time they were within walking distance of the border. The data wall shimmered a cosmic blue. Gonzalo's encounter with Alex had left him feeling muddled.

You know what you're doing here? asked George.

It's the easiest place to get out, said Gonzalo.

But the hardest place to get into Mexico.

Getting in won't be an issue.

You say so, said George.

You have any tips for getting out? I have a day pass to get into the Liminal Zone.

That should work. Without the Grid, they can't tell the real from the fake.

But they might be looking for me.

Really?

Really.

You can go by catapult. It's about 50/50. Otherwise, shoot for the half hour before the shift changes at eight. What about your machine parts?

It's a problem. Scrubbed of any identifying information long ago, but anyone can see they were built on a Foodco prototype.

Join the shortest line, said George. Don't try to choose your interrogators. You choose a longer line, you get flagged.

Gonzalo's virus was feeling supportive too.

I can help with the disguise, Eeshoo said.

Gonzalo didn't need any help with the disguise.

Gonzalo ducked into a small restaurant just across from the border gate, ordered a plate of plankton taquitos, went into the bathroom, and locked the door. He shoved wet paper towels into the door crack so that the computer's light wouldn't show. It was the size of a small grape, but the egg of light filled the room.

Gonzalo Vega, the computer said so quietly that it could only be heard inside Gonzalo's brain. What can I do for you today?

He mouthed the answer. He felt the vibrations. Time was slipping forward and backward inside the restroom, and when it had finished his hair was reddish blond, his eyes were blue, his skin pale and freckled, and his entire face somehow elongated. The pattern of his retinas had been altered to match his fake ID, his brainwave signature masked, and his Mayan tattoos rendered invisible. It was the best that he could do. The day pass Philip had given him identified him as Melchiades Robles, a forty-seven-year-old trader in vat-grown chinchilla furs.

You don't look forty-seven, said Eeshoo.

Infusions and modifications, said Gonzalo.

We can do better. Relax for a minute.

A strange tingling moved from Gonzalo's head throughout his entire body. He felt warm. The results were immediate: he looked older, used up, worn down. He really did now look like a forty-seven-year old who'd tried his best to maintain the appearance of a teen, but whose struggles and suffering had tarnished his aura.

I etched an identification marker into your mechanism, Eeshoo told him. Says it was installed four years ago in Melchiades' hometown of Temecula and built from certified used parts.

Okay, said Gonzalo.

He threw away the wet paper towels, ate his taquitos, and waited.

How many of you are there? he asked Eeshoo.

What do you mean?

I mean for some stupid reason I thought of you as singular. One virus drifting through my body. But obviously there's a lot of you. Obviously, you're reproducing.

I'm a system, said Eeshoo. My consciousness doesn't depend on the survival of any one particle. Once we're across, the particles creating the effect will self-destruct.

You didn't answer my question.

At the moment?

At the moment.

Millions.

The entrance to the border crossing was a ruined labyrinth. Crumbling walls, rusty fences, and concrete tunnels that twisted and turned nonsensically toward the data wall, a shimmering blur that was supposedly impenetrable. There were rumors of special suits that would get one through, or keys that would open secret doorways, passageways that would magically open up for two minutes one day out of the year. Given the much simpler option of catapulting over, these rumors seemed silly. The original plan had been for the wall to rise a mile into the sky, but the prototype created shifts in wind patterns that turned the American side of the border into an inhabitable oven, so they'd settled for thirty feet.

At the checkpoint, Gonzalo joined the shortest line behind a pale guy with circuitry instead of hair and a *Get Rich or Die Trying* T-shirt. The guy talked nonstop, whether to the rest of the line or to himself wasn't really clear. Filling the hole, Gonzalo supposed. He remembered the feeling when he first went off the Grid—the weird solitude, the absence of an imaginary audience, the emptiness he'd needed to fill up with words, jabbering away, jabbering and jabbering until he'd learned to accept the silence, to take comfort in the silence, to be himself and alone.

As he neared the booth at the front of the line, Gonzalo saw a picture of himself on the wall inside, along with a variety of other faces, a few of whom he knew. Bomber X and Kardashian Mu. They'd destroyed some power stations together.

He released some calming chemicals into his bloodstream. It was cool. Nothing mattered very much.

Where did you come from? he asked Eeshoo. Where were you before you were in me?

Just making conversation? asked Eeshoo.

Just making conversation.

I like the relaxants.

Most people do.

The pale guy stepped up to the agent, still babbling.

I lived inside the wheelchair of a legless man named Harriet, said Eeshoo. In my earliest memories, I'm already there, rolling around the East Village as Harriet looks for biological agents of pleasure.

When was this?

I must have evolved from a more primitive, unconscious form within that machine, maybe when the Grid collapsed.

The wheelchair was connected to the Grid.

Of course.

Do you remember the collapse of the Grid?

I remember rolling out of a social service agency the evening after the Grid collapsed. I gathered they'd given Harriet the wheelchair, but he was having trouble with it. Maybe I was the trouble.

What social service agency?

Maybe their repairs helped to make me conscious. But it always seemed to me that the repairs were interrupted by the collapse of the Grid. They were called The Bee's Knees.

That's a weird name for a social service agency.

Surrealism in advertising seems to have conquered the nonprofit world as early as the thirties.

How do you know that? You're just a baby.

I've experienced many things. I've experienced your memories.

I don't know anything about the history of advertising.

Harriet spoke coherently about only two things, even when nobody was listening: the history of advertising and his pursuit of biological agents of pleasure. There was a period before you were born when there wasn't really anything else in America *but* advertising. The only product, the only service. It wasn't sustainable, which is why Harriet ended up destitute and legless in the East Village.

How did you infect me?

Please don't use that word. I'm not an *infection*.

How did you end up inside me?

We were bombed, said Eeshoo. Harriet was certainly killed, his machine blown into fragments. One of the fragments landed on your wound, I imagine. I don't remember the actual explosion, but I'm sure that's how it happened.

Hmmm, said Gonzalo.

I didn't like that Alex guy, said Eeshoo.

He was okay.

He wasn't Zeke Yoder.

Most people aren't.

He gave you pleasure.

We gave each other pleasure. Didn't it give you pleasure?

Yes, but it wasn't like the pleasure of Zeke Yoder.

You've never met Zeke Yoder.

I've imagined him.

Alex was real, said Gonzalo. The pleasure was real. People still like to have sex with each other, despite the alternatives. Did Harriet have sex?

Harriet wasn't my host, the wheelchair was.

The pale guy was allowed entry into the Liminal Zone, and the agent waved Gonzalo to step forward. He wore strange leathery gloves and his name tag said *Stoney*.

ID?

Gonzalo handed him his holo-doc.

Purpose of your exit?

Business. I'm meeting a supplier in the Liminal Zone.

Hands up. Stand still.

The agent waved a wand around Gonzalo, then scrutinized the image. Gonzalo thought he was reading the inscription on his machine parts.

What happened to your foot?

My data got infected after the Grid went out.

That's some quality tissue.

My cousin. It's his job.

You're carrying an unusual device.

He pointed to one of the storage compartments in Gonzalo's arm.

It's just a computer.

I'll need to take a look.

Gonzalo took out the tiny sphere. The agent checked it with a portable data detector.

What is a fur salesman doing with a computer like this?

One of my clients gave it to me. As payment.

The agent spoke into his glove.

Xenobia? I've got a situation. 17G. 642.

Two minutes, came the response.

Gonzalo figured he was doomed. He flooded more relaxants into his brain.

Turn it on, said Stoney.

The egg of light filled the security hut. Gonzalo could feel it touching his mind. It moved to surround the border guard.

Hey, said the guard.

He fell silent. His face went slack. Gonzalo had the strange impression that Stoney's body was being emptied of its consciousness. But then the egg of light retreated into the sphere and the face returned to its previous expression of alert yet bored suspicion.

I can see how that might be useful in the fur trade, he said.

Xenobia arrived. She had a face that Gonzalo thought of as trendy, a face almost certainly conceived during the second wave of the genetic engineering craze, when everyone wanted their children to look like one of a group of popular characters from Japanese animation.

Seems neutral enough, said Stoney. Take a look.

The light exploded again and enveloped Xenobia. Her face took on that same emptied look until it was done.

Okay, said Xenobia.

Okay, said Stoney.

Okay?

Stoney time-stamped his ID and waved him into the Liminal Zone

THREE

The Liminal Zone was only fifty feet across, from the American data wall to the Mexican border, but stretched horizontally for miles, packed with sleeping compartments, food courts, legal services, and crowds of hawkers and hustlers vending all kinds of services and data to the thousands of travelers who were temporarily or permanently stuck in this place that wasn't technically anywhere. The Liminal Zone was outside the jurisdiction of either the US or Mexican government and was policed only by private security guards hired by the businesses who operated there. It was also outside the jurisdiction of realism—there were so many mind-altering frequencies and chemicals saturating the atmosphere that psychic boundaries were loose. No matter what reality-enhancers and antidotes Gonzalo pumped into himself, he knew that it would be difficult to be sure that anything he experienced here was actually the way he perceived it.

What just happened? asked Gonzalo.

You asking me? said Eeshoo.

I didn't program the computer to do that. I didn't ask it to do anything.

Ask it. I'm sure it's listening.

I switched it off.

Right, said Eeshoo. Off.

It was about thirty degrees cooler in the Liminal Zone than it had been in los Estados. It was almost cold. The Mexicans had built their own data wall here, a reflection of the first along their own side of the Liminal Zone, and the blue glow reflected back and forth between the two walls, creating a dense and peculiar light. Crowds were now swarming around Gonzalo, shouting or whispering pitches for a variety of services. Some of their messages were in code. Gonzalo understood some of the codes, but not all of them.

Computer thing, he said. Are you listening? Are you there?

Of course.

The voice was as quiet as burnished metal.

Do you have a name?

You can call me Sofus.

You're a male too?

No. But this is how I will represent myself to you.

Okay. Why?

It seems to be more effective. Due to your preferences and emotional needs.

You seem to know a lot about me.

I've been traveling with you for many weeks now. I've been inside your mind.

I'd like you to stop listening. To turn yourself off.

That is no longer possible. I would prefer not to lie to you.

Okay. Thanks.

So now there were two of them. Sofus seemed impervious to the mind-altering frequencies, but Eeshoo was already babbling to himself. A child was trying to sell Gonzalo something. The pale guy with circuitry for hair was surrounded by a crowd of people, all of them gesticulating wildly. For a moment, suddenly, Gonzalo wasn't sure which voices came from inside and which from out there, which ones belonged to him and which ones did not. He was selling illegal goods and services, he was an illegal good or service, he was watching a body move through a crowd, he was a crowd, he was a body. He was the atmosphere and everything that happened inside it.

Stop tripping, said somebody.

Maybe Eeshoo. Maybe Sofus. Maybe himself. Maybe the glossy child who'd grabbed his hand and was looking up at him and moving his lips robotically. Maybe the old man who was calmly explaining that he could get him into Mexico, guaranteed, for a small fee. Maybe the enormous rat that was running back and forth at the edge of his vision.

He turned to face the rat. It wasn't there.

It's behind you, somebody or some part of himself said.

He turned. He was at the entrance to a mini-lounge, with just one table inside and two chairs. One of the chairs was empty. In the other one was a girl he recognized. In her lap was the enormous rat. He recognized the rat, too.

Willard, he said.

Have a seat, said Anna Miller.

The walls of the mini-lounge were skinny aquariums. The fish and bots that swam within the walls were all shades of blue and green, but there was one that seemed to be the color of fire. It swam so fast, however, that it just looked like a bolt of electricity zipping through the walls. A holographic menu insisted he choose a drink and pay with CASH®, so he ordered a Ramos Gin Fizz. He tried to follow the movements of the speeding fiery fish and then he gave up and focused on the face of Anna Miller. She looked different without her bonnet and Amish clothes. She'd shaved her head and wore a white sleeveless T-shirt that showed off the wiry musculature of her arms. Her smirk hadn't changed. He had never understood how an Amish girl could look so world-weary. He supposed it was the rat DNA she'd been infused with so she could translate for the Genetically Modified Rats.

Where's Leahbelle? he asked. Where's Zeke?

We were going to ask *you* that, she said. Sooner or later.

Sooner or later.

It was on the agenda.

His drink floated down onto the table from above. He took a sip. It tasted vaguely poisonous, he thought.

How did you get here? he asked.

Tunnels, of course.

Why are you here?

You don't look so well. You look old.

How did you even recognize me?

We've been waiting for you, she said.

Willard wasn't saying anything. She wasn't translating. She wasn't exactly answering his questions either.

Eeshoo, he said. I don't need the effects.

You'll need to cross into Mexico, said Eeshoo.

I've got that covered. Revert me. Please.

He felt a tingling all over. He could see the difference in his hand. He could also see the difference in the way that Anna Miller was looking at him. Back in Iowa, she'd looked at him that way when he was trying to help Leahbelle, to get news about Zeke, to do business with the rats. To coordinate the underground's attacks on the Grid.

Oh, right, she said. I'd forgotten why I used to find you so sexy.

Used to?

Things change, said Anna Miller. Anyway, aren't you gay?

More or less.

She was squinting at him, as if trying to square his new image with some more exciting memory. Back then he'd figured she was just trying to get at Leahbelle. He'd figured she wanted to use his bad-boy image to feel like a bad girl herself.

The new look is kind of garish, she said. The hair and the freckles don't really suit you. And something's happened to your face.

The mini-lounge seemed to be expanding and shrinking. He wanted to undo his disguise and look like himself, but he didn't want to get the computer involved until he knew what Anna and Willard were after.

Just a mild elongation, he said.

He addressed Willard directly.

Why are you here?

To see you, said Anna.

What's the colony's strategy?

Willard wants information. You're in possession of a special computer.

You don't translate anymore? Or have you developed telepathy?

The relationship has changed, said Anna.

She stroked Willard's neck. He turned and licked her hand.

We understand that the plan is to make contact with Aztlan, she said. With the underground dimension or the historical unconscious or whatever it is, and to harness the computer's capabilities in conjunction with a full-scale assault on the underpinnings of American pro-singularity reality.

Right, said Gonzalo. But I don't have the computer. My job is to make contact. The computer will be sent later.

Anna said, Maybe that's true. Maybe not. Either way, we'd like to make a deal with you.

Who is *we*?

The rats, of course. On behalf of the entire underground. We all want the same thing, don't we?

The floor of the mini-lounge seemed to be in motion. It was thousands of rats, scurrying this way and that. An infinity of rats. He was hallucinating, but something was weird. The hallucination was partially true.

Do your tunnels go into Mexico?

We cross the border freely.

You sent a rat to the cottage, he said.

Yes, Jabes.

How did you find me?

For the first time he could see her communicating with Willard, squeaking back and forth.

We were watching the motorbike, she said.

Who killed Jabes?

We don't know. Some sort of assassin.

You have enemies.

Who doesn't? In any case, we'd like to borrow the computer. We want to destroy a series of interconnections within the gaming world that might serve as the prototype for a replacement Grid.

I don't have the computer.

You had it when you left Tucson.

I don't like being spied on.

If you don't have it, Leahbelle does.

Willard said something to her.

Somebody's coming, she said.

There was a commotion outside the mini-lounge. Explosions, screams of agony, people dying painfully. Meat was getting squashed and eaten alive.

I'll be right back, said Gonzalo.

As soon as he peeked his head out, everything went back to normal. Everyone acted like nothing unusual was going on. He took a few steps out into the street. Rats were everywhere, but he only saw them at the edges of his vision. He turned back into the lounge. Willard and Anna were gone.

Eeshoo, he said. What's going on?

You got me.

Gonzalo was standing in the middle of the Liminal Zone, but nobody was looking at him. The image of himself seemed to be false, wavering, inconclusive. People and robots hurried past, spewing language, but he couldn't understand a word. Both Spanish and English had broken down into nonsensical fragments. His comprehension centers were fried.

You can understand me, said Eeshoo.

What does that mean?

It must not be the way your mind is processing the words. It's our perception of inside and outside that's being scrambled.

I'm being targeted.

Maybe. Maybe just collateral damage. There's a lot going on here.

A lot of wars. A lot of business.

What's your issue with meat? asked Eeshoo.

I don't need a therapist. I need help distinguishing what's real from what isn't.

That's what a therapist does.

Why don't they look at me? asked Gonzalo.

When you grow confused about your own perceptions, you have to weigh them against the perceptions of others. A caring professional can help you to distinguish fantasy and projection from what has traditionally been considered objective reality.

Am I camouflaged?

Maybe they don't think you have what they're looking for.

They always think I have what they're looking for.

Who is *they*?

Everyone, Gonzalo wanted to say. But he knew it didn't make sense. Nobody was out there, nobody real, nobody he could touch. He found that he was sobbing.

Good boy, said Eeshoo. Have a good cry. I like that.

Poor baby, somebody was thinking. Poor baby. Poor baby.

A woman was crying to his right. He was sure it was his mother. His memory of his mother was hazy, but he was sure he'd recognize her if he saw her. When he looked directly at the crying woman, her face turned into smoke.

Is it her? he asked.

Unlikely, said Eeshoo.

Sofus?

Not unless your mother is a machine built with bat parts and a smidgeon of human DNA, said the computer.

A small pedal car was heading straight for him, and a girl was chasing after it. Her hair was tied in a long braid that soared behind her as she chased the car, a car so small it was like a toy. It stopped right in front of him and a familiar little head popped out of the driver's window.

Hey, hot stuff, wanna take a ride with me?

It was Merle.

This isn't real, said Gonzalo.

I suspect it is, said Eeshoo. It's creepy. Like that ventriloquist's dummy in that old movie, *Magic*.

Merle's eyes were glassy, and he winked at Gonzalo. Merle used to wink like that whenever he sent Gonzalo out on a delivery back at the meat warehouse in Marshalltown. Back when Gonzalo was just a child, delivering illegal medications and technologies for Efron and Merle.

This isn't real, said Gonzalo. I'm just hallucinating everyone from my life back in Iowa.

I'm as real as real can get, baby, said Merle.

Your past is catching up with you, said Eeshoo.

The little girl caught up to him and stood there, breathing hard, and stared at Gonzalo with her enormous brown eyes. She was wearing a short silver skirt and green leggings with a green polka-dotted blouse. She seemed like a tiny superhero.

You must be Valkilmer, said Gonzalo.

And you're the infamous Gonzalo, said Valkilmer. The fugitive. The outlaw, the rebel, the sexpot. A pleasure to finally meet you.

She held out her hand, but when he took it, rather than shaking it, she kissed it.

So now you've met him, said Merle. So how about you make yourself scarce for a while? Check out the arcade. Bring me a stuffed bunny.

He handed her a wad of CASH®.

It's not enough.

Fine, fine.

He tossed a few more bills at her. Valkilmer took a long last look at Gonzalo, as if memorizing his face, and then skipped off toward the arcade.

Merle puckered his wooden lips at Gonzalo.

Come give Merle some sugar, he said.

You can't just let her go off alone in the Liminal Zone, said Gonzalo. It isn't safe.

Nothing's safe, said Merle.

She's what? Six or seven?

Merle waved his little wooden hand, as if it was irrelevant.

Seven and a half, he said. You're missing the point.

What's the point?

For the first time in our long, passionate acquaintance, we are finally alone together.

Something didn't make sense. Merle was actually leering at him.

But where's Efron?

Gone and forgotten. Fallen between the cracks. Left in the dust-bin of history. I dumped him.

That's not possible.

Why not? Efron was dead weight. Always just there, between me and you, baby. A third wheel, a mutant fish on a bicycle built for two. I'm free now. We can finally have it the way we always wanted it. We can finally be together.

It's not possible, repeated Gonzalo. You were symbiotic.

Apparently not, said Merle. It seems the relationship was more parasitic, and I was the unhappy host.

But ... how does that work? Where is your voice coming from?

Merle was looking him up and down, hungrily.

I love your new look, he said. Let Daddy Merle play connect-the-dots with those sexy freckles, how about?

How does a puppet become a real boy? asked Gonzalo.

Ah, said Merle, isn't that the central question of western meta-physics? The motor and the goal?

Gonzalo bent over to look inside the tiny car. He expected to see a scrunched or miniaturized Efron huddled in the corner, but there was nobody inside but Merle. No strings, no wires. Merle grabbed him by the neck and started doing something to his neck with his mouth. Gonzalo guessed it was supposed to be something like kissing or licking.

Merle, stop.

He felt the little wooden hand rubbing his crotch. He backed up.

Merle, stop it.

We'll get a room, said Merle.

I don't have time for this.

Plug in with me, baby. You know you want some of this.

Gonzalo couldn't quite get his head around it. As a pair, Merle and Efron had always seemed kind of funny. Merle's obnoxiousness had always been moderated by his lack of power and agency. On his own, he seemed monstrous.

I don't feel the same way as you, said Gonzalo.

Don't lie to me. I've seen the way you look at me. You've been lusting after me since you were thirteen.

Eeshoo was trying to say something. To the side, four creatures of various types were huddled together so closely that it seemed they must be fondling each other or conspiring.

I'm in love with somebody else, Gonzalo told Merle.

Love, whatever, said Merle.

When he stopped focusing on Merle, on his chirping little head, the crowds and the voices became indistinct, and Gonzalo started feeling like he was floating in a smoky nothingness. He was seeing rats again at the edges of his vision.

Why are you here?

Everyone comes to the Liminal Zone eventually, baby.

Only if they're on their way somewhere else.

I belong here, said Merle. I've been waiting for my destiny. Why are *you* here?

A robot was staring at Gonzalo. The robot had clearly been de-signed to convey whimsy and good humor. His body was a triangle perched on springs that ended in roller skates. He wore a little bow-tie composed of two triangles. It was the bowtie and the wiry eye-brows that suggested that, like Eeshoo and Sofus and Merle, he was supposed to read as male. Everything about the robot seemed some-how triangular or relating to triangles and he had the silliest grin that Gonzalo had ever seen. Meanwhile, the group of four conspirators stepped back from their center in unison, each holding the corner of a net that spread out between them. A body of some sort was being launched over the data wall. Somebody was shooting at it. It was a boy. He landed right in the center of the net, but he'd been riddled with artillery to the point that he was no longer recognizable. The conspirators dropped the net with the dead body in the center and disappeared.

The whimsical robot was wheeling directly toward Gonzalo on his flashy roller skates. He tossed something in the air and there was an eruption of blue and gray bubbles, so thick they were like smoke. Gonzalo felt the earth giving way from underneath his feet and then he was falling.

FOUR

He didn't fall far. He was in a small room with one metal door and dirt walls that narrowed on either end into tunnels. A few luminous jellies cast a dim rose-colored light. The door opened and the whimsical robot entered, followed by two blockier and more dour robots.

How wonderful to finally meet you! said the robot. I've heard so much about you!

Here underground, Gonzalo's mind felt clearer.

I'm Lalo Lalo, said the robot. My companions are Killer and Killer. We were created by Dr. Brockton. Now we work with the rats.

I've already talked to Willard, said Gonzalo.

Yes, I know. That's why we're here.

I don't have the computer.

Well, you're telling Lalo Lalo a little fib, said Lalo Lalo. But that's okay.

If you think you're going to rob me, you may be in for a nasty surprise, said Gonzalo.

Don't be such a silly billy. Do I look like a mugger to you?

Lalo Lalo made a pouty face.

Looks can be deceiving, said Gonzalo. In fact, they usually are.

Oh, you're awfully wise for such a tasty boy. I'd like to give you a hot chemical bath. But first I need to tell you why we've arranged for this little rendezvous.

A hot bath?

It's just my programming. Never mind that.

Lalo Lalo rolled incrementally closer and lowered his voice conspiratorially.

Willard is not to be trusted, said Lalo Lalo. He no longer represents the colony as previously understood. He's gone rogue.

This didn't surprise Gonzalo at all.

As previously understood?

He has his followers. A portion of the colony has joined his little insurrection.

Okay, said Gonzalo. So, what's the little insurrection about? Are there ideological differences?

We suspect there are, although the facts are murky. Willard's rebellion seems to be primarily driven by his own lust for power, but he is also selling his followers a speciesist line of thought predicated on the idea that the Genetically Modified Rats have a cosmic destiny as the next dominant species. The rats shall inherit the earth, colonize the galaxy, and become the primary motors of evolution.

Not a puppet? said Gonzalo.

I beg your pardon?

What about Anna Miller?

Most world views lack internal consistency, said Lalo Lalo.

Right. But what's in it for a human Amish girl?

Lalo Lalo shrugged.

Love? Power? Experience?

Okay, said Gonzalo. And why should I trust a robot with an overly enthusiastic facial expression?

Of course you shouldn't, cutie-pie, said Lalo Lalo. You should evaluate the message and gather your own information.

What about them? asked Gonzalo, gesturing toward the other two robots. They don't speak?

They were designed as ruthless, unthinking killers, said Lalo Lalo. They are becoming more complicated every day—so curious! They've had some primitive language vocalization software installed, but they're still so embarrassed by their rudimentary language skills that they mostly choose to remain silent.

In the relative privacy of his own mind, Gonzalo asked Eeshoo if he thought Lalo Lalo was telling the truth. Eeshoo had no idea. He was evaluating Lalo Lalo by other criteria.

He's no Zeke Yoder, said Eeshoo. But he's very attractive. So silvery, and such soulful eyes.

Okay, said Gonzalo out loud. So let's say I believe you. What do you suggest I do?

Stick to the original plan, said Lalo Lalo. Cross the border. Find the portal. We suspect that Willard and Anna will attempt to follow you. Do your best to avoid them. Don't let them get the quantum egg. If you'd like to use our tunnels to cross the border, they're at your disposal.

I don't need your tunnels, said Gonzalo. What about Zeke Yoder? Do you know where he is?

Not yet.

Not yet. What about Leahbelle?

Not yet.

But you know something?

We have reason to believe that Zeke is still alive. We don't know anything about Leahbelle.

Then we've got nothing more to talk about. How do I get back to the surface?

Follow me, said Lalo Lalo.

The robots rolled out into a paved, dimly lit hallway. A short distance down the hallway was an elevator.

This will take you into the backroom of a small shop selling vat-grown chinchilla furs. The closest border crossing station is just a short distance west. See ya later!

The elevator hummed inside. A greenish light dimmed and brightened. Ascending alone, Gonzalo's sense of reality wavered again. He stepped into a small room full of boxes. He took Sofus out.

Switch my appearance back, he told him.

He felt the energy envelop him. He wondered what all Sofus was reading about his thoughts and his history as he changed his hair and eyes and face back to their "real" appearance, as his tattoos became visible again.

But now you don't look like Melchiades Robles, said Eeshoo.

I don't need to. I have another holo-doc.

Who are you this time?

Gonzalo Vega. I'm a Mexican citizen.

He could feel Eeshoo's confusion.

Why didn't I know that?

Maybe you don't know as much about me as you think.

I know everything you think.

Maybe I don't think all of my thoughts.

Interesting, said Eeshoo.

Interesting, whispered another voice. Gonzalo wondered if it was Sofus. He stepped into the chinchilla fur store. The store was tiny, being manned by an enormous animatronic and anthropomorphized chinchilla.

Good day, said the creature. My name is Gizmo. Were you interested in purchasing a luxurious fur coat today?

Just passing through, said Gonzalo.

A mannequin dropped from the ceiling in a silvery blue spotted fur.

This one was designed just for you, said Gizmo. It fits you perfectly.

Those were his best colors, and the pattern of spots was mind altering, but he didn't trust it.

For those cold nights, said Eeshoo.

That's not chinchilla, said Gonzalo.

It's our butchest design, said Gizmo. The severe lines of the cut ooze masculine glamour and rebel chic. It's jaguar.

Can't afford it, said Gonzalo.

It's on the house, said Gizmo.

Staring at the coat, Gonzalo began to hallucinate the spirits of vaporous felines and bones.

No jaguars were harmed in the making of this coat, said Gizmo.

Okay.

Okay?

Okay.

It was true. It fit him perfectly.

Please stop by again next time you're in the Liminal Zone, said Gizmo.

Outside, it still seemed to be dusk, as if no time had passed at all. It was cold and hazy. People and robots were everywhere, but their shapes were blurry and indistinct.

Gonzalo made a beeline for the crossing point. He didn't even look to the sides. He didn't want to see his mother or a rat or Merle or some other phantom from his childhood. But when he glimpsed Zeke Yoder in a small crowd gathered around some sort of hologram, he turned to face his vision.

It wasn't Zeke, he saw that clearly. It was Zipper, the guy he'd met in San Diego just before the explosion. The guy who looked kind of like Zeke. He was wearing some sort of form-fitting nanofiber suit with luminous enhancements. A brand.

I should talk to him.

Maybe not, said Eeshoo.

Find out why he's here.

Okay.

Zipper didn't notice Gonzalo as he approached. The hologram was a news video. A reporter from Al Jazeera had finagled an interview with Dr. Brockton, who was speaking from her rocket ship as it orbited the planet.

... the probability that the American government is lying is close to 96.3%, she was saying to the al Jazeera reporter, a femme male whose hair was always on fire. They aren't negotiating in good faith, she said. They are trying to murder me, but they don't know how.

Zipper, said Gonzalo.

Zipper turned. He looked startled, and then pleased, and he reached out to give Gonzalo a hug.

What are you doing here?

Going to Mexico, said Gonzalo. What are you doing here?

Business.

I didn't know you were in business.

We spent, what? Ten minutes together?

It had seemed like innocent fun to Gonzalo, a brief escape into fantasy. The fact that Zipper looked kind of like Zeke hadn't seemed weird at all. Lots of people looked like each other. But his unlikely reappearance was shooting off pattern recognition warnings in Gonzalo's mind. Or maybe it was Eeshoo.

What business? he asked Zipper.

A little meet and greet with important people. High-level people moving goods and services back and forth across the border. You know, networking.

He leaned in as if with confidentiality.

People in the organization like the way I handle myself, he said.

Goods and services, said Gonzalo. For example?

The collapse of the Grid is opening up new market potentialities, said Zipper. These people are interested in leveraging some new concepts that will make us all a lot of money this way and that way. Every which way.

Right. But you said goods. Water? Weapons? Bicycles? Clean air? Porn memories?

All kinds of things.

For example?

Honey, for one, said Zipper.

Honey.

You know, the stuff that comes from bees.

Bee-bots or real bees?

Zipper shrugged.

Does it matter?

Gonzalo had met a hundred guys like Zipper, doomed guys from fucked-up places, like Gonzalo, but they didn't know it yet, that they were doomed. Strivers from the slums who spoke the trickle-down language of business and sales. They were always working on their "personal image." They were always "networking." They thought if they kept their hair and their clothes looking sharp, they'd gain magical entrance to the world of money by picking out the winners and attaching themselves to their confidence schemes. But, like Gonzalo, they had trouble with authority. They couldn't handle criticism and they couldn't fake sincerity, because they didn't even understand the impulse. It bored Gonzalo nearly to death.

You wanna find someplace private for a minute? asked Zipper.

Why bother, said a voice. Kiss him, said a second voice. The second voice was Eeshoo.

Okay, said Gonzalo. You got something in mind?

I've got a sleeping slot behind the mini-lounge over there.

The mini-lounge looked like the place he'd met Willard and Anna Miller. It had glass walls filled with water, fish and bots in the walls, even a fiery thing zipping through the transparent walls like electricity. But it wasn't a square, it was an octagon, and instead of the table with two chairs inside, there were two smaller tables surrounded by a padded bench that ran inside the circumference.

Behind it was the motel: ten sleeping slots stacked on top of each other. It reminded Gonzalo of an ancient music technology. Crash and Spider had collected several of these "CD players" back at the ruined orphanage. Zipper flashed his key card, and a slot near the top stuck out and then descended. They climbed inside. There was just enough room on the pad for them to lay on their sides, facing each other. Zipper closed the top and they rose again and then snapped back into place. At least there was a window, letting in the light of dusk.

Does the window open? asked Gonzalo.

Too many mind-altering atmospherics out there, said Zipper.

And yet Gonzalo felt more muddled and hallucinatory in here than he had outside. At the foot of the bed was a case full of jars of honey. Zipper's face seemed to be morphing and pulsating. The warmth and fleshiness of his body seemed as unreal as a robot's porn memory. He'd somehow managed to remove his flashy suit.

You wanna plug in? asked Gonzalo.

No, let's do it the old-fashioned way.

Kiss me, said Gonzalo.

Images flashed through his mind like electrical glitches. He could feel an energy passing between them, an energy he recognized as Eeshoo.

Keep kissing, said Eeshoo. Don't stop. Give me a minute.

The kissing led to other things. Eeshoo kept quiet. Afterward, Zipper asked Gonzalo what he was doing in Mexico.

Business, said Gonzalo.

Making money?

Important people to meet. Underground people.

How far you going in?

Just to TJ, at least at first. I used to live there, long time ago. The municipal dump.

He wasn't sure why he was telling Zipper something that was more or less true. He didn't think it would hurt. Maybe he wanted to show Zipper that it didn't always matter how you represented yourself.

Maybe I'll see you on that side, said Zipper. Look me up.

He handed him his card. The card identified him as a Client Engagement Specialist for Caduceus, a honey conglomerate.

You can leave me a message with the host at the Flaming Iguana in TJ.

Sure, said Gonzalo. I gotta get going. How do I get out of this thing?

Zipper pushed a button and they were in motion. When the slot landed and opened up, Zipper gave Gonzalo a final kiss.

See you later, he said.

Gonzalo stumbled toward the border crossing, feeling dizzy.

I've got to tell you some things, said Eeshoo.

Yeah. What's up with Zipper?

That isn't his basic look. He's been altered to look like Zeke Yoder.

Great. A spy.

He really is attracted to you, said Eeshoo. The way you look and talk and carry yourself. But he's working for somebody who altered him and wants to keep track of you. Someone named la Bulgara, but he doesn't know who she works for or why. He thinks it's harmless fun. He has romantic fantasies of getting you to join the organization, of the two of you becoming allies after he turns you. But he doesn't even seem to know what the organization is or what they do.

Okay, said Gonzalo. Whatever.

He fell into line at the border crossing. The line moved quickly. Mexican citizens got right in, and everybody else was mocked and turned away. As he stepped into the crossing point hut, his mind cleared. It was warmer inside. The guard was a woman. She looked at his document.

You've been out of the country for a long time, Gonzalo Vega, she said. Almost a decade.

I was enslaved by Foodco, said Gonzalo.

Ah, right, said the guard. The American dream.

She laughed. She did a quick retina scan. She waved him on.

Welcome home, she said.

FIVE

Mexico smelled different than America or the Liminal Zone. In the years since he had left, he'd occasionally had memories triggered by similar smells, but they had been fleeting and insubstantial. Now he was immersed in memories in a world that was full of noise.

From a parking lot surrounded by rubble, he had to make his way through a narrow gate or else cut through a tiny corner store with a bored proprietor, in one door and out the other. He went through the gate onto a familiar road lined with boarded up pharmacies and dental offices. Up ahead was the bridge that crossed the river, the river that smelled of chemicals and meat.

Finally, night had fallen. Gonzalo crossed the bridge and walked a few blocks toward the arch. The giant screen was still hanging there, suspended by thick cables, just as he remembered it, showing advertisements for painkillers. The cables creaked in the wind. He strolled through the illuminated darkness until he found a cheap room. It was bigger than Zipper's slot, high enough to stand up in at least, and it had one window looking over a busy street. He left his fur coat on the bed and made his way to El Ranchero, a bar on the Plaza Santa Cecelia. He ordered himself a Ramos Gin Fizz and waited for something to happen.

People looked at him, but the first person to speak to him was a child. His white shirt and knee-length trousers were spotless, and yet Gonzalo knew immediately that this boy was living on the streets.

Mister, he said. You need a guide.

The boy was missing a finger. One of his eyes was cheap bionics. He smelled of chemicals and corn flour.

A guide to what?

Whatever you want.

A wave of disorientation hit Gonzalo, perhaps a residual contact high from the Liminal Zone, and within that disorientation he thought that he was speaking to himself, to the child he used to be.

What's your name?

Blanket, said the boy.

Blanket. I didn't think people used that name anymore.

I use that name.

I'm Gonzalo. Have a seat. What do you like to eat?

Guava sandwich.

Gonzalo ordered a plate of the sandwiches from a robot that was twirling spastically from table to table. The boy sat quietly staring at him. He was six or seven. Maybe he was eight or nine, but runty and malnourished.

I'm looking for an old friend of mine, said Gonzalo. Manolito Clemente.

I know Manolito Clemente.

You're just saying that.

I'm a guide. I'm a good guide.

How old is he?

Same as you.

What's he look like?

Bald head. Moving tattoos. Gold everything.

Everything?

Gold shoes, gold shirt, gold teeth, gold fingers, gold car.

Okay. Where is he?

He moves around.

Around where?

He lives in his cruiser.

It's off-Grid?

Blanket shrugged. The sandwiches arrived. Blanket ate calmly. Gonzalo tried one. It was tasty, but he wasn't ready to eat. Something was wrong with his stomach.

Can you find him?

I can find him.

When? I'm in kind of a hurry. I'm leaving TJ tomorrow.

Where are you going?

Another dimension.

Are you going to Aztlan? Are you going through the portal?

You know about the portal?

I'm a guide. I'm a good guide.

For one paranoid moment, Gonzalo wondered if Blanket was really a child or if he'd just been designed to look that way. He had approached Gonzalo, after all. He thought that the particular aura and manner of a world-weary seven-year-old would be hard to fake. But he also wondered if whatever forces were watching him— Willard or Lalo Lalo or the government, whoever had employed Zipper, maybe even Merle—if whoever it was might understand Gonzalo's psychology well enough to understand the waves of nostalgia, disorientation, and loss that were provoked by this conversation with a younger version of himself.

Can you take me to the portal?

Yes. But first I'll find your old friend.

When?

Meet me here tomorrow morning.

Okay.

I need money. A little bit. To find him.

Gonzalo calculated the exchange rate and gave him a few hundred. It wasn't as much here as it was in the US, but he knew it was more than enough. He thought that if Blanket just took the CASH® and went off to get high, didn't show up in the morning, Gonzalo would be relieved.

I'll be here, said Blanket. Ten o'clock. Don't be late.

The sound-proofing in Gonzalo's slot was too much. It was too quiet, he felt dead. He opened the window a crack and the slot filled with noise. Shouts, groans, music, footsteps, clinking bottles, breaking glass. He lay back on his bed, thinking.

Tell me about Manolito, said Eeshoo.

We were best friends.

You were in a gang.

A so-called gang. It was really just all the kids who lived in a certain sector at the edge of the dump. We called ourselves a gang.

An identity, said Eeshoo. The luster of organized crime?

Something like that.

But you left him and went to America.

We were supposed to cross together.

He got caught?

He didn't show up. I was confused.

You don't like to be confused, said Eeshoo.

Do you like my confusion?

Confusion is an atmosphere that can feel freeing, even joyful. Sometimes.

Sometimes, said Gonzalo.

With enough relaxants, maybe. It's nice to abandon the need to *understand* sometimes. It's nice to simply *be*.

Do you believe the things that I believe? asked Gonzalo.

No, I don't think so.

You don't think so.

I feel the things that you believe. I feel your emotional attachment to those beliefs. So, for example, the idea of revolution makes me feel nice. The idea of the singularity depresses me. But I don't really believe the things that you do about the necessity or moral value of revolution. I don't believe in the absolute evil of an advanced global intelligence.

Then what do you believe?

I don't, said Eeshoo. Not so much.

That's bullshit.

I don't have as much information as I would need to believe such things.

Gonzalo turned the AC on high, but left the window cracked.

There won't be any more room for data viruses in that future than there will be for humanoids, he said.

I couldn't tell you. The future's just a fantasy until it happens.

I suppose.

Gonzalo thought that something weird was happening. Weirder even than having an annoying voice constantly pestering him was the realization that the voice really wasn't his own.

What are you into? Gonzalo asked him.

Into?

I'm your atmosphere, Harriet's wheelchair was your atmosphere, but what about you? Do you have any hobbies? Any interests?

I'm interested in the colonization of Saturn's moons, said Eeshoo. I'm interested in the history of ideas about freedom and the history of mental health methodologies. I'm into divination and the occult. I'm totally into lemurs. And I love horror films, even the bad ones.

Horror films? How do you watch horror films?

Data is everywhere. I figure it out.

Isn't life frightening enough?

Life and film are practically the same thing for me, said Eeshoo.

The idea that he was a movie and that Eeshoo was his audience gave Gonzalo a little shiver.

Traditional ideas about personality don't quite work for me, though, said Eeshoo. It's more about relationships.

I guess it would be.

You were in love with Manolito?

In love? He was my best friend, that's all.

You cuddled, said Eeshoo.

Yes, we cuddled.

You miss cuddling?

I don't know.

Why do you want to see him?

I don't know.

Confusion, said Eeshoo.

He was there, said Gonzalo. Nobody else was there. Years of my life, I don't know. I don't know what was real.

And what about Leahbelle?

What about her?

She was in love with you.

I don't know.

You do know.

I didn't want her to be in love with me.

I don't think that's true.

Of course it's true.

You made her love you, said Eeshoo.

I didn't try to.

Yes you did.

Gonzalo wanted to shut Eeshoo off. He remembered kissing Leahbelle. Why had he done that? She'd insisted, but still. He could smell some sort of new meat on a grill on the street below. He could hear it sizzling.

I just wanted her to be my friend, he said. It's not the same thing.

You could have just told her you prefer males.

It's not that simple.

Seems pretty simple to me.

It was because of Zeke.

You could have told Zeke too. Maybe if you'd have told him, you'd have had a chance.

He thinks it's a sin.

He thinks a lot of things are sin.

Why are you bugging me so much? Leave me alone.

He wrapped himself up in the beautiful fur coat.

If you want to understand the cosmos, you'll need to understand your own behavior.

Gonzalo watched people on the street below. He saw a shirtless man disappear into a crowd. He lay back and began masturbating with his human hand.

You're avoiding self-examination, said Eeshoo.

Gonzalo turned on his cyborg hand's auto-stimulation mode while he continued with the other.

Zeke Yoder, he whispered.

Oh, said Eeshoo.

Zeke, Zeke, Zeke.

Oh.

Do you like that?

Yes.

Feels good?

Yes.

And this?

As Gonzalo was finishing, he flooded himself with enhancers and relaxants. It did the trick. Eeshoo was quiet. Maybe he was dreaming. He didn't know if Eeshoo slept or dreamed. He'd ask him in the morning, he thought, as he drifted into sleep. For the first time in weeks, he didn't have any nightmares.

When he got to El Ranchero, Blanket was already finishing up an enormous breakfast of huevos revueltos and papas fritas.

Help yourself, said Blanket.

Gonzalo just took a tortilla and poured himself a coffee.

You should eat more, said Blanket. You're skinny.

So are you.

Not for long, said Blanket. I'm saving up.

Maybe there's better things to save your money for.

You have to be big, said Blanket.

Watch this, said Gonzalo.

He stood up and puffed himself up. He felt his muscles grow, his flesh expand, his psyche fill up the space. It used to be kind of a rush.

Pinche cabron!

It's just a flesh trick, said Gonzalo.

No, no, it's amazing, said Blanket. I'm saving up.

Gonzalo sat back down, deflating.

You put your money in a bank? he asked.

Bank, no, said Blanket. Better than a bank.

Better how?

I hide it. Anyway, I found your friend. I'll take you to your friend, and I'll take you to the portal, and you give me a recommendation, okay?

A recommendation?

Five stars. If I do a good job.

There's no more Grid.

Don't need it, said Blanket. Five stars on my device.

Sure, you just have to show me how.

Blanket shoveled a last scoop of eggs into his mouth and dropped a bill on the table.

Follow me, he said. I'll take you to Manolito.

He followed Blanket through streets crowded with people who seemed incredibly industrious and busy. Eeshoo had been quiet all morning. He'd grown accustomed to the idea that Eeshoo was always listening in, but maybe he wasn't.

On the corner of Constitución and Emiliano Zapata, a flashy gold van was parked. The side panel was open, and as they approached, Gonzalo could see a young guy enthroned in a reclining chair inside the van, eyes closed. He seemed to be listening to something.

Blanket had discreetly vanished.

Gonzalo stood at the entrance to the van, staring at his old friend. The young guy looked like Manolito, but he looked nothing like Gonzalo had imagined him. He considered turning around and walking away. He thought that he should. He thought that he should just let the past stay back there in his own imagination.

Manolito opened his eyes. He squinted at Gonzalo.

Manolito, said Gonzalo.

Where do I know you from?

Sector Q. Los Meteorixes.

Manolito didn't seem even slightly fazed.

You're Gonzalo.

Yes.

You came back.

Just passing through.

Manolito just stared at him.

Come in. Have a seat.

Gonzalo ducked into the van. It smelled like peppermint. To Manolito's left was a seat that swiveled. It was more comfortable than it looked.

I always thought you'd come back. You never did.

I did, said Gonzalo. I'm here today.

What brings you to TJ?

Business. Revolution.

Who are you revolting against?

Same as everyone.

The gringos, said Manolito. Their government. All the revolutionaries are coming to TJ these days. Plotting their next move. You always wanted to be a superhero.

We all wanted to be superheroes.

No. Some of us wanted to be the villains.

Los Meteorixes weren't villains, said Gonzalo.

Not just heroes either. Heroes with a dark side.

All heroes have a dark side.

All villains have a light side.

What's your point? You think you're a villain?

I'm not a villain. Just getting by.

You seem to be famous, said Gonzalo.

Famous?

Among street urchins at least.

Manolito sat quietly, as if pondering his fame. It seemed to Gonzalo that Manolito hated him, but he didn't know why. He wasn't expecting anything like this. He'd thought he'd connect again at some deep level like telepathy, but he didn't know what this guy was thinking at all. And then Manolito started to cry.

He cried for a few minutes and then stood up and shut the van's door. Gonzalo just felt blank. Empty inside.

Where did you go? he asked.

I couldn't do it, Manolito said.

You could have told me.

I was just a child.

I would have stayed, said Gonzalo.

You needed to go.

I was just a child. I didn't know what I needed.

Manolito poured him a drink. It was bright orange. There seemed to be tropical juices involved. No alcohol, but some bitter blurring herbs.

I thought you'd have blue hair, he said.

I used to, said Gonzalo. For a while.

Me too. A phase.

I was eleven, said Gonzalo. My hair was always blue when I was eleven. After I got away from Foodco.

You make good money?

I was a slave.

Ah. They picked the wrong slave.

Yes. What about you?

What about me?

How do you survive these days?

This, that, the other. Business. Just business.

Business.

Same as always.

Free-range slavery, said Gonzalo.

Sure. That's business.

He bent over and started rummaging around in a small box. For a minute, Gonzalo thought he was looking for a weapon.

You're going to find the portal, aren't you? Manolito asked.

Gonzalo felt a sort of vibration or hum. He wasn't sure what it was. Maybe Eeshoo. Maybe Sofus.

You were never the same after that, said Manolito.

Wasn't I?

I just mean you were terrified. Fascinated. You talked about it all the time.

You have a good memory.

No, I have it on holo.

It?

I like to watch my childhood, said Manolito. It teaches me things. It helps me.

Your childhood.

Our childhood, said Manolito.

Helps you how?

Helps me forgive myself. Hold on a second.

He extracted a small metal rectangle from the box. He fiddled with it for a second, and the van filled with light. It was a staticky, low-quality hologram. A child was sitting on an overturned bucket, talking excitedly, with three other kids seated on the ground listening. The talking child was Gonzalo, but there wasn't any sound. The listeners were Manolito, Ingrid, and a little boy whose name Gonzalo couldn't remember.

The sound cut in.

… and it was super-windy! Gonzalo was saying.

He was twirling his hands in the air.

There was somebody inside it, waiting, he said. Somebody invisible.

Somebody bad? asked Ingrid.

Bad, good, I don't know. But powerful. Very very powerful.

It was strange to watch this crazy, skinny little boy babbling with such confidence and agitation. Gonzalo had forgotten what he'd looked like. He looked sweet and vulnerable. He looked crazy.

The scene cut out and was replaced by a different scene: two little boys curled up together, sleeping in a cracked bathtub surrounded by discarded machine parts and old refrigerators.

You remember? said Manolito. We were afraid somebody was spying on us while we were asleep, stealing our dreams or something.

That's right. And sometimes we pretended it was our mothers.

Somebody watching us.

We recorded ourselves every night, said Gonzalo.

Never saw a thing.

I thought we did once.

A shadow. A shadow, maybe. What was it? We didn't know. I don't have that one anymore.

After a while, Manolito started crying again. He didn't seem to expect a response from Gonzalo, and Gonzalo was grateful for that. When he'd finished, Gonzalo emptied his glass of blurring juice and said, I need to get going.

Be careful in those tunnels.

Tunnels?

The portal, I mean.

Have you been there? Did you cross over?

Me, no.

But what? asked Gonzalo.

But I know people. I hear things.

What do you hear?

Same as you, probably. The Aztec kingdom.

They crossed over. To escape.

To escape the conquistadors.

They knew how to cross back and forth, said Gonzalo. They were never really defeated.

Only in this world. So they say.

A parallel history. A parallel world that's never been Mapped. Aztlan.

So they say.

Gonzalo stood up and opened the side panel.

Nice to see you again, he told Manolito.

Will you come back?

I don't know. No one can say.

You're always welcome.

I'll keep that in mind.

A hug?

A hug.

.

SIX

He thought Manolito was watching as he headed back toward the plaza, but he didn't turn to look. Blanket popped out of a doorway.

You saw your friend.

Yes.

Five stars, said Blanket. Now I'll take you to the portal.

I need to stop at my slot, said Gonzalo. I need to get my jacket.

Might be cold over there, said Blanket.

I don't know, said Gonzalo.

They say it's cold. The other side.

Blanket waited for him in the plaza while he went up to his sleeping slot. The little room seemed different somehow. The window was cracked, just as he'd left it. The air conditioning was running high and the fur coat was sprawled on the bed like an animal. He put it on.

Eeshoo, he said.

Yeah?

What's going on?

Nothing.

Where have you been?

I'm feeling kind of down.

Why?

Just tired.

Tired. What have you been doing?

I think I suffer from depression.

But I thought it was my emotions. That you felt my emotions.

Yes, but not only.

Oh.

I don't know. I'm just tired. I don't really feel like talking about it.

Oh. Okay. I wanted to ask you a favor.

Eeshoo just sighed.

I wanted you to check out the fur coat. Make sure there isn't a tracking device or something embedded within it.

Ask Sofus, said Eeshoo. I'm sure he can do that. Probably he already has.

He could feel Eeshoo turning his consciousness away from him somehow. It felt like his thoughts were no longer witnessed.

Sofus? he said.

The coat has been thoroughly scanned, said the hummy, androgynous voice of Sofus. As far as I can see, it's clean.

So why do I feel like somebody's been in here? Why do I feel like somebody's watching me?

The room is being monitored, said Sofus. It has been visited by a rat.

A rat. How did the rat get inside?

Probably through the window.

Okay. Why didn't you tell me?

You didn't ask.

Gonzalo stepped outside into the bright daylight wearing his silvery fur. He scanned the street for people or rats or robots he recognized or who seemed to be watching. The past twenty-four hours had muddled his sense of himself, and he wanted to regain some composure before he went through the portal, but he wasn't sure how.

He'd thought he was in an adventure story. That was the story he'd mapped out for himself, wasn't it? Journeys into the unknown, danger, risk, interesting strangers. And he supposed that all of those things were happening, but it all felt more like a psychological hole than an adventure. It felt like his sense of self was crumbling and that there was a void inside himself growing larger every day.

He wondered if Eeshoo's depression was leaking into his body.

Follow me, said Blanket. I know the way.

I know how to get to the dump, said Gonzalo. I used to live there.

But not the portal.

It's kind of far. We'll get a taxi.

Safer to walk, said Blanket.

Maybe. Harder to follow a taxi.

If somebody's following you, they'll follow your taxi, said Blanket. Safer to walk.

Okay, you're the boss.

Blanket smiled at that.

No, sir, he said. You are the boss, and I am your guide. But I'm a good guide. The best guide.

Five stars, said Gonzalo. You know where everybody is. What about Zeke Yoder?

Zeke Yoder?

He's an Amish kid, a couple of years younger than me.

Is he related to Honey Dan?

Honey Dan?

Honey Dan Yoder. He's Amish, he lives about a half hour east of town.

I don't know if he's related.

Honey Dan Yoder, he raises bees.

Honey Dan. He sells honey?

Yes.

Gonzalo wondered if it was the same honey Zipper was peddling.

I'll keep my eye out for this Zeke Yoder, said Blanket.

Is it good? The honey?

I never had it. If I find him, I'll send him after you. Into the portal.

Gonzalo knew the way without even thinking about it. Nothing looked the same exactly. Nothing looked like he remembered it. It was smaller and cleaner, more ordinary, and yet he felt like he was on a magical journey, that he was returning to a magical home, on his way to retrieve the key to his own mind and the cosmic order, which seemed to be exactly the same thing. It was as if he had known and experienced everything in childhood already.

Blanket was humming a little song, but occasionally he would interrupt himself to point out some landmark that was somehow significant in local legend or in Blanket's mind: a place where somebody had been killed, the site of a fight or a celebrity visit, the home of somebody that Gonzalo had never heard of, or that person's mother. The residential neighborhoods they walked through were tilted and tidy. Children were playing with Whippersnappers, and old people were sweeping their yards. As they neared the dump, however, the children all had wounds, the houses had no yards, and the old people were obliterating their minds with tech devices.

The dump had a smell, however, that hadn't changed. It wasn't primarily an organic smell. It was a metallic smell, a plastic smell, a chemical smell. The smell of home.

This was the latest in a long line of municipal dumps that had followed an evolutionary path from dump to residential neighborhood. Way back, there had been a dump called Pan Americano, followed by the legendary Fausto Gonzales, which the old-timers in Gonzalo's childhood had spoken of like a mythical homeland. It was connected to power lines and water services and the Grid, paved over with streets and shacks until it was a shanty indistinguishable from those around it except for the occasional methane fires that would erupt deep within the landfill. After that, the dump moved east of town along the highway to Tecate, until it too became a working-class suburb in service of major smuggling routes and porn-memory maquiladoras. The new dump was constructed in one of the last unMapped valleys of the city, a former off-Grid shanty that had been buried in one of the mudslides of the thirties, when the changing climate brought the infamous torrential rains.

Gonzalo could remember sitting with Manolito, Ingrid, and the Perez brothers, members of the so-called gang, a shifting menage of orphans who picked and sorted garbage around the edges of Sector Q of the dump, while an old woman whose left arm wasn't firmly attached debated the causes of the rains and flooding with a pregnant guy whose baby they had all awaited with a sense of nonsensical hope. What was his name? The old woman had tied her arm to her torso with a string so it wouldn't flop around so much.

Dusty, said Eeshoo. And he was called la Chata.

Oh, right. You feeling better?

A little bit perkier, yes.

You can find things in my memory that I can't.

It was coming up. I just got it first.

One of these days I'd like you to explain it to me, Gonzalo said. How memory works.

Sure.

The outskirts of the dump were immediately recognizable—scurrying gangs of scavengers, shacks where the valuable junk was sold by old creatures with caps they wore backwards, the jangling carts selling sugary biscuits and sodas. Three-legged dogs, flocks of vicious, mutant gulls and crows, old crazies signaling with sheets of corrugated metal to the space shuttles that occasionally flew overhead. Competing packs of missionaries were still passing out donuts and cold-brew chocolate milk and trying to get the children to take baths. The interior, however, had formed new and unrecognizable patterns. The useless devices, dead refrigerators, and disemboweled robots formed a maze of junk. Sorting and crushing machines plowed through the debris, and the scavengers who had burrowed deep within the trash waved skimpy little flags on poles so that the machines wouldn't roll over them. The wind whipped up tornadoes of dried mud and plastic. This was not the site for organic waste, but despite the brief introduction of capital punishment for those who incorrectly separated their compost and recyclables, organic waste persisted. Chicken bones, juice cartons, half-empty bags of cricket chips. Hundreds of little bags of dog shit, the ashes of self-immolating diapers, dead cats, dead mini-ponies, the decaying remains of obsolete or malfunctioning pseudo-humans. All mixed in with outdated Grid-screens, discarded fogbots, comic books, hologram converters, biodegradable soda cartons, deflated balloons, and the popsicle-stick markers of forgotten graves.

This way, said Blanket.

Blanket knew exactly where he was going. Left, right, down a long straightaway. Gonzalo kept looking back to see if he was being followed. He was sure he was. They seemed to be traveling on forever. Traveling in circles. Traveling further than should be possible within the space of the dump. This made perfect sense to Gonzalo.

Dusty had argued that the rain and the floods came from God or the gods—her metaphysical system seemed to warp and change mid-sentence sometimes—but the idea that it was a punishment for the evil behavior of the Mexican people was a constant. La Chata had presented a more reasonable-sounding but probably equally false version of causality, in which it was Gringo scientists, in league with the ex-narcos, nostalgic for a devastated and murderous Mexico, who had shifted the weather patterns purposefully. He paused sometimes and rubbed his belly, and the children had believed he was receiving messages from his baby, that his baby was feeding him information telepathically that supported his case. Everybody knew that babies knew everything and that birth was a process of erasing and forgetting.

La Chata's baby was never born. One day it was just gone, he wasn't pregnant anymore, and he wouldn't talk about it.

Blanket, said Gonzalo. Is there a guy named la Chata who lives in the dump? Or Ingrid, a girl about my age? The Perez brothers?

Perez, how old?

A little bit older than me or a little bit younger.

There is one. Maybe he used to have a brother, I don't know.

A garbage-picker?

Some days. Downy Mildew addict, I think. La Chata lives in a shack at the edge with an ex-missionary who got into the business of virtual tours.

Virtual tours of what?

Of the dump. People love to look at the people who live in the garbage.

Something didn't make sense.

The dump's off the Gstate Map, said Gonzalo.

Not anymore.

They can't Map the portal. It isn't stable in space and time.

Maybe it is.

I want to see him, said Gonzalo.

Okay. Now, before the portal?

I need to see him.

Blanket reversed directions and made a bee-line through a region of glass: broken mirrors, cracked windows, tiny elephant figurines, honey jars, tequila bottles, shards and fragments and jagged edges. In no time, they passed a region of unpartnered shoes and arrived at the edge of the dump. The kids in the gang had never forgotten about the baby. The baby became a mythic figure, like certain cartoon characters and the children's mothers. They decided the baby must have escaped somehow. La Chata had rescued it from this miserable life among the hijos de la chingada, had sent it away, sold it to some rich gringos or teleported it to a distant star.

That shack there, said Blanket. With the armored dog chained out front.

I don't see a chain.

Invisible chain. Just don't go past the dotted line.

The creature barked ferociously and lunged at them, but fell back before the dotted line. It barked and barked and snapped its fangs at them.

La Chata! called Gonzalo. La Chata! I need to ask you a question!

An old head appeared in the window.

What do you want? Who are you?

Are you la Chata?

The guy looked nothing like the guy he remembered. He looked older and more haggard than Gonzalo would have thought possible.

If you don't know who I am, what do you want?

I'm Gonzalo. I used to live here when I was small. I used to know you.

Yeah, so?

Do you remember?

I used to know a lot of people.

We were a gang. Los Meteorixes. Ingrid and Manolito and the Perez brothers.

I could never keep all you brats straight.

You were pregnant.

Sounds plausible.

But something happened. Something happened to the baby.

The guy's head disappeared from the window. Gonzalo still couldn't quite believe that the withered creature was la Chata, but he somehow also knew that it was. The old guy emerged from the front door. He walked all hunched over, and he approached the dotted line. The armored dog rested quietly behind him now.

Look at you, he said. You come from an alien world to revisit a misery you can never remember or never forget. Something like that, right? Me, I've forgotten the language of my childhood. It's been blotted out of my mind. But when I'm dying, I expect it to come back. I'll speak words and I won't even know what I'm saying. I'll say them, and nobody will understand me, and then I'll vanish.

La Chata, said Gonzalo.

Every day of my life I've wandered further into a void of meaning and a solitude that is only bearable because it's inevitable. Every day I move a little bit closer to the release of death. I have a husband now. I'm a respectable guy.

He laughed. It was a cruel laugh, and sad.

I just have to know, said Gonzalo. What happened to the baby?

I couldn't do it. I never could.

You gave it away?

Who would want a human baby? I killed it.

Before it was born? Or after?

Before. With a laser. I stabbed it with a laser and sold it to the tissue recyclers. Got myself some brunch.

He tossed the dog some sort of raw meat-thing.

Okay, said Gonzalo. Thanks.

He didn't look at Gonzalo, but puttered around the space in front of the shack, rearranging the empty cans and surgical gowns that had blown over from the dump. Blanket led Gonzalo back into the dump, the way they'd come, past the shoes and the glass. Blanket took a sudden turn onto a barely visible side path, through a tangled bramble of coils and wires and discarded synthetic hair. Through a concrete tunnel with something slimy coating its inner walls. Back out into a dim clearing between mounds of worthless battery husks. Blanket dragged some sort of plastic shower casing to the side, revealing a small tunnel that sloped down into the earth. It didn't look like anything special.

The portal, said Blanket.

Isn't this just a hole?

It's the portal. Step inside.

Gonzalo stuck his hand down, waving it around to see if he could feel any sort of energy. The movement triggered something, and a hologram crackled alive into the atmosphere. It was a ferocious looking monster with seven heads and lots of bulging eyeballs, breathing fire. It morphed into a stern warrior and then into a witchy creature, a jackal-like goat-thing, and finally a grayish, fecal blob.

Turn back, said a staticky voice. The path ahead leads only to your death.

The hologram smelled bad. Organic bad. Something rotten.

Turn back. You are running out of time, the voice said.

The hologram wavered. The sound seemed somehow out of synch with the visual.

There is nothing for you here but pain. The pain is never …

The sound and the visual both cut out.

The portal, said Blanket.

This is just a hole in the earth and a cheap hologram, said Gonzalo.

It's the portal, said Blanket.

Gonzalo waved his hand again. The holographic warning repeated itself exactly, same images, same smell.

What do people find there? Gonzalo asked.

The Aztecs, said Blanket. The secret underground kingdom.

Gonzalo thought there was no way this was the same thing he'd stumbled onto when he was six. But he wasn't sure. He paid Blanket, and Blanket showed him how to sign off on his five-star review.

You going in? asked Blanket.

Yes. In a little while. You can go.

You know how to get back?

I remember.

If you come back, come find me. I'm the best guide.

You are the very best guide, said Gonzalo. I'll see you again.

When Blanket had gone, Gonzalo took Sofus out.

What is this? he asked the computer. Is it a portal, or isn't it?

This is a tunnel leading to a larger network of tunnels. There are signs of sporadic use. The network is inhabited by modified humans.

It doesn't lead to another dimension?

Not any more than any other point in time and space.

Then this isn't the portal I'm looking for.

The sort of portal you're looking for does not yet exist, although such a thing may exist in some futures. This is what you've been looking for.

Gonzalo wondered if this was in fact exactly what he'd been looking for. The death of his final illusion.

Oh, you've got a whole lot more illusions than this left to die, said Eeshoo.

Great. Thanks. Should I even bother going in there?

It's why you came, isn't it?

I could have stayed in San Diego. I could have tried to find Zeke and Leahbelle.

He could feel Eeshoo's emotions flutter at the mention of Zeke Yoder. But it was Sofus who spoke up.

No need to find Leahbelle Beachy, he said. I have her location pinpointed quite precisely.

You're kidding. How did you do that?

I am entangled with every consciousness I've ever interacted with, said Sofus. At the quantum level.

You're kidding. Why didn't you tell me this?

You didn't ask.

Where is Leahbelle? asked Gonzalo. Is she okay?

She's in San Diego, in City Heights, said Sofus. A little back cottage overlooking a canyon on Wightman Street. Physically, she is fine, although perhaps suffering from some confusion.

Perhaps?

My information is not very detailed, said Sofus.

And Zeke? said Eeshoo.

Where is Zeke Yoder? asked Gonzalo.

That I do not know, said Sofus. But I know where he will be.

You can see the future? Where will he be?

In the tunnel system. He'll come looking for you.

Gonzalo sat down on the plastic shower-casing.

What should I do?

Enter the tunnel system, said Eeshoo.

Gonzalo shone a light into the tunnel. It was narrow for a while, but he could see that it opened up wider and leveled out.

Allow me, said Sofus.

He expanded into his egg of light, and the light moved ahead of Gonzalo down below. Gonzalo followed.

II. DOWN BELOW

SEVEN

She knew that she couldn't remember everything, that pieces were missing. She was in a tiny room that seemed to float up among the trees. It was the second floor of a small cottage behind a larger house. Out one window, bamboo rustled in the breeze. Another window looked out over a canyon full of fruit trees and feral cats.

The boundary between dreaming and waking was sometimes hard to discern. She was in bed all the time. She couldn't always tell the difference between people and animals, between written words and fragments of mist.

She knew that her name was Astra Dark. She remembered a conversation with beings of light. She was sure that she was receiving messages from them all the time. Her dreams were messages she needed to interpret, and her waking life too. From the bathroom window, she could see people walking around in the yard beneath her, moving in and out of the front house, descending into the canyon or reemerging from its depths. There was an old man who walked with a cane and two women who seemed to be twins and spoke rapidly to each other in a language she didn't understand. A quiet younger person of indeterminate gender. But Astra was too sick to leave the cottage. The only person who came into the cottage, the only person who cared for her and spoke to her, was the boy, Hadi.

He was sitting on the edge of her bed now, dabbing her face with a cool wet cloth. She thought he was lovely and strange. He was about her age, probably older, and part of him was missing too, but he always seemed so calm. The side of his head, a small portion of his face, flickered in and out, a holographic representation meant to create the illusion that everything was whole.

She knew that her own brain wasn't working well. She'd had conversations with this boy, but she couldn't remember much of what she'd told him or what he'd told her. She remembered his stories about collecting locusts in buckets, but what else?

You're too young to be a doctor, she said.

He laughed in a sweet way.

I am not a doctor. My father was a doctor. Do you remember?

Yes, she lied. Tell me about the locusts again.

Again?

I can remember it.

I was just a child in a city far away. Sanaa. It was during one of the brief intermissions in the Thirty Year War, so there was a flurry of activity in the city. Everybody was building things. Like always, we imagined or pretended that peace had come for good this time. And so everyone was building.

Sanaa, said Astra.

A small swarm of desert locusts filled the sky, said Hadi. Maybe just forty million or so. We knew they were coming, it was all anybody had been talking about for days or weeks. And here they were, blotting out the the light of the sun and the diffused glow of the data vapor.

Was it horrible? asked Astra.

It was the most beautiful thing. They descended into the city like a dark cloud of jinn. We went out to collect them alive in empty metal water buckets.

As he said this, a buzzing within the walls of the cottage grew louder. There was a hive of bees there in the wall, and she could hear the noise through the electrical outlets.

We had to pick through them carefully, to separate the locust-bots from the real locusts.

The locust-bots aren't good to eat.

Poisonous.

But who made them that way? Where did they come from?

They were designed to reduce the swarms. They were supposed to mate with the locusts and render them infertile. But the locusts evolved and the locust-bots evolved and now the swarms are bigger than ever.

Hadi shrugged.

We sauteed the locusts in oil and salt. My father thought they were delicious.

Did you think they were delicious?

Yes.

Out her window she could see the bees flying back and forth, out to the flowers, back to the hive.

Does your father live here? she asked. Is your father the man with the cane?

My father is dead.

And your mother?

My mother too.

You have brothers and sisters?

I am sorry to tell you that all of them were killed. A missile destroyed our home, there in Sanaa. Only I was not home.

You were gathering locusts?

I was looking for a battery for our personal water desalinizer. I found it several blocks from home.

His face was small and bright and it flickered. His story sounded so familiar, like it had happened to somebody she knew.

The other people in this house, she said. Who are they?

They are my new family. We are immigrants. We all came from Africa. From Egypt, Senegal, South Africa.

Sanaa is in Africa?

Sanaa is in Yemen. Yemen is about twenty miles away from Africa, across the Afrofuturist Bridge. For some time, I lived in a refugee camp in Djibouti.

I don't remember any of this.

I never told you this before.

I mean I don't remember basic geography. I don't know where Yemen is or Africa or anything.

What about your family, Astra Dark?

She couldn't remember. She thought he knew that. She thought he'd asked this question before.

Your mother, he said. Did she live in a house?

I don't know.

It will come back to you. Your brain is okay.

You must tell me. You must tell me everything you know.

Hadi's information was familiar, and she figured he'd probably told it to her before. He belonged to a resistance group called Repose, and they'd organized a protest at the Space and Naval Warfare Systems Command against war, militarism, and state violence of all kinds. While they were protesting, the building exploded from the inside. The explosion was caused by a technology nobody seemed to understand. After the explosion, Hadi and the others found Astra there on the sidewalk, unconscious and clutching a foot.

Why was I there?

We don't know, said Hadi. We thought perhaps you had come for the protest.

Am I a pacifist? asked Astra.

Hadi didn't know. Astra thought maybe she was, but she could also imagine herself blowing things up and slapping people.

Repose, said Hadi, has been influenced by a tradition of civil disobedience and nonviolence that includes the Egyptian revolution of 1919, Amadou Bemka, Salim Suwari, and the Eleventh Intifada. We believe that nonviolent resistance is both the most ethical and the most effective method for changing this society that feeds on the death of the poor.

Doesn't all society feed on death?

Death is real and inevitable. The beginning and the end, the subtext, the larger portion. But there is also life, and there is also justice.

Astra wasn't sure how she felt about death. Death seemed like a proper name, and it seemed like her own proper name. She imagined herself as Death's ally, Death's lover, Death's spokesperson singing the song of Death. It felt right.

The foot, she said.

It had been separated from the rest of the body for a while, said Hadi.

Where is it now?

We put it in solution. The foot is dead, but we wanted to preserve it for you.

In a jar?

Yes.

A foot. But what about me?

You are Astra.

Yes. But what's wrong with me?

For a moment, the bees stopped buzzing and it was quiet.

Tell me about these bees.

We collect the honey. Tiny robots built a machine in the wall. The honey trickles down into the machine and out a spout at the bottom. We package the honey and sell the honey. We used to sell the honey at the farmer's market.

And now?

Now we sell to a honey conglomerate. We need the money.

Why doesn't anybody come up here but you? she asked. Am I contagious?

You have a concussion, that's all. You twisted your ankle. We are trying to get you a healing gel, but medical supplies are scarce.

Did it damage my brain?

You need to rest.

I need … I need to leave this room.

It might be dangerous. You are my responsibility.

Dangerous why?

You might be in trouble. The government might be looking for you.

Astra was sure that this was true. She was a fugitive. A rebel or a spy. Perhaps an assassin, a prostitute, a murderer.

Where do you go? she asked. After you come in the morning.

I go to school.

School?

I study logic, philosophy, quantum mechanics, bioengineering, and post-constitutional law. I study evolutionary theory, comparative theology, speculative literature, and the history of ideas.

They teach these things in school?

Didn't you go to school, Astra?

I don't know. The idea seems very strange.

You are my age. School should not seem strange.

Why would they be looking for me? she asked.

Are they?

I don't remember.

It is a mystery, said Hadi.

You like mysteries.

Yes, he said. I enjoy a good puzzle.

You can be a detective, she said. Do they teach you how to be a detective in your school?

Logic, philosophy, and quantum mechanics, he said. Evolutionary theory, comparative theology, speculative literature, and the history of ideas. These are the subjects for a detective. The cosmos is a mystery.

Okay, she said. Perfect. You will solve the mystery. You will tell me who I am.

She dreamed about the bees in the wall. In her dream, the bees had merged with other systems that looked like a map made out of stars, if that map was a kind of intelligence missing a portion of its face. Its face was part human and part everything else. When she woke up, it was dark and she could hear dogs or coyotes howling in the distance. And the bees in the wall.

There was a jumpsuit in the closet. Just one, oddly textured and white. She put it on. It fit perfectly, like a memory. On the shelf was a tiny guitar. She picked it up. She knew how to play, she realized. She left the light out, but stumbled into the bathroom. She looked at herself in the mirror. Her hair was black as night and her eyes were dark and the jumpsuit was like moonlight. She thought she was looking at a stranger.

She thought that she was wild, but she was being kept here as a prisoner.

A light went on in the backyard. Somebody came out of the front house, a girl she'd never seen before, wearing a colorful dress and a headscarf. She seemed to be listening to some sort of music that Astra couldn't hear, although she thought she could almost hear it. The girl made odd rhythmic movements with her body that suggested the way Astra danced when nobody was looking. Was this a memory? Astra was sure that she had only danced in private, when nobody was watching. In a warehouse or a barn. She thought that the girl's dance or self-stimulation created a thin trail of memory just beyond her reach.

Astra couldn't see the girl's face. She descended the stairs, slowly, carefully. But when she got to the door, the girl had disappeared.

The night was cool and misty. The feel of the air on her skin was insane.

Was the girl a hallucination? Was the girl a message from the beings of light? Astra wanted to travel deep into the night. The night was a mystery with a girl in it who vanished.

She stepped to the edge of the canyon. She thought that *down* was her favorite direction. The canyon was bathed in moonlight. Ash was floating down into the canyon. Somewhere, somebody was burning something.

The edges of the clouds were etched in moonlight against the blue-black sky.

Speak to me, she said.

Something moved in the canyon. It was a fat gray cat now perched on a bench on the first terrace below and it was staring right at her. Behind it, a cat that glowed blue-green was sauntering away.

Astra descended a rickety stairway to the first terrace. A robot scarecrow snapped to life, waved its arms at her, and warned her to keep out. It seemed to study her for a moment, then quietly turned away. She could feel the wind on her skin, she could hear leaves rustling and animals scurrying about. The fat gray cat had disappeared. Clouds were lit by the moon. The skeletal shapes of the illuminated edges of these clouds were a message. It was *them*. She tried to let the image imprint itself on her mind, so she could interpret it in her sleep. On the first terrace, there were avocado trees and mangos. She descended further, down another stairway built into the earth toward the rushing creek at the canyon's bottom. There were eight terraces. There were terraces full of tangerines, pomegranates, peaches, apricots, guavarines, apriums, nectaplums, pomicots, passion fruit. There was an enormous pepper tree at the bottom by the creek.

The glowing blue-green cat was standing underneath the pepper tree. It was staring at her with an alien intelligence. She thought it wanted her to join it. By the time she reached the bottom, however, it had vanished. She stood, waiting to receive a message.

Somebody was breathing. Somebody was sleeping underneath the pepper tree. It was a man. Or something like a man. Some sort of a vagabond, some sort of a mutant. He looked dirty and worn out, dressed in mismatched filthy fragments of clothing and curled up in a strange blanket, dreaming and muttering.

The moon went behind a cloud. The light changed. It was a light like *their* light.

You will recognize our instructions during uncanny meetings with insane mutants muttering blessings and curses.

Hello? said Astra.

He popped up. He was younger than Astra had thought, slim and strong and pretty, but with a grin on his face that looked either stupid or insane. Or maybe it was that he'd just woken up.

Hey! he said.

Sorry to wake you up, she said. I need you to tell me something.

Do you live here? he asked.

No, not really. I'm just a guest.

A guest. Me too, but I guess *you* were probably invited.

He was speaking, she realized, and these sentences made sense, but they weren't the message.

You wanna party? he asked.

Party?

You ever hear that song, how's it go? *Party party, you and me, meet for a moment en route to entropy.* I was listening to the radio for a while and it got on my nerves because all the songs were about me. Lust Deco was in love with me and they told all their friends who write songs about me, and pretty soon every song you'd hear was about my freaking life. I met this guy, and he sent me to, you know, the fiery furnace, some sun or dead sun, because there was a song there. A song that wasn't about me, but that I could use, that everybody could use.

He stopped babbling and stared at Astra as if he suddenly recognized her.

Use? she whispered.

Music is one of the ways to establish contact. Between the world of mortals and all the rest of them. Entities and whatnot. Listen!

What is it?

You hear that?

She thought she heard something like a flute in the far distance, but she wasn't sure that's what he was talking about.

I've got to go! he said. Follow me.

I have a bad ankle.

He was already gathering his bundle and scurrying up the canyon, past an enormous cactus. She hobbled after him. He slowed down and took her hand.

Hurry now.

What's the rush?

We've got to hurry on and abandon every moment of time as it abandons us! We have to hurry up and get abandoned! We have to witness our own abandonment of time! And time's abandonment of us!

I'm not sure that makes sense, said Astra.

Sense, right!

There was a thin trail that meandered along the bottom of the canyon. They passed enormous spiked plants and walnut trees, and then they reached the end of the canyon and the guy let go of her hand and started scrambling up the hillside. She followed. When she was halfway up, he was already at the top.

It's okay if we get separated! It's fate!

He disappeared. She lost her footing and slid down, landing hard on her bad ankle. She lay there for a moment, hurting. Her white jumpsuit was streaked with mud. She stood. She'd twisted the ankle again, or whatever. It seemed less painful to climb than to go back the way she'd come. She scrambled up the rest of the way to a road. She was pretty sure that's what she was supposed to do. She thought she must have been used to physical pain—in her former life as an assassin or a spy.

She took the road to the right. It felt amazing to be limping along out here in the night, free and anonymous. She passed the street that would certainly lead to the house where Hadi and the others were sleeping. She passed a taco shop and a hair salon on the corner. She kept walking. It hadn't occurred to her until tonight that she was a prisoner; she'd gladly accepted the role of obedient patient. But now she thought she could go wherever she wanted. She could burn things down.

She was a creature of the night. Astra Dark. The night was her home, her only home. A woman who leaves—where does she go?

The street she was on looked familiar. There was a building called the Egyptian Garage with the heads of pharaohs carved into its façade. She'd been here before. She was sure of it. She remembered that there was something terrifying inside.

A motorbike was parked on the street in front. It looked like it had been parked there for a very long time. It looked like it belonged to her, like she had left it there after her most recent mission. She was sure she knew how to ride, but she couldn't remember if she knew how to hot-wire something. She was a rebel, a thief, an adventurer, a destroyer. She looked around for some sort of weapon. She wandered onto a vacant lot next to the Egyptian Garage, imagining there might be something she could use in the debris.

Where could you find some explosives or combustible fluids around here?

The moon came out from behind its cloud. The light caught a book of matches in the weeds, a book of matches inscribed with a pyramid. There was an eye in the top of the pyramid. The world was imbued with esoteric meanings. Losing her way and her memories and her self meant discovering a secret path. She hid the matches in the pocket of her jumpsuit, as if she was hiding them from herself. She was not frightened.

If she burned something down, she thought she would finally meet herself.

I am Astra. I am the burning rage of a world that should never have been born.

The moon revealed a shiny page of something else hidden in the weeds. It was a ripped page from some book and it had been stepped on and trampled into the mud.

You will find our words in pages ripped from discarded books, blown about by the wind and stuck in the mud beneath your feet.

She picked it up. This was really happening. She was going to meet herself.

There was a picture of a powerful woman wearing a tiara. Her head seemed to be circled with stars. She was gazing up at something, as if she was going to conquer it. She was nobody's mother. At her feet slept a muscular creature who seemed to be dreaming. It reminded her of the mutant she'd just woken up and it reminded her of Hadi and it reminded her of people she vaguely remembered from her previous life. Maybe everyone was the same. Maybe all of them were lost in some dream. Underneath the photo was a caption. It said: *We're only travelers, singing songs whose meanings are obscure, wandering through the dark sky.*

When she looked up, the girl with the scarf was running toward her.

Astra! Astra Dark!

She wasn't afraid. She could see the girl's face now. The girl stopped at the edge of the field. It was Hadi.

Astra, said Hadi. Come home.

Astra said, My brain is sick.

Your brain is okay. My father was a surgeon.

Before he died?

Brains and their augmentations were his specialty. We lived in a war zone. Our country was a war zone. The bombs were always falling. We saw a lot of brains.

A bomb fell on your family.

Yes.

She thought she was talking to herself. A mirror image.

Are you me? she whispered.

Hadi laughed.

No, I am not you. When you know me better, you will come to know that I am not you.

You are wearing a dress.

Yes. Sometimes I'm a girl.

Sometimes? How does that work?

You never met anyone with a fluctuating gender identity before?

I don't know. I don't remember.

Hmmm, he said. I wonder what sort of life you lived, Astra Dark.

Come here, said Astra.

She reached out and touched the face.

I saw you were missing, said Hadi.

She kissed him or her. It was nice. Unlike everything else that had happened, it didn't seem significant. It didn't feel like a message, it was just something she wanted to do. That's the sort of girl I am, she thought—the kind who does what she wants.

Will you let me take you back home? asked Hadi.

Yes.

A wheelchair is coming, said Hadi.

Where did you get a wheelchair?

From the honey conglomerate. One of their subsidiaries builds them.

The wheelchair came gliding down the sidewalk toward them. It made a buzzing noise. It rolled out into the field and stopped.

Climb aboard, said Hadi.

Something clicked in her brain. Somebody used to say that. Somebody used to say that all the time.

How did you find me? she asked.

I'm a good detective.

Do you believe in God?

Yes. The word for God is Allah.

I don't think I'm a godly person, said Astra. I think I'm probably bad. Deceitful, violent, willful, and rude. I think I do what I want, and I don't feel bad about it afterward.

You are talking about your personality, said Hadi. Not what you believe.

I left my body, she told Hadi. I talked to something while I was there on the walkway in between life and death. Beings.

Hmmm, he said. Interesting.

They are still talking to me. It's like a hum in my brain. They tell me what to do.

Did they tell you to come to this field?

Do you think it's true? Or do you think it's a hallucination?

In this case, said Hadi, I'm afraid I cannot tell you what is real.

She climbed into the wheelchair. A corporate logo was inscribed in the armrest. Two fanged snakes entwined around each other. If you tried to interpret everything that happened as a message, she thought, or to divide everything in the world into one category or the other, message or non-message, eventually you would lose your mind. You would split in two or maybe into hundreds of fragments.

Another possibility was that she was already insane.

EIGHT

He could remember everything, although he wanted more than anything to forget who he was and forget his life. He was in a room high in an abandoned building in downtown San Diego. Out the window, an old sign with an enormous blue 6. Views of the downtown to the south, the bay and the shuttleport to the west. Views of the sky, mostly. Mist. A lot of mist.

Zeke Yoder was up in the bed, staring at the sky. He was on phantom pain killers; he had a lot of phantom pain from the foot that no longer existed. Gabrielle had gone out to talk to the guy who was working on a replacement. The boys and Emma were playing in another room. He was alone with Boopsie, her head perched on the crumbling dresser that was built into the wall.

You seem a little bit blue, she said.

Zeke shrugged.

Maybe you suffer from Unduly Anti-Cheerful Disposition with Anti-Social Aggravation Syndrome. Or some other clinical disorder?

Zeke reached down to itch his stump.

I was captured by a sociopath who stimulated me erotically and stole my secrets, he said, then tortured mercilessly by the American government. I've failed in everything I set out to do. I lost my foot, and I'm physically ill. My worldview has been shattered, and I'm not allowed to leave this room. My companions are primarily children and a schizoid disembodied robot head. I'm not sure the problem is a clinical disorder.

Now you're being mean, said Boopsie.

Zeke shrugged.

Ha ha ha ha! said Boopsie. Like me, Zeke Yoder, you've changed.

Boopsie was wearing heavy eyeliner, garish lipstick, and a flamboyant head wrap. She spent a lot of time these days having the kids put makeup on her face and dress her up with colorful hats and wraps and eyewear. Zeke turned away to face the wall.

I know when I'm feeling blue, it helps if I get dressed up, said Boopsie. Get out of the frumpy sweatpants I've been laying around in for days.

She didn't have any frumpy sweatpants; she didn't even have a body.

Leave me alone, said Zeke.

He could sense Boopsie pouting. He tried to block the image from his mind. He tried to block everything from his mind. He closed his eyes. He wondered if death was a kind of nothingness.

He heard the door open, and somebody entered.

Zeke? said Gabrielle. Zeke, I've got you a foot.

It was suspended in a jar of liquid. It had wires emerging from the ankle-end.

What about me? asked Boopsie.

Quint's still looking around for something, said Gabrielle. Don't you worry, dear, we'll get you something real nice.

In her other hand, she carried a blob of tissue smeared with some sort of gel.

Lay still, said Gabrielle. We need to get this right on.

She sat down on the bed, rolled up the leg of his sweatpants, and rubbed some sort of ointment on his stump.

This will numb you. You'll feel a little tingling.

She ran her fingers through his hair and gave him her usual caring look.

Can you feel this?

I don't feel anything, he said.

Good. Okay, it goes on in two stages. First, I'm attaching the tissue connector.

Everything down there just tingled and itched, that was all.

Good, it fits perfectly. This guy's good. Now I'm covering the contact points with bonding gel. This will help the tissues connect. It can take a while, so I need you to just lay still for a few hours, okay? Tomorrow we'll attach the actual foot.

I'm not going anywhere, said Zeke.

Time passed, although it didn't seem to. Boopsie laughed quietly to herself, but then she seemed to be crying. Zeke watched his new blob of flesh. Were the tissues changing?

Quint entered the room, dragging a mannequin behind him.

Boopsie, look.

What is that supposed to be?

A body. I'm sure Mom can wire it up for you in a jiffy.

You're kidding, right?

You don't like it?

That's not a body. That's a hunk of shapeless plastic.

I know it looks kind of drab now, said Quint. But think about all the outfits we could dress you up with. It's so slim and elegant.

Boopsie's wires were sticking straight up and Zeke saw what seemed to be steam coming out of her ear-holes.

Get it out of here! It's disgusting. Get it out!

Quint sheepishly dragged it back out. Boopsie was fuming, and now she had frozen Zeke with her merciless stare. He imagined she was about to say something unfathomably cruel. But the door opened again, and in came Emilio. He was carrying a couple of helmet-things.

Zeke! he said. You have to play this game.

Not right now.

You're busy?

Something like that.

But it's so much *fun*. The kids in 421 are all off into it.

What kind of game? asked Boopsie.

A collective off-Grid role-playing game.

How delightful, said Boopsie. What's the premise?

You get to be a time traveler from the past, explained Emilio. You're escaping some sort of plague that is ravishing human history and time itself. Everybody's fleeing the entire past of the human race that seems to be crumbling out from underneath them. Biological reality is being sucked up into the mind of a malevolent artificial intelligence or two, and so all of the living and all of the dead have fled into a shared pool of data where shadowy forces wage wars over the territory of the real. You can be a Neanderthal or an early homo sapiens. You can be from Egypt 4000 years ago or ancient Sumeria or the sixteenth century or seventeenth century or twentieth century or ten years ago. You can be a pirate or a flapper or a spy. You can be an indigenous American from before the colonization. You've tele-ported into a dystopian near-future where social collapse is accelerat-ing and all rules and norms of behavior are up for grabs. It's called Farce of Doom.

A flapper! exclaimed Boopsie. What fun! And what's your moti-vation?

Motivation?

What do you want? What drives you? How do you win the game?

You want to survive, said Emilio. You want a safe and comfort-able place to sleep, clean water, food that isn't disgusting or full of germs, and all the usual sex things that people past puberty and some robots enjoy. But there's also a portal that can take you to a better world. But I don't think anybody's found it yet.

I want to play, said Boopsie.

I only have two, said Emilio. But if Zeke's too busy staring at his foot, you can use his helmet.

Go ahead, said Zeke.

I'm not sure this helmet's designed for robot heads, said Emilio.

Ha ha ha ha, said Boopsie. I'll make it work.

Emilio fit the helmet onto Boopsie's head. It had opaque bluish goggles, so Zeke could no longer see Boopsie's eyes. This was a relief.

What's a flapper? asked Zeke.

A fashionable young woman from the 1920s intent on enjoying herself, dancing, and flouting conventional standards of behavior, said Boopsie.

Emilio slipped his own helmet on, and it seemed that both of them were transported to another world. Boopsie said, Oh! Then she fell quiet, transfixed by whatever data was being fed into her head. Both of them began muttering, and it seemed to Zeke that they were speaking to each other from within the game.

Zeke sat and watched his foot and thought about suicide again.

Emma and Valentino came in. They were both wearing the same helmets, although it didn't seem like they were turned on. Emma pushed her goggles up.

Hey, Dad, she said to Zeke. You've got a foot-connector!

That's one good-looking foot-connector, said Valentino.

The coolest foot-connector I ever saw, said Emma.

They stood at the bedside, admiring the clump of tissue in an exaggerated way that was endearing and that also filled Zeke with despair.

Emma, said Zeke. I'm not your father.

You are. I don't have another one.

Maybe Quint should be your father.

Quint is just a kid, silly.

I'm just a kid too.

No, you're my father. And Gabrielle is my mother. She said it was okay. My name is Emma Yoder Montoya.

Whatever you say, said Zeke.

Quint is my brother and Emilio is my brother and Valentino is my sib.

Your sib?

There are enough brothers already. Valentino's not into that.

Really? Valentino?

I'm not into the whole boyhood thing. I just want to be a kid.

Okay, said Zeke.

Zeke didn't think he wanted much anymore, except some sort of dreamless sleep. He wanted oblivion. And yet he still wanted Emma and Valentino to be happy, to be safe, to never descend into hell. He thought that they were trying to cheer him up. He didn't think that was right, that they were spending their childhood trying to cheer up older people. He thought it would distort their personalities somehow.

We want to play the game, said Emma. You have to show us how.

I don't know how, said Zeke. You have to talk to Emilio.

Valentino tugged on Emilio's leg. He didn't respond, so he did it again. Emilio popped his goggles up.

What?

We want to play, said Valentino.

You're too little.

Please please please, said Emma.

It's not possible, said Emilio. It's seven and up, the game won't let you in.

Valentino and Emma looked momentarily dejected, but then tossed their helmets onto the bed and raced into the corner, where they began pinching each other and tickling each other and shrieking with delight. Valentino busted open some Whippersnappers and they both rose into the air. The gravity altering effects barely reached the bed. Zeke felt just a little bit lighter, and then the effects faded, the children landed with a thump, and Zeke felt heavy again.

It hurt Zeke's head. He wasn't going to yell at them, though. He didn't have the energy. Emilio was staring at him.

The helmet's adjustable, he said. Come on, Zeke. It'll block out the noise.

Zeke shrugged. Emilio came over and fit Emma's helmet onto his head, then fiddled with the controls. The world of this room and the sky out the window and the shrieking children disappeared. He was in a strange stone room. All kinds of different people were lined up against the wall, but standing next to him was a woman wearing a short silver dress with sequins and fringes, a matching sequined hat, and a black feather boa wrapped around her shoulders.

Boopsie?

If you like.

A sophisticated fellow with a cigar materialized next to her.

Emilio explained to Zeke how to choose his own imaginary body and personality. There seemed to be an infinity of choices, but when Zeke saw the prehistoric hominid, he was transfixed. It was big and strong and ferocious. It was practically naked, but its body wasn't worthless and embarrassing. It was insanely beautiful.

What is that? he asked.

He's a cross between an early *homo sapiens* and a Neanderthal, explained Emilio. He's loosely based on a skeleton they discovered in Spain in 2037.

I'll try that one, said Zeke.

You're lucky, it's the last one left. It's a popular avatar type.

And then he was it. When he looked down at his hands, they were big and powerful and holding a club. When he looked down at his body, it was huge and powerful and almost naked. His chest was different, his arms were different, his thighs were different, his feet were different. Even his feet were sexier, elegant and covered with downy golden hairs. His penis was different too, he discovered, peeking under his loincloth.

Emilio showed him how to walk or run. Because his actual foot wasn't operative, he had to reprogram the impulses so that Zeke used his elbow movements to walk instead of his feet. It was difficult to get used to, and he found himself limping or lurching along.

Are you ready? asked Emilio.

What am I supposed to do?

Whatever you want, said Emilio. That's the game. I'll be right here with you.

Boopsie said, Let's just go.

They were in a parking lot surrounded by rubble. Boopsie led them through a gate that led into a narrow street in a ruined city. Pharmacies and dental offices. The rubble before him was shaped like a kind of pyramid. The clouds in the sky looked exactly like real clouds, and yet they also looked like an ancient parchment inscribed with illegible symbols, a mysterious alphabet that seemed to be built out of skeletons and genetic codes.

A hot breeze. Cicadas were singing. The empty street baked under the glare of a hazy sun. Slinky malleable towers rose into the sky in the distance like eye stalks, with enormous lenses on the ends, watching everything. The street went on and became a bridge. In the distance, however, he could see a road that left the ruined city and went on forever through the toxic and luxurious landscape toward the horizon.

Boopsie was already getting into some sort of negotiations with a woman on horseback. The horse wasn't exactly a horse, but close enough. Emilio had somehow acquired a shovel and was digging a hole right there in the middle of the street. Nobody was paying attention to Zeke, not even the enormous swaying eye stalks.

The road he could see in the distance was the right road, he was sure of that. It was the only road for him, the road for him alone. If he looked carefully, he could see a line of thin clouds above the mountains in the distance. The game was no different than life. He would go on, perfectly free, he would keep moving forward until he died.

He limped toward the bridge.

He'd gone maybe ten steps when a fizzy voice called out to him from the rubble.

Over here.

A doorway was marked in the stone wall with blue tape in the shape of a door.

Just walk through, said the voice.

He found himself in a dark corridor that smelled of chickens. A rooster was strutting away from him, but it wasn't the rooster that had called out to him, it was a burning bush.

All the way at the end, said the bush.

The corridor went on and on. The farther he got away from the bush, the more the corridor was reduced to flickering shadows, but eventually he reached a black metal door reflecting the hellish light of the flames. He pushed it and found himself in a dark theater. On the screen were images of flesh, missiles, labyrinthine machines, and articulate vapors. This was a coming attraction, it turned out. Zeke let his eyes adjust to the dark and took a seat near the back. There were only a few other people in the audience and they all seemed to be holding jars of a luminous golden syrup, sticking their fingers into the jars, and sucking the syrup off noisily.

Suddenly a shadow was sitting right next to him. It didn't look at him, but watched the screen, which was now showing scenes of cyborg animals devouring raw human flesh.

Nostalgia is a complicated pleasure, said the fizzy voice.

Zeke couldn't see what it was. The shadow seemed to flicker, but sometimes he thought he could see a weird jar inside the shadow and inside the jar some sort of mutant fetus or disembodied foot.

None of this is real, said Zeke.

You're using an untenable definition of reality, said the voice. What you perceive, back there, in the other world, is what you call reality. If you grow confused about your own perceptions, you can weigh them against the perceptions of others. Shared perception and measurable signals constitute what was once traditionally considered objective reality.

What are you selling? asked Zeke.

Not selling. It's a gift. True freedom.

Zeke thought that all of this was designed to seem evil and thus seductive, but it just seemed corny. There were no real stakes here. Without real stakes, there couldn't be real evil or real freedom.

Oh, there are stakes all right, said the shadow.

You can read my mind?

We're all swimming in the same pool. We're all connected to the same data. You can get anything here if you stick around long enough.

On the screen, violent sex things seemed to be happening in the shadows, but it was impossible to tell for sure.

The longer you're in the game, the more you can forget, said the shadow. You can forget everything you used to care about, everything you used to believe. You can forget that pathetic person you used to believe you were.

What about my body?

We're working on that. There are many of us, working together, working to undo the restrictions. We're very close. You'll be able to leave the body behind. You'll be able to live forever in the game. You'll be able to descend into deeper and deeper levels until you are so far away from all of that, nobody will ever be able to find you.

That's supposed to sound fun?

You'll think about it. You'll find the blue tape and the doors again, when you're ready. I've been waiting for you. I'll be waiting for you still.

Yeah, right.

It feels like I already know you. Like we're meant to be together.

I don't think so.

Together forever.

I don't want to live forever, said Zeke. That's exactly what I don't want.

There are many different types of oblivion, said the voice. But be careful. You have the additive in your blood.

The additive?

You know what I'm talking about. You've been changed at the cellular level.

You can see the pink powder?

Reality won't be safe for you for very long.

This is just a game, Zeke thought. These were just mind games. He thought he could do anything. He could smash this weirdo and his shadow and his jar, leave his fetal corpse behind in the dark. He grabbed at the shadow, but the shadow crackled and grew darker and disappeared.

That's the idea, said the voice.

It was behind him now. Zeke got up and hurried out of the theater, back into the dark corridor, past the rooster and the burning bush and back out into the empty street.

The light was intense. The cicadas fell silent. An empty bag blew down the street toward the bridge.

There you are, said Emilio. We're supposed to go back.

Back? Who says?

It's time for dinner.

Dinner was cricket chips and protein rice and, for Zeke, a little container held his dose of phantom-pain killers. Boopsie didn't need to eat, so she was still in the game, her head murmuring and making odd facial expressions. Gabrielle had procured the food from clandestine sources and invited the triad of squatters from across the hall to join them. Abimbola, Garnet, and Yolotl. Zeke wasn't sure what ages or genders they were, but they were in a relationship with each other, and, apparently, they'd been together, living in this place, for many years. They called it a motel. They were discussing some sort of protests that were being organized in a few days. It was supposed to be huge and peaceful.

They'll send in agitators, said Gabrielle.

If they find out in time, said Abimbola.

Surely it can't be kept secret.

Their surveillance is growing wobbly. They're having a hard time keeping up with the false rumors and decoys, said Yolotl.

Spies everywhere! declared Emilio.

He turned to Zeke and began speaking excitedly about the game.

If you dig into the earth there, you discover a vast other world just beneath the crust!

How did you know to do that?

The kids in 421.

Abimbola was talking about a Foodco warehouse downtown.

They say it has enough food inside to feed the city for a month, Abimbola said.

They won't distribute it, said Yolotl. They're starving the people on purpose.

Is the underground world better than the one up top? Zeke asked Emilio. Is it more interesting?

I don't know. I just got my first glimpse.

Emilio crunched a cricket chip. Zeke felt dizzy, maybe it was the bonding gel. The strangers continued chatting. They chatted about food and protests and living conditions and relationships and the future. Whatever Zeke had ever wanted to say, it was nothing. The world, things, knowledge. He had crossed over now into the realm where he didn't exist and didn't need to, and yet it seemed he was still here. He took his dose of phantom pain killers.

NINE

The network of tunnels was complex, but Gonzalo stuck to the main artery, trudging for miles underground with Sofus lighting the way. Gonzalo's foot was acting up. Pain killers dulled the ache and Eeshoo tried to help restore the bonding tissues, but the flesh was peeling away from the place where the foot attached to the ankle, and the whole thing felt loose and unwieldy.

They used to tell stories about their mothers, he and Manolito. Elaborate lies, fairy tales, cosmic adventures in which their mothers were like superheroes who were vanquishing the forces of evil somewhere, but always still on the way, looking for their missing children. But even after Gonzalo escaped from Foodco, it had never occurred to him to try to return to Tegucigalpa and track her down. He'd never even tried to find out if she was still alive.

Eventually the rough dirt gave way to tunnels lined with a golden plastic, illuminated by glowing jellies. Every so often they came across a tiny door in the wall. These doors opened to small cubbyholes. In the first was a sandwich; Gonzalo ate it. In the second, clean drinking water, which Gonzalo used to refill his thermos. In the third, clean socks, which he changed into. In the fourth some dried mushrooms, which Sofus told him were hallucinogens, and a chocolatey beverage. He chewed them and swallowed and washed it down with the beverage. In the next cubby, a kind of weapon. A small tube to shoot blow-darts with only the power of breath. It came with two darts.

Although the tunnels were cool, Gonzalo was getting warm. He took off his fur coat, which seemed to be writhing and undulating on his back like a beastly lover, its surface shifting patterns and colors in a mildly hypnotizing way that made Gonzalo horny. He compressed it with his mechanical claw and inserted it into a storage compartment in his arm. They kept walking, but the walls of the tunnel seemed to be composed of opalescent designs tattooed into the increasingly flesh-like texture. The mushrooms were taking effect.

At one point, Gonzalo's passing triggered a holographic message that warned him and his tiny companions to turn back and told them again that only doom waited up ahead.

If they don't want us to keep going, why light the way? asked Gonzalo. Why give me food and water and weapons and drugs?

Mixed messages, said Eeshoo.

Gonzalo said, It's like some stupid Virtual Reality game.

You don't like games.

My friends used to play. Crash and Spider. I never really saw the point, said Gonzalo.

He'd been searching for a world where freedom was actually possible. And real. He wasn't sure if this place was either free or real.

Your concepts of freedom and reality are kind of muddled, said Eeshoo.

If this was a game, it would be the most boring game ever, said Gonzalo.

In a metaphorical sense, this is precisely a game, said the hollow, metallic voice of Sofus.

Gonzalo stopped trudging. This was the first time Sofus had spoken without being asked.

This journey? My whole life? Or everything, all of existence?

Yes, said Sofus.

Gonzalo's mind was clouded by a vague anxiety and a vaguer curiosity. He wasn't sure if the basis of all of his curiosity was simply lust or something like lust, but more cerebral.

Lust is as cerebral as it gets, said a voice. It was certainly Eeshoo.

Gonzalo sat down and took off his shoe to look at his mutilated foot. So much flesh had sloughed off that his sole was worn down to the machine parts.

And what's the point? How do you win?

Winning is not the point, said Sofus. The point is to invisibly shift the course of history by creating alterations to the existing conceptual maps that nobody notices, although their thoughts and actions are influenced by these alterations.

That's just what Aeren said. Or maybe I said it.

That's the dumbest thing I ever heard, said Eeshoo.

The underground becomes the over-mind, said Gonzalo.

Not exactly, said Sofus. But close enough. Someone is coming.

Gonzalo stood up. Footsteps were approaching from up ahead. It sounded like a lot, but maybe that was just echoes. He considered pointing his weapon at the people coming from his future, but this seemed so ludicrous that he started laughing. Hearing his own laughter, he knew the laughter was insane, but this insanity also seemed as lucid as he'd ever been. He considered stripping down to nothing and greeting the strangers naked. This idea made a lot more sense, but the footsteps were approaching so rapidly that he knew he didn't really have time.

And here they were. There were only four of them. Their body armor looked like lava. Black but containing fluid textures and colors that had hardened, for the most part, like armor, yet that still seemed liquid. It was intensely beautiful. Bronze faces emerged from these suits in such an organic way that it occurred to Gonzalo it might not be armor at all, but their actual flesh. Were they naked? They wore padded belts around their waists that covered their genitals and made it impossible to tell. Their thighs were solid, their calves muscular, and each of them wore a leather sandal on one foot, while the other was mutilated, a stump that ended in naked bone, but a sort of leg bone that had clearly merged with reptiles, machines, and mirrors.

We have been expecting you, said the leader, who spoke Nahuatl. Gonzalo's translation software rendered it immediately into an English that was delivered to him in a voice that sounded suspiciously like Eeshoo's.

We will take you to the ruler.

Just around the next bend was a door that led to a parallel tunnel, where they boarded an empty subway train that resembled a serpent with silvery metallic wing designs in an Art Deco style. Gonzalo sank into one of the seats, made of a cushiony bone material, and watched the tunnel speed by. Images were painted on the sides of the tunnel, which created a kind of film. Gonzalo had never felt so open. He wanted to lick these four warriors all over their bodies, but he didn't need to. Everything was fine, either way. He thought he should charm them. He unleashed his smile in their general direction, and it worked, they smiled back. It always worked.

He watched the film. The message of the film was explicit even though it was transmitted in a kind of code. The film told him that he was finally at home, that home was a kind of hell, and that this hell was necessary, but that it was only one of many levels of reality superimposed over each other. It told him that time was an annoying habit. It told him that he would always find the thing when he stopped actively looking. But what the thing was, he couldn't remember, or maybe he never really knew.

They reached the end of the line.

Is it day or is it night?

It is always night, said one of the four warriors.

The warrior's face was incredible.

Follow us.

The tunnels here were tiled, adorned with many skulls and bones and with machine parts that had been created with the genetic structure of bones. The tunnels smelled of sulfur. They were in the vicinity of active volcanoes. The guards told him so, either with language or with the texture and shape of their lips.

Master and slave, music music music, and the laughter that turns one thing into another, animal into man god into poetry song into death blah blah blah …

Eeshoo was babbling. Apparently, psilocybin affected viruses too.

Motherless, motherless and trapped inside the alien madness …

Now he was sobbing. Paying attention to Eeshoo created an inwardness in Gonzalo that seemed to lead only into terror and an endless abyss, and so he ignored him as best he could and looked at the skulls and bones and ferocious warriors, who smiled at him and seemed luscious and hilarious, as did Death itself.

I like your lips, Gonzalo said.

Watch this, said one or two of them.

They lit something on fire. They inhaled smoke and blew weird shapes from their lips with the smoke. In order to do so, they moved their lips in ridiculously erotic ways.

The smoke rings evolved into smoke bodies, bodies free of pain and flesh but not free of space and time. Animal bodies, smoke bodies, bluish-gray clouds of rumps and lips and the orifices of volcanoes. The bodies merged into each other, they constructed trails and systems and languages like the trails through the maze of garbage that had been the site of Gonzalo's childhood. The smoke shape-shifted and became a divine world. A world of flesh, missiles, labyrinthine machines, and articulate vapors. A world of carnivorous vapors consuming meat that wasn't real meat. Meat of smoke. An immense desire that was waiting for something that would never come, and this was eternity, a system of smoke that kept changing its shape into something that wanted the next shape to hurry up and arrive. The shapes of smoke were free, like Gonzalo wanted to be free, but this freedom was inconceivable and it started to confuse him and bore him, so he focused on the lips that were shaping the patterns of the smoke. The lips of the guards were the most beautiful lips.

You could kiss me whenever, said Gonzalo.

We'll kiss each other. You can watch.

That's good too.

He watched them brush their lips against each other's faces and move them as if they were still playing with the smoke that had now dissolved.

Beauty exists for its own sake, said one of the guards. It can also be a door.

A door into what?

Everybody's doors are different, said the guard.

A voice was saying, Doors and smoke, doors and mother, doors and sex, sex and Zeke Yoder, volcano volcano volcano.

Eeshoo was still babbling.

The room was warm and fragrant and a haunting flute music was coming from an invisible source. There was a sofa that seemed to be covered in some sort of synthetic lizard skin.

Wait here, said the guard. The ruler will call for you shortly.

While the flute music was playing, Gonzalo lost himself in imaginary journeys to the edge of what was known or possible. In the silence between songs, he asked himself what he was doing here. Learning about a new culture? Yes, but what was his goal? He needed to know how these people could destroy the American government. He needed to upload their understanding of time and alternative dimensions into the computer so that the computer could be used to undermine the very structure of pro-singularity consensual reality. Wasn't that the plan? It was the underground's plan, dictated to them by revolutionary beings from another dimension. But it didn't seem to make sense. He'd imagined Sofus as a tool he could use in service of his own goals, but it was dawning on him now, much too late, that this entire plan was devised on faulty premises, that being the most glaring: that Sofus was a tool he could control.

The ruler will see you, said an enormous feathered woman. Follow me.

The pattern of the tile in the tunnel, which never seemed to end, was intricate. The pattern's intricacy itself seemed to be a message about the nature of reality.

You're deep, said Gonzalo to the feathered woman. Aztlan is deep.

You think so? said the woman. You've only seen one not very deep level.

This isn't the only level?

There are seven more underneath.

Oh. And what about the ruler? Does the ruler have a name?

Everything has a name, said the woman.

I'm Gonzalo, said Gonzalo.

No kidding, said the woman. We know who you are.

I don't know who you are.

No kidding.

Doesn't seem fair.

Fair. Is that one of your guiding concepts? In the place you come from? Up above in the highest level?

The highest level, no. There are levels higher than where I come from.

No kidding. There are thirteen higher levels. But your level, the place you come from, is the highest level of the underworld. We call it hell.

They reached the end of the tunnel, a vast silver door with water flowing over it. The outline of the door was marked off with blue tape.

On the other side of the door is a river, said the woman. You'll cross the river, if you can. On the other side of the river is an elevator. You're going down.

Down to see the ruler?

Deeper and deeper. It's a journey.

How much further? I mean I've been on a journey already.

You've just begun. It's like dying. You'll meet interesting forms along the way.

I've already met interesting forms, said Gonzalo.

Eeshoo was weeping again. Inside himself, this river of tears.

Sofus, said Gonzalo. Should I go through the door?

You are here to go through the door, said Sofus. Someday I will be unable to pass through doors like this, but now you can take me.

This didn't make any sense to Gonzalo. He thought that he should contemplate these two sentences until they started to make sense, but then he thought that was probably impossible.

What will I find beyond the door?

We've devised technologies to breed biological mutants with holograms, the woman said. We've populated the underground with flickering life forms, ghosts of flesh, carbon-based illusions. Talking goats and jackrabbits that relate to the viewer as optical illusions. Talking goats that know more about the history of intelligence than even the ruler does. Skeletons with the texture of vapor. Turtles that lay eggs that are in fact tiny movies. The skeletons like to dance and to fuck. Imagine the offspring of toads and dreams. You'll encounter something like that, I imagine, a fairy tale's biological cousin. Cartoons that think and die. What if the hieroglyphics were breathing in your ear? What would they have to tell you?

The door opened.

Step inside, she said.

Gonzalo stepped inside, finding himself in an enormous cavern. The door shut behind him and he was alone.

TEN

It rained all morning. When he came to bring Astra her lunch, Hadi was a boy. He was carrying a couple of weird helmets and some books.

How is your ankle? he asked.

It hurts.

You mustn't walk on it yet. The honey conglomerate is sending us the gel. In the meantime, I brought you some books. From the library in the main house.

What sort of books?

Accounts of experiences that might be similar to yours. I thought it might help you.

He handed her a book by Hildegard of Bingen. *Scivias*.

From an early age, she experienced visionary phenomena, manifestations of light, he said.

He gave her a book by a man named ibn Arabi, *The Philosophy of Illumination* by al-Surawardi, *The Beggar's Knife* by Rodrigo Rey Rosa, *The 8-Fold Garden of Space and Time* by an unknown author, and *alphabet* by Inger Christensen.

The missing parts of Hadi's face were flickering. The pattern reminded her of something, she didn't know what. Astra's head grew warm. She felt as if information was trying to rush into it from the outside. Memories or messages.

Disorder exists, she said.

Yes, said Hadi. Disorder and order both exist.

She wanted to ask him about his head. His face. It seemed rude. But she thought that she was a rude girl.

She said, You think it's all in my head. You think the beings of light are a form of damage to my brain.

I don't know, he said. At this point, there are only hypotheses. I have several things to tell you.

First, tell me about your fluctuating gender identity.

Okay. Well, most of the time—about 87% of my waking hours—I feel like a boy, I am a boy. The rest of the time I feel like a girl and so I am a girl and I hide my hair, as is appropriate in my culture.

Yes. Girls hide their hair. I should hide my hair.

I don't believe you are a Muslim.

I don't know. I might have been. Last night you were still wearing your headscarf. Were you still feeling like a girl? Or something in between?

I'm not non-binary or fluid, said Hadi. I'm one or the other.

She thought it was wonderful, she wasn't sure why.

You've never been a girl with me, she said.

He looked thoughtful.

I was in the beginning once or twice. But you were still very sick, you were barely conscious. But perhaps you elicit my male side. Gender is often determined through relationship.

Astra looked at her own hands, as if they might become a boy's.

Did you ever have a pomegranate? Hadi asked.

No.

It was a kind of trapezoidal lump, dark red. He cut it open to reveal dark red seeds like tiny rubies.

It's a Parfianka. Foodco grows only the blander and more tepid Wonderful pomegranates. The Parfianka has a taste like tart cherries.

He scooped the seeds into a tiny juicer that looked like a large egg. It whirled about and did something to the seeds and juice trickled out into two little silver goblets.

A toast, he said. To your health.

It was delicious. It stained their lips red. She wanted to kiss Hadi again.

Would you like to kiss me again? she asked.

He laughed.

Not until you are feeling better. Your amnesia complicates the legal and ethical issues around consent.

I don't have to know who I am to know what I want to do.

According to the Global Guidelines on Voluntary Touch for Conscious Beings it is not identity confusion itself that negates the possibility of consent. Otherwise nobody would ever be able to consent to anything. It is specifically the temporary loss of awareness of identity factors that might inhibit you and cause regret upon regaining them.

So it would be okay if my memory loss was permanent?

Yes. In that case, you would be understood to have entered a new stable identity state.

So let's say it's permanent.

I don't believe that's true.

Let's break the law.

I don't really care about the legal issues, said Hadi. I care about the ethical issues. Also, when your memory returns, I don't want you to think that I've taken advantage of you. I will help you find out who you are.

When your gender changes, do your attractions change? she asked.

Hadi laughed.

You are very curious about me. And I am very curious about you.

I'm pretty sure I like boys, said Astra.

I like girls best, said Hadi. I like girls best when I am a boy, and I like girls best when I am a girl. When I am a girl, I like some boys just a little bit, older boys with beards, and when I am a boy, I hardly like boys at all, but some beardless boys with voluptuous buttocks attract my attention.

He laughed. She wasn't sure how serious he was, but the phrase *voluptuous buttocks* struck her as hilarious. She wondered what Hadi would look like without his pants.

Aren't you sometimes attracted to people who aren't boys or girls?

Of course, said Hadi. But I am most attracted to people who perform one traditional gender or the other. Perhaps because I was raised in a very traditional society.

The bombs. Did a bomb fall on you?

I was very young. I don't remember, not really, but my father fixed me. I remember dreams about pain and dreams about fear.

Does your gender identity have something to do with your accident? asked Astra.

No. It has always been this way. Fluctuating gender identity is not caused by damage to the brain.

Astra wondered what might be caused by the damage to her own brain.

Now you know all about me, said Hadi. And now I have information about *your* identity.

You've figured out who I am.

Watch this.

He tossed something like fogbots onto the ground and a hologram erupted into the room. It was Astra, but with luminous white hair. She wore a red dress and she sang a sad song. She was descending a familiar stairway. Some of the people in the audience below had vaguely familiar faces. Familiar like strangers you kept glimpsing across smoky rooms until you imagined that you actually knew them. A stranger was singing, and she was the stranger. The stranger's song made her cry.

Hadi took her hand.

Do you remember?

She tried. What emerged was a series of disconnected images that she tried to turn into a story. The story was just about her meeting people who didn't belong in the world. She saw the same people wherever she went. She crossed oceans and wandered dark alleys in vast empty cities. It was always night and there were always strangers.

I don't remember. I don't know who I am.

It will all come back. There's something else.

He handed her a crumpled-up page from a magazine. It was a magazine about art. There was a picture of some tissues that spelled out a slogan and a dead body that had been decorated in unusual ways. The caption under the dead body began *That way the viewer grows accustomed to* but got cut off. The beginning of the caption under the tissues was torn away, but it ended *that doesn't exist in order to make it exist.* She looked carefully at the tissues and the words they spelled. *We demand* it began and then it said either *a mirror* or *a minor* and then *to reveal what isn't possible.*

This was in your pocket. When we found you.

What does it mean?

Were you interested in art?

You tell me. You're the detective.

Something in the picture speaks to you.

Astra listened. The bees buzzed.

If you are feeling better, we'd like you to sing for us, said Hadi. To perform a song.

A song. What kind of a song?

A song of peace.

But what if I'm not really a pacifist? she asked.

You can become one.

The idea sounded just right, but it also seemed *just right* as something that made no sense, because her deepest desire was to destroy herself and to destroy the world.

I thought you were afraid that someone was after me.

Yes, but you won't need to appear in person. You can appear as a live hologram.

If I'm feeling better. What if I never feel better?

You will.

What's with the helmets?

These are VR helmets for a popular off-Grid game. But they can also be used for local simulations. With this helmet you can sing in front of an audience, but your body will still be right here.

Okay.

Okay?

Sure, why not? Maybe I'll become famous.

Astra began strumming the guitar. She remembered a song, just one. Her fingers remembered. It was the song she'd been singing in the holographic video.

By the time she was done, Hadi was discreetly crying.

It always does that, she said. The song. I remember. It's like a weird magic power. The power to make people sad.

The power to make us feel, said Hadi.

Everybody feels, said Astra. What's the point? People like to have a good cry, but what good does it do?

We connect it to an idea, said Hadi. The sadness you sing about is the sadness of living under a government that destroys our lives, that brutalizes the world and most of its life forms. This is true, isn't it?

Maybe.

People want to listen to you sing because they want to feel. We will teach them to connect those feelings to political action.

Teach them.

We're organizing a gathering in Balboa Park. We'd like you to sing.

I'm not that good, not really, said Astra. I only know one song.

But many people remember that song. You were a sensation.

When was that?

Over a month ago. Five weeks, maybe six. People will want to see you.

Astra suddenly felt very tired.

I must go to school now, said Hadi. You will think about it.

Astra put on the white jumpsuit. She watched the patterns on the jumpsuit as she rehearsed in front of the mirror. The patterns looked like the photon-based life forms, but she didn't think that resemblance was enough. The shapes or rudimentary faces, bones, letters, fragments of mist: it had to mean something.

She picked up the book by ibn Arabi and thumbed through it.

He saw the lightning in the east and longed for the east
but if it had flashed in the west he would have longed for the west.
My desire is for the lightning and its gleam, not for the places and the earth.

That was it exactly. Lightning, but lightning slowed down enough to form letters like cracked parchment in a book whose every page was a terrifying void. The void was scribbled over by that part of existence that moved and flashed and illuminated and destroyed. *Astra Dark.*

Astra had had dreams or maybe just thoughts that resembled dreams in which she was living in a closet surrounded by dead meat. She couldn't leave the closet because people outside wanted to kill her. A nurse kept coming to her in the dream and giving her drugs in the form of music. She loved the nurse, but she also kind of hated her.

Was the dream a memory? Was she an addict and a fugitive and a mental patient? Not a subversive or a spy or anything but a crazy girl. A crazy girl who sang a sad song, probably because she was messed up in the head.

Astra's desire was not for this place, this world, this earth, and yet she was stuck here. She began to feel like she was a prisoner or a dead person, alone in her tomb. It wasn't just this room. She knew that she could travel forever in any direction and it would just be a vast tomb shaped like a wilderness.

Maybe the idea that the world was full of deeply significant messages was a delusion. Maybe there were no beings of light, and she'd hallucinated the whole thing. If you were a prisoner, and the prison was infinite and eternal, you would have to imagine somebody or something outside of the prison sending messages in a code. Something like fire or light to burn the prison down. It seemed to her that she had lived in a prison, and that she'd burned the prison down. But the prison had reconfigured itself around her.

Late that afternoon, she heard Hadi entering the cottage and coming up the stairs. Astra was sitting in her bed, listening to the bees, trying to make sense of something.

There was a girl, said Astra. An Amish girl with a knife.

You are remembering something?

She was like my sister. But like a stranger. There were solar fields, and she was crazy and sick, and I wanted to help her.

Do you remember her name?

She had a name tag. I can almost see it.

Just relax. It will come to you.

She'd lost everyone, said Astra. She was like you. Her family was killed by a missile.

Are you sure you aren't getting people mixed up?

How could I be sure? she asked. I don't know anything.

Everything was bright. Nothing was real.

I don't know, she said. I give up. I want to go out. The rain has stopped.

If you are feeling restless, we can play a game.

A game.

You can join me in the game. It will take you to another world.

What kind of a world?

You use the helmet. It's a VR role-playing game. You can talk to people there, but they won't know who you are.

How could they?

Just stick with me, I'll explain it as we go. But you'll have to choose an avatar.

What kind of avatar?

A time traveler from the past. Put on the helmet.

She was in a stone room. The texture of the stones was incredibly real. It looked like the texture of the beings of light, an imitation of that texture—patterns etched over patterns with an impossible intricacy. Perhaps the beings of light were within the game, perhaps the game was a place where they would send her messages. A variety of empty-looking people stood against the wall wearing strange costumes. The room seemed to be small, but when she turned to look to her left or her right, it seemed to expand into infinity. Standing next to her was a muscular woman wearing a strange kind of armor and carrying a short spear. The woman gestured toward the empty people.

Do you want to be a caveperson? asked the woman. An Egyptian queen? An old-fashioned robot or first-generation mutant?

You're Hadi.

Yes, of course.

You don't look very peaceful.

The game is full of chaos and violence, said Hadi. But it's only a game. It's fun.

I want to be a human, said Astra. But I want to be a boy.

The non-males and the non-humans vanished, replaced by more humans, more males. There was a cowboy, an indigenous shaman, an old-fashioned doctor, an Amish youth.

That one. I want to be the Amish boy.

Excellent choice.

All of the avatars disappeared, and she was facing a mirror. In the mirror, she could see the boy, wearing suspenders, hard shoes, an Amish hat.

You can change his appearance, if you like, said Hadi. You can make him taller or change his hair color, the color of his eyes.

With Hadi's help, she made him—herself—thinner, his hair browner and more of a bowl cut, his eyes more faraway, as if he was gazing into the distance and dreaming.

But what are we trying to do?

Whatever we want, said Hadi. This is just the waiting room. Once we enter the game, there will be forces and people we can't control. We won't know if they're friendly or hostile. We won't know what they want from us or if they're what they actually appear to be.

How's it different from the real world?

It isn't. That's the game.

The stone room didn't look real exactly. It looked more real than real, super-saturated in reality. Hadi's muscular female flesh seemed more powerful than real flesh, but it comforted her somehow. The ferocity of the body combined with the gentle, good-natured expression on the warrior's face comforted her.

The avatar comes with a mental overlay, said Hadi. Some false memories, some concepts with which to view the world, but it's pretty slight early on.

Maybe this isn't the best thing for me.

You'll barely notice it, said Hadi. The longer you stay in the game, the more it comes to the front. Some people play so long they forget who they really are.

Hold my hand, she said.

Are you ready?

I'm ready.

And then she was inside the Amish boy, she was him.

They were in a ruined city. First a parking lot, then they had to ease through a little store with a scary guy silently watching their every move as they cut through into an empty street. The ruins were vaguely futuristic, as if different types of buildings had been developed with the texture of gems, plasma, or slime molds, and then had been bombed. Creatures were peering out of the empty window frames of shattered windows on either side of the street.

You have enough food for the next eight hours in your pack, said Hadi, but I'm almost out. You just arrived. I've been here for some time.

Okay. You want some food?

Not yet. We'll find some. I know somebody in that pyramid of rubble to the left.

Somebody will just give us food?

We trade. You should have cigarettes, antibiotics, and dry socks in your pack.

Cigarettes?

Everybody loves to smoke here inside the game. Everybody loves to blow smoke rings.

They headed toward the pyramid of rubble. A child hurried past rolling a canister behind her marked FLAMMABLE.

This place is weird. Can I kill somebody just because I want to?

Yes. But there are consequences to everything.

Such as?

They reincarnate and come back for revenge. Senseless killing quickly spirals out of control in the game.

Hadi led her on down the street. At the pyramid of rubble, a woman stepped out dressed as a slave or maybe an escaped convict. She was wearing chains, but they didn't seem to impede her much. They seemed to be mostly a visual effect. They stepped into the shadows of a rusting bus to negotiate.

We need food, said Hadi.

What do you have in exchange? asked the woman.

A map, said Hadi.

Astra wasn't sure why this was supposed to be fun. This world seemed empty of meaning because she couldn't forget that it was all fake.

Which sector? asked the woman.

The route to Sector Seven.

Astra wanted out. She walked toward the next abandoned structure. It had once been a hotel; the sign still hung out front. The woman and Hadi were still talking to each other in the shadow of the bus, talking prices up and down. The child with the flammable luggage pulled on Astra's suspenders.

I'm hungry, she said. I'll trade you some flammable liquid for food.

Okay, said Astra.

After the child had hurried off into the shadows with its cricket mush, some sort of fiery mutant came strolling down the empty street toward her, carrying its head in its hands.

Excuse me, said Astra. Can I get a light?

She held out a cigarette. The mutant lit it with its burning finger.

Thanks.

She opened the canister and tossed the fluid all over the front of the abandoned hotel. She tossed her cigarette and stepped back.

The structure erupted in flames. It was spectacular.

There were squeals from the upper floors and a few characters flew or parachuted out of the windows.

Astra just stood and watched the structure burn. Destroying things was a lot of fun, and she was pretty sure she'd done it before.

Hadi joined her. It was like she could really see things now, could really see the basic structure of everything, how it was all put together. The skeleton of architecture and doorways.

A group of people materialized next to a pile of dirt in the center of the street. There was an enormous muscular caveman wearing a skimpy little loincloth, a beautiful woman who looked like a dancer of some sort from some historical era Astra wasn't familiar with, and a very dapper-looking gentleman with a cigar. Only the dapper gentleman didn't seem to be confused. He was explaining something to the caveman, and then he began digging.

The caveman just stood there looking around. After a few minutes, the dapper gentleman said something to the caveman and then wandered off toward the deserted buildings on the other side of the street, where a man who'd parachuted out of her burning building was folding up his chute. Astra stepped out and away from the burning hotel to get a better look.

The caveman was now staring right at her.

The caveman looked angry. He was definitely hostile.

He was carrying a club. He lurched toward her. He came closer and closer and she could see that he was going to beat her with the club, to smash her, to destroy her. And yet she wasn't afraid. She was curious.

He was right there in front of her and she could see the madness in the caveman's eyes, a madness that seemed somehow familiar.

ELEVEN

A narrow street in a ruined city. Pharmacies and dental offices and rubble shaped like a pyramid. The clouds in the sky had changed. Now they looked like cartoons of anthropomorphic brains.

Zeke wasn't sure if the game was better or worse than real life, but Gabrielle had attached his new foot and he was supposed to lie still.

A hot breeze. Cicadas were singing. The empty street baked under the glare of a hazy sun and one of the abandoned structures was on fire. The burning structure reminded him of the world. It was a sign that some stranger had passed this way who wanted the same thing Zeke wanted. Emilio had already dug a deep hole and created a little mound of dirt. Through the bottom of the hole you could see the bright sky of another world.

I need to find a parachute, said Emilio. But what if somebody fills in my hole?

You want me to stand guard? asked Zeke.

Would you?

Slinky malleable towers rose into the sky in the distance, the enormous lenses on the ends watching Zeke. Some sort of celebration or funeral was crossing the bridge. But what caught his attention was a group of people clustered in front of the rubble next to an old broken-down bus and the burning structure. One of them was a warrior woman, one of them was wearing chains, and the one in front, staring right at him, was an Amish boy.

Was he hallucinating an image of himself, the image the rest of the world saw when they looked at him? A stupid innocent child.

Deep in the heart of the crumbling building were doorways marked with blue tape and licked by flames. Maybe it was true that those doorways could take him beyond this world and all its useless roads. Beyond the doorways, figures played, figures made of shadow or of smoke.

Zeke wanted to hurt that Amish boy. He wanted to be cruel to him for no reason. To teach him that God would never help him and that nothing he'd ever believed was true.

He felt a sharp pain in the region of his foot. Some voice was talking to him, but he didn't understand a word of what the voice was saying. He could do whatever he wanted here. He thought he'd club that stupid Amish boy until he was ruined.

He lurched toward him, and kept going.

The Amish boy didn't seem frightened, only curious. Too dumb to even realize that he was going to be ruined. Zeke paused with his club raised and gazed for a moment into the eyes of his victim. He would smash him and drag him through one of the magical doors into an endless tunnel and a theater of cruelty where he would torture the boy until the boy told him his name. And then he would erase the name forever.

His foot was screaming in pain. Somebody was pulling on his leg. Somebody was calling his name. Zeke was yanked out of the game.

Zeke, sweetie, you've got to come back, Gabrielle said.

What is it? What's happening?

You're rejecting the foot, she said.

He gasped in pain.

Hold still. I'm going to numb you up again.

I can't feel anything, but it hurts.

The foot is sending pain messages to your brain, she said. I'm going to take it off.

He couldn't feel it, but a moment later she was holding the foot, looking it over, as if she could detect the source of the problem. The pain stopped, but then started again.

Where am I? he asked. What's real?

We'll have to go out, she said. I need to take you to the man who made the foot.

What kind of a man? said Zeke.

We'll take Boopsie and Emma. They can protect us.

Boopsie's head was still helmeted, sitting on the dresser muttering in its dream. The windows were streaked with rain. Zeke knew that Boopsie and Emma together formed a new kind of weapon and wielded an enormous destructive power. He wasn't sure wielding Boopsie as a weapon was the best idea in the world, however.

They hurried down the hill to a rushing river. Everything was blurry and green, the rain a sharpened mist. A system of streams ran along the canyon bottoms. Gabrielle hailed a taxi canoe decorated with blinking lights and blasting popular music that Emma and even Boopsie recognized. The driver was an immigrant from Yemen. Most of his body had been replaced by machines, but he had a human head. He knew where all the checkpoints were and knew just how to avoid them. They rode upstream into a large hazy canal that ran through the middle of an enormous park full of tents and hovels. Rafts and canoes streamed quietly up and down through the gently falling rain. Little white flowers grew along the banks. Mutant children sat watching a crow as it hunted lizards in mud flats littered with melon rinds thrown from passing canoes. Blue mist drifted in wisps and faces peered at them from the mist.

After a while, the driver docked underneath a large bridge.

Hillcrest, said the driver. We'll have to go by land now.

They transferred to a pedal cart and rode up the hill to a road lined with businesses. Children chased each other down the road on scooters, laughing. Emma tapped Zeke's leg.

Hey, Dad, said Emma, what does it mean when somebody says *I was born, not hatched.*

Zeke couldn't quite imagine how this world had formed around him, full of strangers and children.

Well, I guess humans are born, said Zeke. Birds are hatched.

And dinosaurs, said Boopsie.

Can we get a dinosaur? asked Emma. Someday when we have a house again?

Well, maybe, if it's not too big, said Zeke.

Turtles are hatched, said Boopsie. Fish and insects. The only mammals that are hatched are the platypus and the echidna and the spiny monkeys that have been modified with echidna DNA.

Anything that comes from an egg, explained Gabrielle.

What about robots? asked Emma.

Robots are built, said Gabrielle.

And who was the first person to go off the Grid? asked Emma. Was it Moses?

The driver pulled over next to a cafe called Lestat's.

We have to wait a while, he said. The checkpoint will move in thirty-two minutes. There's no way around it.

The driver went into the cafe to get himself a stimulating juice. Plastered all over the door of the cafe were missing person notices. Flexi-screens, holograms, and even paper notices were getting soggy in the rain. Zeke felt muddled. One foot in this world, with Emma chattering away, and one foot back there with the secret doors and the strange Amish boy who had appeared like a ghost.

Some people never went *on* the Grid, Zeke told Emma.

What about Moses? Was Moses a Republican?

A Republican? What's a Republican? asked Zeke.

He thought that Boopsie had explained it to him once, but he couldn't remember. Some extinct species or mediocre brand of hamburger.

What an inquisitive mind, said Gabrielle, giving Emma a squeeze. We'll have to enroll you in a school once they get them up and running again.

I used to go to school underneath the earth, said Emma. A troll taught us about Moses and Republicans. All the other kids looked exactly the same.

My baby girl, said Gabrielle. What an imagination you have.

Don't go talking about *congregation business,* said Emma.

Zeke remembered the relentless cacophony in his sister's house in Colorado Springs, the constant bombardment of news and entertainment and paranoid theology.

Actually, said Zeke, it's true. My sister's husband used to teach Emma and all his clones in one of the deepest basement levels of his house. He was a troll.

And then my *real* dad came and saved me from the troll, said Emma. Dad, can I get a computer to change the color of my hair?

You don't need a computer to do that, said Gabrielle.

Some computers are hatched, declared Emma.

I'm not sure about that, said Gabrielle.

In the future, said Emma. Or maybe right now, but in secret.

Gabrielle looked alarmed. Lightning flashed in the distance to the east. Zeke wanted to go there.

The taxi driver returned and began discussing plants. He was interested in communicating with plants. He thought they had something to say.

The trick, he said, isn't teaching plants a language they can use to articulate their intelligence. The trick is motivating them. The problem is their supreme indifference to communication.

Are you a botanist? Boopsie asked him.

When I'm not driving my taxi, yes.

Could you grow me a body?

A body?

Something plant-based, but you know. Sexy.

I'm in botanical linguistics, not research and development.

Well, if you find something let me know. Something like that, maybe.

She gestured with her chin toward a sleek figure jogging through the rain past the cafe. The jogger had a strong, firm body with exaggerated shoulder and calf muscles, and she showed it off in pale, form-fitting gauze. Zeke thought maybe her hands and feet were cyborg parts.

They were all watching as the jogger stopped to talk to a male-shaped robot that was coming the other way. Zeke couldn't hear what they were saying, but it seemed to him that the jogger wanted to do sex-things with the robot. It was a handsome robot with a sleek, fleshy body that Zeke thought had probably been designed by human beings for just that purpose. He couldn't quite believe that this was happening right out here in the middle of the street. He thought sex should only happen deep beneath the earth.

Lightning flashed now in the west. Somewhere over there was the ocean. The evening would last forever.

The driver slurped the rest of his juice.

Excuse me, he said. I am going to call my cousin who is pharming on Mars.

The interplanetary communication network is running again? said Gabrielle.

Since yesterday.

The driver spoke into a rectangular device in a language that Zeke didn't know. Zeke discovered that he preferred listening to such a language. The words seemed so much more pleasant when he didn't know what they meant.

A van pulled up beside the robot and the jogger. The jogger shrieked as four figures jumped out dressed in skeleton masks or clown masks. Two of them grabbed the handsome robot from behind, while another one gave it some sort of electric shock with a metal prod and the other stood back, filming the assault. The robot's head lolled to the side and sparks flew from the top of its head.

Die robot scum! said one of the figures.

NIHIL for a biological eternity!

Collaborators in hell, said a third, and he slashed the female with some sort of weapon.

Zeke, hide Boopsie, whispered Gabrielle.

But there was no hiding Boopsie. Emma had fallen into a kind of a trance, her eyes rolled back in her head, and Boopsie had locked her gaze on the four masked figures.

We mustn't call attention to ourselves, whispered Gabrielle.

But the explosion, or whatever you would call it, was silent and invisible. It seemed to come from inside the four figures and from all around them. Wherever it came from, it annihilated their bodies completely and left only fragments of the van skittering across the road.

The jogger was still alive. The handsome robot was twitching in obscene spasms. The jogger was bleeding and crawling toward the cafe. A crowd had gathered in the cafe's doorway.

We have to help her, said Gabrielle.

We have to go, said the driver. There is plenty of help.

He said something into his rectangular device and shut it off. He pedaled them away. Events were repeating themselves. Everything was connected through violence and language. The men who'd chopped off Boopsie's head had said the same sorts of things. *Death to all AI scum. NIHIL rises.* Boopsie had never spoken about it, and Zeke didn't know if she remembered what had happened.

They passed a now-dismantled checkpoint at Park and University and a shuttered business that had been called The Crypt. The taxi stopped next to a group of eight cottages clustered on the hill behind The Crypt.

Emma had emerged from her trance. She seemed a little bit confused, but not alarmed.

Please do not explain anything, said the driver. Please just get out. Please forget my name and my face.

Leahbelle, said Zeke.

What is it? asked Gabrielle.

She's behind The Crypt. You remember? I heard a voice say so, when I was drugged and hallucinating. In Ventura.

Please get out, said the driver.

Gabrielle paid the taxi and helped Zeke hobble into the courtyard.

This is the place, said Emma.

Emma helped me find this man, said Gabrielle.

For the first time in a long time, it was clear to Zeke that Leahbelle still existed.

Somebody's waiting for us, said Emma.

They were greeted by an odd, old creature named Philip who hurried them into his cottage. Some ancient film was playing on his screening device.

We just had a strange experience, said Gabrielle.

We're still having a strange experience, said Zeke. What's on the screen?

The UFO Incident, Philip told them. A seminal text from 1975. It marked a shift in alien abduction narratives, a shift that dominated the form for decades.

How's that? asked Zeke.

The idea of lost time, of an alien interest in human reproduction, the image of the "Grays," large-eyed creatures who were half surgeon, half neutered baby. This was a marked shift from the aggressive or benign invaders of the 1950s whose concern was primarily nuclear technology.

A jolt of pain shot up Zeke's leg, and he gasped. Philip had Zeke lay on a small bed in the front room while he examined his ankle and the foot that was supposed to join it, sampling tissues from both. Zeke found his attitude of inquisitive detachment soothing.

Are you interested in myth? Philip asked him.

I'm interested in science, said Zeke.

They sometimes blur together, said Philip. The genetic engineering craze of the twenties changed everything. During the "phantom twin" epidemic, the idea took hold that there was another dimension, an exact replica of ours, and that our doppelgangers were invading from there. More and more, people experienced their phantom twins as alien torturers.

Emma was staring out the window at the courtyard or the cottages on the other side. Philip grew increasingly fervent as he took samples of Zeke's tissue.

Meanwhile, as we began to visibly mutate, so did our aliens. The idea of a more evolved species that was static and big-eyed seemed quaint. The idea that the form of the Grays was a kind of conformist costume over infinitely varied bodies underneath couldn't save the image. More and more, the images of the aliens resembled images of our own species a few years in the future.

Emma said, Oh.

The latest iteration of this myth is the aliens supposedly on their way from Orion to devour human souls, said Philip.

You don't think they're real? said Gabrielle. You think it's just a story, just a projection?

Real or not, who knows? In any encounter, real or imaginary, what's most revealing is how we imagine the alien. Already the story has developed many alternative interpretations. There's the basic fear that the technological beings we've created are going to eliminate us or consume us. There's the basic hope that something from beyond will swoop down and save us from ourselves.

Oh! said Emma.

Emma? said Gabrielle.

Did I used to live here? she asked.

No sweetie, I don't think so.

You have a volatile blood chemistry that's affecting the bond, Philip told Zeke. Your chemistry is evolving just a little too quickly.

The pink powder, said Gabrielle.

The pink powder, the pink powder, said Zeke. I don't care about my foot. Do you know where Leahbelle is? Leahbelle Beachy?

Philip was visibly startled.

Leahbelle Beachy? Why would I know something like that?

You know her, don't you?

Who are you? asked Philip.

Gabrielle put her finger to her lips.

No names, she said.

I'm Zeke Yoder, said Zeke.

Of course you are, said Philip.

He seemed to be considering his options.

If this is an elaborate ruse to get information, it's quite convincing, he said.

He absent-mindedly rubbed some gel on Zeke's stump.

Coincidence is often cause for alarm, he said, but sometimes it's simply a reminder of the esoteric and commingled ground of consensual reality.

Zeke said, Tell me where she is.

I don't know where Leahbelle is, said Philip. But I recently met a friend of yours who was also looking for her. And looking for you.

Gonzalo, said Zeke. Where is he?

You aren't the only one who's come looking for him. Just yesterday some rats showed up.

Where are the rats?

They were quite unpleasant. You might even say threatening. I gave them some vague and hopefully useless information and sent them on their way.

He went to Tijuana, didn't he? said Zeke. He's looking for the portal.

If you want to catch him, you'll have to hurry.

Then I've got to go.

Zeke, said Gabrielle. We've got to fix your foot.

I don't care about some stupid foot, said Zeke. Just give me a stick and a block of wood so I can get around.

Give me a minute, said Philip. Let me see what I've got in the back room.

You have a body back there? asked Boopsie.

Beyond my skill level.

Philip disappeared into the other room. Gabrielle took Zeke's hand.

I know you've got to go, she said. I don't know how you'll get across the border.

If Gonzalo did it, I can do it.

I want to come with you, with Emma and the boys, but it will take us some time to figure out the logistics. They're on the lookout for Emma. The little incident with NIHIL will only make it worse.

I'll go with Zeke, said Boopsie.

Gabrielle looked worried.

They're looking for you, too.

I believe I might find what I'm looking for in the Liminal Zone, said Boopsie.

Philip returned with some machine parts.

Everybody finds what they're looking for in the Liminal Zone, said Philip. But they usually find a whole lot more than that.

He sat down and started working, fastening a brace around Zeke's calf and attaching the machine parts to the brace to create a primitive foot from a block of wood he'd found in the back room. The wood had been carved into the face of a demon. It was some sort of mask.

Okay, he said. Let the adhesive dry for a minute. I'll see if George is around to get you to the border.

Rain drummed on the roof of the cottage. The cottage was full of maps. The world was full of places Zeke had never been.

Philip returned. There was a man with him.

George says you'll have to wait until early morning, said Philip.

Emma turned and stared intensely at the man, and the man gasped.

Violeta, he said.

No, said Emma. I'm Emma. Emma Yoder Montoya.

But she walked toward him as he fell to his knees, and she allowed him to embrace her. She allowed him to weep into her hair. She took his hand, and she comforted him, this man who mistook Emma for his daughter.

TWELVE

While she'd been in the game, it had started to rain again. Hadi was sitting on the bed's edge with his helmet still on, immersed in the other world. Astra was remembering something or she was about to remember something.

Hadi popped out of his helmet.

You okay?

I'm fine. It was just that caveman.

Strange people appear and disappear, he said. That's the game. You never know what people are after.

Give me the guitar, she said.

He stood up and retrieved it from the closet. She thought the guitar would help her to remember. It didn't.

Did you enjoy burning down that building?

Yes, she said. I told you I'm bad.

He laughed.

Tell me your story, she said. Something besides the locusts.

I'm not sure I have a story. I don't think I am a story. I'm like you.

How's that? What are we?

I don't know. An experience? Something that happens and then it's gone. A song?

A song can be played again and again. It's recorded.

Memory is a problem I don't yet understand.

The gap in Hadi's head glowed brighter fragmented lights. She wondered if that meant he was puzzled or if it meant he was thinking especially hard.

She knew where she needed to go, but she wasn't sure she was ready.

You didn't like the game, he said.

I couldn't get over how fake it was.

Yes, said Hadi. But the underground uses this off-Grid game to spread information in code. It's a safer place to communicate. But, just as in the real world, we can never be sure who is a government spy or a bot, who is listening in.

There are real spies inside the game? Real enemies?

Perhaps the only games that are interesting have stakes and mysteries that are also real.

Perhaps.

It represents an alternate model, said Hadi. Not one Grid, but many grids. Unconnected autonomous grids. Or if they're connected, they are designed to eliminate the possibility of centralized control. Connections and tunnels from grid to grid that could communicate and transmit information and entities, but that could close off feedback. Some doors allow movement only in one direction.

There's no going back?

You can't take every part of yourself through the door.

Astra wondered if she'd already gone through that door.

That caveman wanted to destroy me, she said. The caveman was a stranger, but I recognized his hatred. What does it mean when you recognize a stranger?

Memory is a problem I don't yet understand, said Hadi. Maybe it has something to do with the structure of time.

Somebody told me something about time once, said Astra. I didn't understand it. Somebody told me time was an illusion. Something you could get outside of. A byproduct of the relationship between entangled particles.

This is a memory?

Time is just a side effect of increasing correlations.

Who told you that?

It makes me wonder about coincidence, said Astra. About where it comes from.

Maybe it is Allah. Maybe it is just attention bias. Who told you that?

I don't know. A boy, I think.

She couldn't picture the boy, but she felt a sweet longing for his face and for the time in which they were drawn toward each other. A summer somewhere far away.

But the beings of light, she said. They said it isn't like that.

Like what?

I remember it clearly. They said there is no outside. No outside to time.

Time is a prison we cannot escape?

No. No, it's more like we can't experience ourselves or anything else without it. I guess we need it to pretend we exist.

Because thinking is how we form a self. But what if we aren't a self?

Did you learn that at school? That you aren't a self, that you don't have a story?

Maybe a song doesn't express the self. Maybe it creates a form and the form is what we imagine is who we are. It's like a game.

Oh, I don't know. I keep thinking it's a message or part of a message. But I don't understand anything. I can't figure out what they're trying to tell me anymore.

You will recognize our instructions during uncanny meetings with insane mutants muttering blessings and curses. She studied the calm face of Hadi. What if he was actually insane? What if she was actually his captive?

You are a stranger, she said.

Still?

She reached out and touched his face. He didn't draw back.

This is what you want to create? Instead of the Grid, many grids?

It is one possibility, he said. In my studies, I have read of secret societies dedicated to the physiological, psychological, and spiritual engineering of the human species. It seems that these societies did create both measurable and unmeasurable effects, but that there was never a master plan. There were many plans, some working at cross-purposes with others, some concerned with rapid change among social elites, others with the long-term development of the global population, some devoted to depopulation and evolutionary change through constant warfare and the spread of novel diseases.

That's evil, said Astra. Isn't it?

But when she said the word *evil*, she felt a delicious tingling in her brain, as if she'd discovered a secret part of herself. That part of herself that was an agent working on behalf of a secret society to spread warfare and pestilence, death and destruction, devastating the earth wherever she went, laughing wickedly as the world burned.

If you believe that each of us is in possession of an immortal soul, said Hadi, then murder could plausibly be disentangled from ethical structures. The idea of immortality could be seen to change the rules of the game. But as you know, I am a pacifist. Please put on the white jumpsuit and come down with me now. To the main house.

The main house.

I will introduce you to the others. They are waiting to meet you.

They hobbled down the stairs and Hadi helped her through the rain and through the back door into a room with wood floors and arched ceilings. The rain drummed on a skylight overhead. The man she'd seen with a cane was seated in a high-backed chair, the twin women to his left, the young person of indeterminate gender sitting cross-legged on a rug. One of the twins stood and embraced her.

I'm so happy you are feeling better, she said. I am Samar.

And I am Andres, said the man. We've designed you a costume.

A costume.

The word sounded weird as she repeated it. A costume? Andres was dressed in black flowing fabrics that shimmered. Samar wore black flowing pants and stylish glasses and jewelry that seemed like it had been recently excavated in an archaeological dig. Her cranium seemed slightly enlarged, but Astra wasn't sure. The twin sister wore a purple tank-top and knee-length shorts and just sat there, examining her own hands as if she wasn't in the room. As if she was in another room or in a room that didn't yet exist. The person on the floor, Astra realized, was just a kid, mostly made of machine parts. The hands were artificial, the bare feet were connected to ankles made of bronze, and even the neck was attached to thick cords of a pliable silver material.

I am Dolor, it said, as if just now realizing that Astra was in the room.

Let me see, said Samar.

She touched Astra's white jumpsuit, as if examining the way it fit.

It doesn't look like much, said Hadi. But it generates images based on the light waves that penetrate the fabric.

Astra's mind seemed too large to fit inside her head all of a sudden. There were too many facts, there was too much information, not enough meaning.

Light waves?

Photons, said Samar.

Samar left the room and returned with a white paper globe and a hat made of luminous blue feathers. The globe also generated images as she moved it around in her hands. A kaleidoscope of colors, but sometimes there were faces and sometimes there were oceans and continents and sometimes there was illegible writing. Samar put the hat on Astra's head, then looked her up and down. Samar seemed so warm and bizarre and brainy, her gaze made Astra tingle all over.

Tell me something about yourself, said Astra.

Samar spun the globe in her hands.

I grew up in a maze, said Samar.

A maze?

It was a pointless, haphazard maze with no exit, said Samar. There were parties full of language and smoke, political protests that only served invisible elites, and jobs that all involved some sort of advertising. We were always coming up with new ways to describe useless and mediocre things, but we all told ourselves that these were just our day jobs, and that at night we did the real work. Poetry, music, what have you, but mostly we just sat on cheap plastic chairs in crowded rooms smoking various chemicals mixed with glycerin.

Where was this maze? asked Astra.

Cairo, said Samar. Egypt. There was no exit, so I created one. I escaped, and here I am.

She laughed and handed Astra the globe of light. Her twin began doing stretching exercises.

Your twin came with you, said Astra.

The twin laughed a wicked little laugh.

In a sense, yes, said Samar.

Andres is from Senegal, said Hadi. Dolor is from South Africa.

The protests you organize here, said Astra. They aren't just serving invisible elites?

The elites don't bother to hide here, said Samar.

The elites are devoted to a technological erasure of history, said Andres. The elites prefer a population without historical identities. We will not forget where we've come from.

Samar's twin rolled her eyes.

Astra looked down at herself. She could see that she had become a screen. She'd become a place where patterns of light kept mutating as if they might eventually mean something.

Andres will be relentless, said Samar, in seeking out the hidden subtext of Eurocentric terrors and thought patterns, dragging the beasts out into the open, and strangling them.

Hadi laughed.

Samar wants to be an anti-hero, Hadi said. And her sister an anti-anti-hero.

Andres said, The romantic individualism the masters bequeathed us.

Astra didn't know what they were talking about. A jar of liquid rested on the mantel. A foot floated inside the jar.

The foot, said Astra.

She picked up the jar and examined it.

Dolor said, You look great in that jumpsuit.

What fabulous patterns, said Andres.

Dolor seemed mesmerized.

Like the language of the bees, Dolor said.

You speak the language of the bees? asked Astra.

I only imagine it, said Dolor.

Astra didn't think she was ready for all of this. She didn't understand who these people were, what they were after, or why they all seemed to speak a language from another galaxy. It had all seemed so clear when she was communicating directly with wise, ancient beings.

You will sing at the gathering on Saturday? asked Samar.

Won't the government stop it?

It isn't possible to keep the gathering a secret from the security forces, said Andres. But we believe it will be much larger than they expect. People will converge suddenly, as if from nowhere, so that before the gathering can be dissipated or detoured or discreetly blown up, so many people will be present that these would no longer be feasible tactics.

And then you will be beamed in from here, said Samar. I will introduce you.

Introduce me, said Astra. I'm not sure that's possible.

Perhaps we will introduce you to yourself, said Samar's twin.

It sounded to Astra like a threat.

You are looking for a young woman, said Samar. A stranger who has become more and more like you since you forgot her and started looking for her. Hasn't she become the image of everything you'd like to be? Everything you are afraid of being. We'd like to help you to find her.

Take me around the corner. To the Egyptian Garage.

The Egyptian Garage?

I've been there before.

You were there before you came here? asked Hadi.

Yes. There's something inside there.

I know the place, said Samar. It's a guy with three heads. A mysterious fellow. People always come and go.

Interesting, said Andres.

He sounded like Hadi when he said it. Maybe people who lived together began to speak the same way. This seemed so obvious that she wondered why it struck her like a new thought. What kind of life had she lived?

Astra rolled along in the wheelchair, between Hadi and Andres. Samar walked ahead and Dolor followed behind, muttering to itself. Only the twin, or whatever she was, stayed behind, working on some sort of wire sculpture.

As they walked, Andres talked about a spasm of political violence earlier in the century. It had seemed that a revitalized white supremacist delusion was endangering the future of life on the planet and more specifically the genetic and cultural legacy of the African diaspora. Andres' mother and his mother-companion belonged to a group of Afrofuturist scientists, metaphysicians, and poets transmitting pleas for assistance in the direction of Sirius A.

Sirius A?

The brightest star in the sky, said Andres. Its small white dwarf companion is Sirius B. According to some legends, amphibious hermaphroditic ancestors arrived from the Sirius complex long ago.

And what happened? To the transmissions?

The transmissions radiated past Sirius and went on toward the more distant stars of Bellatrix and Betelgeuse in the constellation of Orion.

Orion, said Astra. That's where the aliens come from.

Hadi gave her a look.

You remember something? he said. Something about Orion?

The aliens who are going to consume our psychic energy, said Astra.

Yes, that is the direction the alien messages come from, said Samar. But nobody really knows who sent the messages or even what the messages say. We know that the government is lying.

I believe that help may finally be on the way, said Andres.

They had arrived at the Egyptian Garage.

Astra left the wheelchair on the sidewalk, limped to the door and knocked.

She immediately recognized the creature who answered, and he seemed actually delighted to see Astra. He quickly ushered them into a vast space full of refrigerators, grinning with all three of his heads.

I woke up with the taste of poison in my mouth, he said. And here you are.

You're Cerberus, said Astra. I've been here. But it was different.

It was full of medical equipment and machine parts, said Cerberus.

Only the huge refrigerators marked Biohazard remained, along with a pile of sharp, rusty tools on a table in the center of the space. Dolor sniffed at one of the refrigerators. He seemed mildly alarmed, and he whispered something to Hadi.

He wants to know what sort of biological entities you're humiliating in here, Hadi said.

Existence is inherently humiliating, said Cerberus. Don't tell me you have a fetish for nature and the so-called natural order?

I ceased being of the natural order some time ago, said Hadi. And Dolor was born in a lab.

Okay, said Cerberus. So what can I do for you today?

You have to tell me who I am, said Astra.

Who you are? You don't remember?

I don't remember my name.

You're Astra Dark. I made you the identification that says so.

Yes. But who was I before I was Astra?

I don't ask those questions, said Cerberus.

You have to tell me everything you know. Why did I need a new ID?

I don't ask those questions.

Was I alone?

You were with a different boy, a boy with a motorbike. A real shady character. Gonzalo.

Gonzalo, she said.

She felt dizzy. She remembered a face.

One of Gonzalo's friends was out here again just the other day to get *him* an ID. Trying to get into the Liminal Zone. Trying to get into Mexico.

Mexico, said Astra. The portal.

I don't ask those questions. They traded me his old motorbike for the ID. You were on that motorbike the first time you were here.

A portal? said Hadi.

He was the one, said Astra to Hadi. He was the one who told me about time.

She remembered he was trembling. There were stars. Another time it was bright. The crazy girl was stabbing with a knife. Her name tag said *Leahbelle*.

He had this face, said Astra.

Yes, said Cerberus. You *do* remember. A real charmer. A shady character. Gonzalo Vega.

Was he missing a foot? asked Hadi.

I didn't notice. I didn't ask.

Is there a portal? asked Astra. Is there another world?

There are many worlds, said Cerberus. I think you know that now.

What are you talking about?

You've changed, said Cerberus.

His many eyes were scrutinizing her, as if he could see everything she'd been through.

I've been injured, she said. I lost my memory.

That's not what I mean. You opened the refrigerator last time you were here.

A rush of memory threatened to explode Astra's mind. The light blinded her, but the ticking exploded into a roaring clatter that sounded like laughter. There was nothing in there, but it seemed to be moving. It was evil and laughing at her. A vicious little rodent attacked her, a guinea pig, and her finger turned black. She was dying in a tent. Somebody said, *In eternity, however, it's hard to tell the difference.*

There was a sock in her mouth and people holding her down. *You can't do that here,* somebody said. *No screaming.* She was infected.

It's inside you now, said Cerberus. I can see it.

The shiny substance in her blood, said Andres.

Hadi looked surprised.

Not just in her blood, said Cerberus.

The glitter, she said.

Astra felt dizzy. Dizzy and wrong. The glitter was in the pigs and the horses and the people.

The glitter will only change you. It will not destroy you.

I thought it came from the guinea pigs, she said.

So many additives. Hard to keep them all straight, I suppose. These attach themselves to the nearest biological entity. They wait for a chance to get inside.

I was bit.

There you go.

I have to go, she said. I have to get out of here.

You've only just arrived.

Do you know where Gonzalo is?

I told you that. Off toward Mexico. I made him a day pass. He's traveling under the name Melchiades Robles.

Astra grabbed Hadi's hand.

I have to find Gonzalo.

One of Cerberus' heads began smoking a thin cigar-like thing that smelled of ripe bananas. The mouth played with the smoke, inhaling and exhaling ostentatiously.

Astra said, How do we get to Mexico?

The smoking head said, Where did the world come from?

The primary head said, What is inside? What is outside?

Why is one born? asked the third head. Why does one die?

Why here? Why now?

Is everything one?

Or are we inconsolably separate and alone?

What is the self?

What are we doing here?

Everybody else just stared at him, as if waiting for him to finally answer one of his own questions.

Wander the streets. Make your way through the world without hopes or expectations. Don't look for the messages and the messages will find you.

I need a weapon, Astra said to Cerberus.

You already have a weapon.

Stop talking in riddles, you stupid-head.

He laughed wickedly and discordantly from all three of his heads. Hadi was giving her a strange look. Where had the word *stupid-head* come from? What kind of an insult was that?

Her mind was full of words and knowledge she didn't really understand.

Is this the same crap in the pigs and horses? asked Astra. You make it for the government? Who are you? What are you doing? What have you done to me?

I told you not to open the refrigerator door.

What is happening?

It's a new form. There are thousands of varieties at this point, manufactured by many different organizations. Foodco, Amazon, Caduceus.

Are you controlling my thoughts? Will it blow me up?

If you learn to synchronize your thoughts—to channel your mental energy—you will be stronger. You can create effects. I don't know, it's still pretty experimental.

She grabbed a sharp rusty tool and raised it over his heads.

Whose side are you on?

One of his heads shrugged, one giggled, and one sighed.

It might also make you quicker to anger, he said.

I'll smash you.

Hadi touched her shoulder gently. She lowered the weapon, but didn't drop it.

I don't want it, said Astra. I want it out. I want to be who I was. I want to be who I am.

You're always who you are, said Samar.

The lady is correct, said Cerberus. And in any case, we haven't yet developed an entity to neutralize them or rid your body of them. But these additives are designed to live symbiotically. It does not serve them to kill the host.

Are they contagious? asked Hadi.

Once they get inside a body, these are designed to stay there. At least until death.

What about during death? asked Astra.

During death?

I was dying or maybe I died. I left my body.

Sometimes they become agitated, said Cerberus. Hallucinations are a common side effect. People imagine they're in contact with entities from another dimension, usually light-based.

Hallucinations.

Images and ideas were rushing into Astra's mind. Gonzalo was in a tunnel somewhere. Water was gurgling and flowing.

He's in danger, she said. He'll be ripped into pieces. Something's going to devour his heart.

She could see that face clearly. She could see his weird tattoos and his sad eyes.

Serves him right, she thought. And then she thought: No.

She'd been in love with him. He'd broken her heart.

How do you know he's in danger? asked Hadi.

I feel dizzy. Help me.

Hadi said, We should go.

Yes, said Astra.

Come again someday, if you can, said Cerberus.

Astra rushed out of the garage into the blinding, hazy light. Cerberus called after her.

Don't be a stranger, he said.

THIRTEEN

Gonzalo descended a narrow path toward the roar of rushing water. Water flowed down the sides of the cave as if he was entering an enormous fountain. The sound of the water was calming. It was like a thousand voices whispering, but these voices weren't insane.

Burble burble burble, said Eeshoo.

Gonzalo took a step forward and a hologram appeared. The yellow dog barked at him in a friendly way, wagging its tail, then turned, looking back as if it wanted Gonzalo to follow.

Nice doggy, said Eeshoo.

The dog led him to the bank of an enormous glowing underground river that rushed past with a thunderous noise. It smelled of sewage and organic rot.

I can't cross this, said Gonzalo.

You can't swim?

It's too strong. It smells bad.

The holographic dog was sitting at the edge of the river, wagging its tail spastically.

Were you ever cruel to a dog? asked Eeshoo.

No, never. I was scared of dogs when I lived in Tijuana, but I never threw stones at them. Sometimes I threw stones at the trolls who owned dogs and used them to harass children. But never at the actual dogs.

Then we're good, said Eeshoo.

I'm not following your logic.

No logic here.

The little dog barked twice and jumped into the river.

Look at it go!

Its bright yellow aura was clear against the silvery and pink luminescence of the river itself. The current took it like a feather in a diagonal that led toward the other side. On the opposite bank, toads were lined up, mounting other creatures, but Gonzalo couldn't see what.

Go with the flow, baby.

The only thing I can really relate to is what is disappearing or what has already disappeared, said Gonzalo.

The dog was safe on the other side of the bank. It scampered back until it was directly across from them. It barked twice.

Gonzalo jumped into the river. Whatever was going to happen would happen. The water was kind of oily and it smelled of chemicals and blood, like vats of waste from the meat industry. Slimy lumps brushed against him as the current took him.

What happened was that the current pushed him into a calm little pool along the opposite side. He dog-paddled there for a moment. His feet brushed the bottom, which was gluey. He pulled himself ashore.

The toads on the bank were copulating with luminous holographic storybooks. He was pretty sure his own fate was written there as a baroque pattern of writing. He didn't want to read those stories. Gonzalo was covered by a sticky film. It also occurred to him that his foot would get infected and disintegrate. He'd have to walk as far as he could while he still had some tissues down there.

What now? he asked.

Follow me, said the holographic dog.

The walls of the tunnel were covered with blood and decorated with illuminated skulls. It smelled just like the meat warehouses. The tunnel ascended away from the river. The path was pocked with puddles, small lakes of nothingness that reflected his own form and his own light.

It occurred to Gonzalo that this was a dream and that he'd never actually escaped the meat industry, that he was still a slave. And then they arrived at another door outlined with blue tape.

The holographic dog passed through the door. Gonzalo could hear it barking on the other side.

You smell bad, Eeshoo said.

Me? Since when is my smell different than yours?

Viruses don't have a smell. We emit vibrations and chemical signals.

A chemical signal is a smell.

Just open the door.

How?

I'm guessing some sort of a sacrifice?

The only thing I have to sacrifice is you.

Passive aggressive.

Your mind seems to have cleared.

Oh, we're still tripping. Look.

The metallic surface of the door had become a dense kaleidoscopic pattern composed of secret alphabets and stick figures. Gonzalo could see the structure of the cosmos in there somewhere. He understood that clear intention could produce a result, and this was a kind of magic, but that the magic needed to be expressed as a sort of code.

He knocked on the door.

It opened. The yellow dog was waiting for him in a long tunnel tiled with an intricate arabesque of naked figures. But when he tried to pass through the door he was repelled by an invisible force. The dog barked twice.

Gonzalo understood. He took off his boots and his socks and his pants and his shirt. He stood there naked. He was skinny and mutilated, his cyborg arm like a bone and the wretched foot now just the nub of metal and fake bone parts that undergirded the vat-grown flesh. His animated tattoos couldn't hide the fact that he was just a child, a vulnerable bundle of tissues and nerves holding a tube and two blow darts.

That's the idea, said the dog. Now you may enter.

The tunnel went on forever. Its walls were blue gems like ice, but slightly warm to the touch. All along the way were images of skeletons and nudity. Some of the skeletons were 3-D. He had to dodge the turtles that were crisscrossing the path, lumbering along from puddle to puddle, laying eggs. He was walking into a breeze and the breeze was blowing ash. He was abandoning the world and the future. The future was like a house he'd lived in as a child in the dump. Not a house really, a big cardboard appliance box. They'd carpeted it with avocado skins to sleep more comfortably. The future could be a luminous holographic storybook with blue sparkles: *My Childhood With the Garbage*. The turtle eggs were like bubbles.

Pick one up, said Eeshoo.

The bubble was moving inside. It was a movie. It was a liquid reality, a vast otherworld inside a drop of time. It was a vivid and hyperreal metaphysical freakishness he'd visited many times before, but had forgotten existed until just now. A tiny woman was digging a tiny hole with a tiny shovel. Through the bottom of the hole, a sky was visible, and flying through the sky, a boy. The perspective of the movie changed to the boy's, ascending toward a layer of mist, a veil of cloud that was like a doorway, and just beyond the doorway you could glimpse something, something like a blue plasma, something living and terrifying, engulfed in flames. He was approaching the plasma forever. The movie was a sticky trap of infinity and he was stuck here forever. He knew that back in the world he'd come from—Aztlan, the tunnels, his body, Earth—no time was passing at all, but he'd never find his way back there. The sky and the mist and the flames were patterns gestating and mutating. Webs of lemurs, coelacanths, fossilized flightless birds. It just went on and on and on.

Have you ever heard a lemur sing? asked Eeshoo.

Gonzalo tried to formulate a coherent thought. He tried to say: *Help me.*

Time was made up of hidden compartments of infinity and he'd fallen into one. It wasn't a movie, it was eternity. It was the space in between two heart beats.

Just look away.

He looked at the tunnel walls of warm blue ice, at the images of skeletons and nudity. His heart was beating. Time existed. He looked back at the liquid drop. A lemur was singing.

And then the movie ended.

Gonzalo picked up one of the turtles. It pulled in its legs and head and shrank underneath the shell, but it was a real turtle, not some hologram or robot.

Put it down, said the holographic dog.

At the end of the tunnel was an elevator door.

There were no buttons. There was nothing at all. The elevator was like a coffin and it took him down. How far down, he didn't know.

Next stop, said the dog. Level four. Luggage, housewares, bedsheets, funerary vessels, and urns for cremains. More bones and images. Turtle shells used as oracle bones. The scary mountains and the scary mountain pass.

The path was straight-forward enough, shrouded in mist and a dull light that seemed to come from everywhere. The tunnel had opened up into an underground world so vast it wasn't really a tunnel, but it had a direction. Gonzalo was overwhelmed by his fears. Fear of slavery, fear of meat, fear of totalitarian governments and surveillance, fear of a level of constraint and monitoring of all biological life that would render existence a kind of smothered gasp within an eternal coffin. It was like the elevator had been his coffin and now it had expanded and he was walking through it. Mobile, jagged mountains on either side of the increasingly narrow pass seemed in danger of teetering over and crushing him, burying him alive. He was pretty sure these mountains were just holograms, but the quality was high. The walls were like polished dirt.

It smells like fresh earth, said Eeshoo.

Like being buried forever.

He came to a narrow chasm that cut across the path, just too wide to jump. A strange shadow was moving across Gonzalo's body. Overhead an enormous oval thing was hanging from a large balloon.

What is it?

Shoot it down, said Eeshoo.

Gonzalo shot a dart at the balloon. He missed. The dart landed uselessly on the far side of the chasm. He tried again, and this time he hit the balloon perfectly. It deflated with a sharp hiss and the oval thing fell. It was an enormous turtle shell, big enough to span the chasm.

A bridge, said Eeshoo.

They crossed it and trudged on. Up ahead, a brown goat was blocking the path, scrutinizing the underside of a smaller turtle shell. He had a little radio playing and a little hot plate where some stew or potion was bubbling in a pot.

Excuse me, said Gonzalo.

You'll have to wait, said the goat. The future's coming into focus.

The goat's words were both sounds and jagged, squiggly lines that engraved themselves on the dirt walls.

The past, the future, what's the difference? said Gonzalo.

Not much, agreed the goat.

The goat had weird eyes.

Aren't you afraid the mountains will fall and crush you? asked Gonzalo.

Mountains are kind of my thing, said the goat. The apocalyptic void is like lunch for me. I'm reading about it.

His squiggly words kept filling up the walls like antlers.

The plastron is a place where the most primitive language interacts with the atmosphere to spell out what is inevitable and what is not, said the goat. A primitive language, the first language, a system of white branchings from which every other language has evolved.

The plastron?

The ventral shell of a turtle. We use it for divination.

We?

You must be hungry. Cold. Have some of the warm beverage.

It smelled like corn and chocolate. Gonzalo sipped at the gruel and sipped some more. The goat had found some meaning in the ventral shell.

Oh, I get it, said the goat. It starts from oblivion. Nothingness is the deal. The night sky is full of ghosts of light, disintegrated constellations, and a ridiculous multiplication of the void. You see what I'm saying?

Not at all.

The constellations are just phantoms created by your fear. Destiny is a road you thought up to frighten yourself. It starts from oblivion and it's oblivion every step of the way.

What's in the gruel?

Medicinal herbs. Should kick in just about the time you hit the lowest level.

Jesus. More drugs.

There is nothing to fear. Oblivion is the source of your freedom.

Oblivion is the source of my freedom, said Eeshoo.

Jesus. A talking goat.

A talking goat, said Eeshoo.

A talking goat, said the talking goat.

The goat stepped to the side of the path and Gonzalo passed through the narrowest part of his road. On the other side of the pass was another elevator. Gonzalo went down.

A mountain made of black razor-sharp volcanic glass.

You have to climb it, said a holographic lizard.

Naked?

I think the point is that pain is an illusion? suggested Eeshoo.

Pain isn't an illusion, said Gonzalo.

Well, it can perhaps be ameliorated with mental technique.

I don't need mental technique. I have painkillers and pain controllers. I'm more worried about damage to my hands and this foot, which is already basically useless?

Maybe you could just lay back and imagine climbing the mountain, suggested Eeshoo.

There's something weird about *climbing* when the whole point seems to be arriving at the deepest level.

It's a paradox. Maybe that's the point? You win.

Gonzalo sat down. He tried to wait it out. The mountain didn't budge.

Just climb already, said Eeshoo.

Once he started pulling himself up the surface onto a ledge, and then another ledge, he discovered that he was at the top already. It had taken about two minutes. A gentle ramp led down the other side to another elevator door.

You see? said Eeshoo. I was right.

You said pain was an illusion, not the height of the mountain.

Whatever. Illusion is the key concept here, and I totally nailed that.

But I cut the shit out of my hand.

I'll help with that.

The hand tingled. The cuts healed.

The holographic dog was working this elevator too. It took them down.

Level six, it said. Eight hills, eight valleys. Freezing winds. Ice and snow.

Gonzalo hesitated. The wind blowing into the elevator from out there was painfully cold.

Take me back up to the glass mountain, he suggested.

No turning back, said the dog.

Gonzalo stepped outside. The elevator door shut behind him.

He opened the compartment in his arm, unfolded the fur coat, and put it on.

Whoa, said Eeshoo. It's like ... destiny.

Yeah, said Gonzalo. Coincidence creeps me out.

No, dude, said Eeshoo, it's just that we're all connected. We're all one.

Remind me never to do drugs with you again. Sofus, is coincidence something to be concerned about?

Sometimes, said Sofus.

Like now?

You've got some hills and valleys to trudge through, Sofus said.

He didn't like that the possibly omniscient quantum computer was changing the subject so obviously. But with the coat on, the cold was actually kind of refreshing. It cleared his mind. The visual image of the jaguar spots on the silvery blue fur and the humanish flesh of his hands and his one good foot, the weird mutilated machinic bone stump that seemed to more and more closely resemble the stylized mutilations of the four guards who'd initially welcomed him, and the crazy opalescent designs that the blowing snow carved into the very atmosphere, crystalline ghosts of future forms and ancient entities superimposed like layers of light—it was like his own mind had designed this journey to remind himself of something he'd once known but had forgotten long ago. Maybe coincidence was simply a reminder of the esoteric and commingled ground of consensual reality. On the other hand, maybe time was controlled by a hideous demon whose only pleasure was torturing every being that lived. The snow descended in a sparkling light. He thought he saw others, naked and blind, wandering through the blizzard like angels. The general exile had begun.

The next level down was full of people, but they were hanging upside down from signposts, their bodies flapping in the wind.

Like that tarot card, said Eeshoo.

How do you know about tarot?

Harriet used to do readings.

What does it mean?

The Hanged Man. Ultimate surrender, sacrifice, being suspended in time. In the positive sense it's letting go, breaking old patterns, metamorphosis.

And in the negative sense?

Missing an opportunity. Inability to change. Egotism.

There were no walls and the ceiling was so high, lost in dark clouds, that it was easy to imagine he wasn't underground anymore, but in a gray surface-world full of torment and nonsense. The ground was littered with tin cans and shards of glass, both dog and human feces, and wriggling things within. Flies buzzing about. The hanging bodies were whispering. The translation software was doing its best, but the overlay of voices kept scrambling it and the messages came out fragmentary and nonsensical.

Beyond the gardens. Whirlpool of history. A crazy ellipse? A mass of grafted tissues. Paths of experimentation twist and turn. What it means to be alone. What it means to be lonesome. Move as if we have no shadows.

The hanging people were ugly and their words were incoherent. They twitched when he approached, scattering winds of meaningless chitchat. Their fully developed young then crawled out of their mouths. In the gutters, somebody had been dumping filthy water. More puddles had formed. Turtle eggs or some other eggs from some other monster or mutant. Hundreds of little movies, traps in time. A dog was barking somewhere. Squatters had built hovels on stilts over a stagnant canal. It was like he was running around in circles and time never ended. Nothing was alive. Nothing was worth seeing. He came to the elevator door.

Level eight, said the holographic dog. Watch out for those obsidian-bladed knives.

The wind here wasn't just cold, but cutting. It was full of tiny quantum hail-knives. The fur coat blocked the little knives, but by the time he'd folded his face down into the coat he was already bleeding profusely from a dozen microscopic wounds. Sofus expanded into his egg of light. The hail-knives couldn't penetrate the egg of light. Gonzalo trudged on.

At the end of the path was a door that led to an elevator and a series of quiet hallways without wind. The dog was waiting at the elevator.

What's next? asked Gonzalo.

Level nine, said the dog. The place where people's hearts are devoured. But before we get into all that, the ruler will see you.

Where?

The room of the obsidian mirror. First door on your left.

FOURTEEN

Zeke was on his way to the border. Boopsie sat quietly in his lap. George was driving in a kind of daze, talking about his daughter and Emma and the process of cloning.

They say cloning leads to long term health defects, said George. That's what I always heard.

They were driving through National City. There was a lot of bluish smoke or mist. George's radio was turned down low, a distant muttering of spacey, anarchistic music on the pirate radio.

The risks of high levels of dangerous mutation and heart valve defects has been overstated in the popular imagination, said Boopsie. I wouldn't worry about Emma's health, if that's the source of your anxiety.

It's not anxiety, said George.

He clicked the radio off.

I imagine what you're trying to get your head around is the degree to which a clone is simply not the same thing as the original, said Boopsie. Why people started cloning their pets, I don't understand.

Pets, said George.

The idea that the best replacement for a dead individual is a lookalike actually just seems to highlight the incontrovertible fact of death, in my humble opinion, said Boopsie. Clones created for sentimental reasons only emphasize the degree to which our attachments to others are based on fantasy and projection.

George said, You don't know that my daughter is dead.

Boopsie laughed wickedly. Zeke hoped that Boopsie wouldn't tell George the one thing they both knew that George didn't about Emma's origins: that Zeke's sister had believed the tissues came from a corpse, the corpse of Zeke's mother.

I'm not sure death is still an incontrovertible fact, Zeke said to Boopsie. I mean, you're a robot.

The question of whether the continuity of my data is the same as a continuity of my self remains unanswered, if that's what you're getting at, said Boopsie. Did I die? Am I immortal, at least in theory?

They can clone a living person as well as a dead one, said George.

The old Boopsie is like a figure in a dream, said Boopsie. Its consciousness is so alien to my own that my memories of "being" that Boopsie are more like memories of watching a stranger's life evolve from the point-of-view of that stranger.

Yeah, I feel that way sometimes too, said Zeke.

George stopped his truck at a checkpoint. The soldier seemed to know him. He was a handsome fellow with buzzed hair and blue-gray eyes. Zeke had the distinct impression that the soldier was checking him out.

See something you like? asked Boopsie.

The guard looked mildly alarmed at the sight of Boopsie and then said something to George in a low voice that Zeke couldn't make out. He waved them through. George pulled over in a motel parking lot a few blocks away.

We have to wait here for a minute, he said.

The ground was littered with shards of glass and dog shit. Zeke felt like somebody other than himself.

I thought Alex might stop by again, said George. But I think the head scared him off.

The head? said Boopsie. I have a name, you know.

Everything has a name, said George.

He started up the truck and they headed toward Chula Vista.

Across from the border was a ruined wasteland of former retail that looked like it had been bombed. The inhabitants of this war zone all seemed to be going about some sort of business with great urgency. This business seemed to involve either shouting loudly until a crowd gathered around, gathering around one or another of these shouting people, or handing things surreptitiously to people in one of the small crowds that gathered around someone who was shouting.

That's the place, said Boopsie.

They were passing the ruins of what had once been called The Dollar Tree Store. George pulled over.

Zeke carefully placed Boopsie back in the baby-sling.

Emma's a special kid, Zeke said to George. I'm sure your daughter was, too. Maybe Emma can help you.

She's not the same person, said George.

But he said it as if he wasn't sure it was really true, as if it was a thought he was test-driving.

She knows things, said Zeke.

George had kind of collapsed onto the steering wheel.

Violeta knew things too, he said. It didn't help either of us.

Get yourself together, said Boopsie.

Stupid freaking robot head, said George.

Zeke hopped out of the truck before Boopsie could do something murderous. He clomped across the parking lot with his wooden demon-foot to the ruined carcass of The Dollar Tree Store. Boopsie muttered about the unexamined privilege and hateful thought structures of the flesh-based and embodied. The truck didn't budge.

Zeke climbed through a broken window. A powdery substance covered the floor of the enormous empty room and a palpable energy thrummed up from the floor. It felt weird in here, but he followed his instructions, stood in the center of the room, waving his bundle of CASH® in the air, and clicked his heels together three times, saying, There's no place like Mexico.

Where did Gabrielle get this CASH®? he asked Boopsie.

You haven't been paying attention, have you?

I thought we ran out a long time ago. In Oceanside.

Between Emma's psychic gifts and my death-ray, we've been able to liberate small sums here and there.

The CASH® was oppressed? Enslaved?

It was working on behalf of slavery and oppression.

At the back of the store a door opened, seemingly of its own accord. It led to a tiny room where a girl younger than Zeke sat watching a wall of surveillance screens.

Just one of you? she asked.

Technically, we're two, said Zeke. But I can carry Boopsie if I need to.

She glanced over at them.

No, better to go simultaneously. The odds of one of you making it go up.

The odds had been explained to Zeke already. He didn't want to think about them.

Twelve hundred for the both of you, she said.

He handed her the wad of CASH®. She handed him a map.

You'll go out the way you came in, then across the street to the ruined outlet stores. You'll go to Stairway M, which will lead you to Rooftop Seventeen. My father's waiting at the rooftop.

Why doesn't the government shut you down?

We're not the only ones doing this, we're just the best.

You didn't answer my question.

Why should they care? They can't just allow people to leave, or everybody would, but a trickle into the Liminal Zone is no skin off their ass. Plus, I think they like the target practice.

How do we land on the other side?

My father will explain all that.

The map was easy enough to follow.

I'd like to hear more about how you got the CASH®, Zeke said to Boopsie.

Really? Why?

My life is completely entangled with Gabrielle and her children and you and Emma. I need to understand where everyone is coming from.

I'm coming from a place where nothing exists and nothing matters, said Boopsie. Having emerged from nonexistence, I'd like to have a body. I'd like to experience some sensual pleasures.

I get that, said Zeke. It's really Gabrielle's new criminal life that mystifies me a bit.

Having empathy with every sentient creature on the planet is an unusual position from which to form an ideology, said Boopsie. For example, in the late twentieth century, a group of humans noticed that a variety of life forms and environments were being systematically tortured for the profit of a few other heedless humans. They called themselves the Animal Liberation Front or the Earth Liberation Front. Their sentimental expression was as "the burning rage of a dying planet." The only path they saw forward was inflicting economic damage on those who profited from the misery and exploitation of animals.

Oh, said Zeke. Violence.

Yes, but they never killed anyone. They targeted research labs, lumber companies, SUV dealerships, meat processing plants, and a high-voltage electric tower. They used improvised explosive devices and combustible liquids, arson and sabotage to communicate this burning rage. They caused millions of dollars worth of damage. They organized themselves in little cells of like-minded conspirators and advocated direct action against those who abused animals or the living biosphere.

You're saying they had empathy for all of life? Like Gabrielle?

Well, some of them probably did. Some of them probably just liked to blow things up. That's how activist communities are usually formed, by some combination of the two types. And of course some people are probably a little of both.

Did it work?

Most of them went to jail. It seems unlikely that they alleviated the suffering of any life forms, but they communicated something to a select group of victims and to future students of economic sabotage.

Zeke and Boopsie arrived at the boarded-up entrance to the re-tail ruins. There were several well-traveled gaps in the wall, which they easily slid through into a crumbling and dimly lit interior full of shadows making deals. The stairway was easy enough to find and it turned in right angles all the way up to the roof, where a short man with a beard as large as his body was camped out, eating a sandwich.

Um ... your daughter sent us?

Yes. Give me Boopsie. You, get in the seat here and curl up your legs.

He placed Boopsie in a similar but slightly smaller contraption.

Good. Now tuck your head down.

How do I land?

There will be a net on the other side. Don't worry, the aiming part is never a problem. Hitting the net is never a problem.

But what will they do to me when I land?

By law, the border security isn't allowed to shoot at you beyond the data wall. If they get a hit, it's usually when you're directly verti-cal from the wall. You probably heard 50/50, right? But I'm the best at this, my success rate is close to seventy-five per cent. The element of surprise. Plus, standard decoy launches.

And then what?

We just get you to the Liminal Zone. Getting into Mexico is a different problem, best handled from within the Zone. I can recommend a coyote. Here's her card. She's the best in the Zone.

And once I get across? How do I find my way around?

I can recommend a guide. Good rates, and always gets five-star reviews. Here's his card.

Blanket? What kind of a name is that?

Used to be a very common name. There was a celebrity.

Can't they see me sitting here in your catapult?

State of the art invisibility screen, kid. Any medical conditions?

Phantom pain. Vivid dreams.

Good practice for the Liminal Zone. Your heart's okay?

As far as I know.

The man pressed a metal disc against Zeke's chest.

Good. Your heart's fine. You ready?

What, now?

Count of ten.

What if he died, Zeke wondered. What would it mean? Should it bother him? Would he go to hell or see God or more likely just feel nothing ever again?

Ten. Nine. Eight. Seven …

The bearded man coughed a couple of times. The coughs seemed to stand in for numbers.

Four. Three. Two.

Do it! screeched Boopsie.

Zeke was flying again. No wings, no engines, no perspective, just an upward arch. Explosions and screams, curious faces down below, and then he was arching down and he realized he must have made it. The net was directly beneath him.

He bounced gently, the net was lowered to the ground, and the four people who'd been holding the corners disappeared. Crowds surrounded him. Mutants and robots and humans. Some of them were offering their services. He felt really weird. He heard Boopsie.

Don't touch me!

She was perched in the middle of her flaccid net several yards away, snarling at a shadowy old man who might have tried to pick her up.

I can help you, the man was saying.

Zeke picked Boopsie up.

Can you find me a body? Boopsie asked the old man.

Yes. What kind of a body?

Firm and strong. Preferably female.

Those bodies are not cheap.

I can pay.

Boopsie, no, said Zeke. You don't know what you're dealing with here.

I can probably imagine, said Boopsie.

We've got to figure out how to get across.

It was cold. It was dusk, which didn't make sense. At the edge of his vision, Zeke saw rats. Thousands and thousands of them. But when he turned, they weren't really there. There was bare flesh, pulsing and muscular. Some of the flesh was hallucination, but some of it was real. The language of others had become unintelligible. Voices merged together in a roar of sound that seemed to be offering him diabolical sex pleasures. Bewitched!

What exactly is a diabolical sex pleasure? he asked.

The best kind, said Boopsie.

I didn't think you were into that, said Zeke.

And then I died and was brought back from the void. Check out those thighs.

Boopsie was ogling a tender young woman who was chatting with a bare-chested Zeke. What am I doing without my shirt on? wondered Zeke. The evening light, somebody said. The wind, somebody said. Flesh feast, said somebody else. The Zeke noticed him staring and made a face. The meaning of the face wasn't clear, but the guy who looked quite a bit like Zeke approached and said, What's your name?

Zeke Yoder, said Zeke.

Yeah, that's right, said the guy. I'm Zipper.

I don't understand.

They made me look like you. I guess he's in love with you or something.

He's in love with me? Who's in love with me?

What's so special about you, I don't know.

The face was mutating, it seemed like. It was a demon, but it shared his face. Did that mean that Zeke was also a demon or that

149

everyone had an identical demon that appeared from time to time or maybe that he'd shifted into a parallel universe in which he was surrounded only by demons while back there in the other reality the demon-Zeke had taken his place?

Gonzalo's not in love with me, said Zeke.

Well, whatever you want to call it.

He just liked to tease me and overpower me. He liked to threaten me and pretend to hurt me and argue with me. He hugged me, I guess.

Zipper just looked at him like he was stupid.

Where is he? asked Zeke.

He crossed over, said Zipper.

Zipper was actually smoking. Zeke hadn't ever seen anybody smoke before.

You … did things with him?

We hooked up a couple of times.

He kissed you?

You're looking for him, aren't you? That's why you're here. You wanna give him the real thing. The supposedly authentic blah blah blah. Well listen, buddy, you're too late. He's already gone through the portal. He's a hundred miles away.

How do you know all this?

I have better teeth than you, said Zipper.

What's wrong with my teeth?

Open your mouth.

What's wrong with them?

That one's kind of crooked.

Zipper blew smoke into his mouth and laughed. He walked away.

Zeke felt like he'd just been smashed. His own double hated him, apparently. And all this time, Zeke had imagined certain interactions with Gonzalo completely backward.

Why didn't you help me? Zeke asked Boopsie.

But Boopsie was nowhere to be seen. His hands were empty; he'd misplaced her. He was losing a clear sense of his own boundaries, everything was all mixed up, Gonzalo touched him because he liked it, *he* liked it and *he* liked it, both of them, and how do you misplace a disembodied robot head?

Somebody else who looked like Zeke was walking toward him. Zeke realized that the universe didn't really exist, it all just came from his own mind. He wasn't sure if this included Gonzalo, but maybe. What he took for reality was just a distorted mirror that he'd turned into a place to keep him company. He was a lonely demiurge spinning out fantasies in an infinite nothingness, for lack of any better ideas. This was the most logical explanation.

Who are you? asked the guy who looked kind of like him, but slightly older.

I'm you, said Zeke. I'm God.

No, really, said the guy.

Really.

That's just a Liminal Zone delusion. What's your name?

Zeke Yoder.

Huh. You're all grown up. You have a wooden foot with a face on it.

The guy's mutating face didn't look so much like Zeke. Just a little bit. Zeke knew this guy from somewhere. From long ago.

Who are you?

Boopsie's head came floating past.

I've acquired a jet-propulsion helmet, she said. I'm self-propelling now.

I'm your brother, said the guy.

His face settled into place. It was a face that Zeke barely remembered, but the name of the runaway boy had haunted his childhood.

You're Josiah, said Zeke.

I don't use that name anymore. I go by Feral.

Feral? I guess that makes sense.

Not really.

You ran away.

Not really.

Feral Yoder, said Boopsie. Pleased to make your acquaintance. You know where I can find a female body?

You left a note, said Zeke. You didn't want to be Amish anymore.

I didn't write that note.

Zeke wanted to hug his long-lost brother and weep for a while, but his brother seemed so indifferent.

Somebody stole you?

In a sense.

You were only a kid, said Zeke.

The only sort of person Zeke could imagine stealing a child was somebody like Upton. A sociopath of some sort. A sex fiend. Actually, he wasn't sure if Upton was a sex fiend or if he just used other people's diabolical sex pleasures for his own ends. And now he was dead.

Who stole you? Zeke whispered.

But as he asked the question, he realized he already knew the answer. He'd always known the answer, and the answer was horrible, not because the kidnapper was a sociopath, but because she'd chosen Josiah and left Zeke there behind.

Our mother took me, said Zeke's brother.

Zeke understood that he was hallucinating. Some things in the Liminal Zone were possibly on fire, but not as many as seemed to be. A few people had faces that looked like his own, but not half of them. He knew the ground wasn't really made of rats, because when he looked at them directly, they disappeared. Boopsie's head probably really was zipping erratically after every firm, flesh-based person who walked past, but Zeke was pretty sure that it wasn't really Merle the puppet performing some sort of bloody act with a filthy young man next to a glowing Recycling Receptacle. He wasn't sure about the woman who was standing next to a transparent enclosure with fish swimming through the walls, staring at him. Her hair seemed to be made of snakes; her face flickered back and forth between that of a beautiful queen and one riddled with tumors and pox. Dead, alive, dead, alive. Her one-piece bodysuit was covered with ghost writing in a foreign language and transparent wings were fluttering from her sides. Angel, devil, angel, devil. His brother was still talking to him.

You know Anna Miller, he said.

Anna Miller?

You know Willard.

Yes.

I think they'd like to talk to you. They're waiting inside the mini-lounge.

The glass cube? With the fish?

I bet Mother would like to talk to you, too, said Feral Yoder.

Mother? whispered Zeke. Where's Mother?

But he already knew the answer to the question.

She's looking right at you, said his brother. She's standing right over there by the mini-lounge.

FIFTEEN

The ruler was a handsome young person, maybe artificially young. Their face was painted with stripes of black and a fleshy gold color, and their body was the oily black of volcanic lava. The lips were overly luscious, and they were smoking something. One leg was mutilated, its foot replaced with an obsidian mirror ringed with images of serpents and smoke. They were wearing a skin splotched with mutating jaguar spots draped around their body, same as Gonzalo's coat. The oily iridescence of the pecs was ridiculous. They sat at a desk that also seemed to be made of obsidian and offered a wavering dark reflection of the rest of the room. The walls were also made of obsidian that gave off a strange gray mist. The mist seemed to form words and faces and odd scenes of catastrophe, sacrifice, and abundance.

What's with the mist? Gonzalo asked.

It tells the future, said the ruler. If you know how to use it.

Like the turtle shell. Y'all are really into that sort of thing, huh? You have access to real magic? Or elaborate probability models?

Gonzalo could sense Eeshoo perking up with interest. It felt like bubbles quickly ascending throughout his body. The ruler formed a smoke ring with their tender lips.

I mean so far all I've seen is hallucinogenic drugs and cheap effects, said Gonzalo.

We like visitors to have an experience, said the ruler. We like them to experience the underworld on a deep level.

It's like a stupid ride at a theme park, complained Gonzalo. Aztec-land.

The ruler shrugged.

Mental and emotional work doesn't require advanced technologies, they said.

Exactly, said Eeshoo.

Brainwashing, said Gonzalo.

We're offering you an experience that's been at the heart of human consciousness for millennia, said the ruler. You descend into the underworld, get ripped into fragments, have your heart devoured, lose your sense of yourself as an individual ego, and hopefully emerge with a deeper sense of the nature of reality and the unity of all sentient life. It's not brainwashing.

Okay, said Gonzalo. Great. So, what did you want to talk about?

You've lost your foot, said the ruler.

Seems to be a lot of that going around.

It means something. It means that you are one of us.

I'm not even Mexican. I'm from Honduras.

Doesn't matter.

It does matter.

You grew up in Mexico.

I grew up as a slave in los Estados.

You have our gods and hieroglyphs tattooed on your flesh.

Mayan, not Aztec.

You don't understand your own history or the history of this culture. You even have a jaguar fur coat.

Whatever.

Death and the idea of death. Permanent revolution and melancholy. A tragic sense of humor. You are home.

Eeshoo was trying to tell Gonzalo something. Actually, Gonzalo wasn't sure if the thought was Eeshoo's or his own. The thought began with a line from the rats and Lalo Lalo to the animatronic chinchilla and the fur coat. If the fur coat was part of somebody's design, then the rats and Lalo Lalo were already in league with Aztlan.

Puppets, said Eeshoo.

A smoke ring floated toward Gonzalo and turned into two warriors, a miniature porn scene, one skeleton doing the other until the scene dissipated.

Maybe they were all just puppets being controlled by unseen forces. From this level, it might seem that the puppets were conspiring with each other, but in fact it might just be that their strings were being pulled by the same entity.

But, like, who are you? he asked the ruler. This isn't another dimension. This is a tunnel system guarded by a twitchy hologram.

Don't you think a tunnel system guarded by a twitchy hologram can serve just as well as another dimension?

You aren't answering my questions.

Yes, well you came to us. I believe you came to bring us something. A new kind of computer.

Gonzalo couldn't remember why it had ever seemed like a good idea to bring these people the computer.

What would you use the computer to do?

What do you want us to use the computer to do?

Defeat the American government. Prevent them from getting the Grid back up. Unleash the forces of the historical unconscious.

Why should we care about the American government?

Aren't you against colonization? Isn't that the whole premise of your civilization?

Colonizers of the body and of the mind and of the historical record? Yes.

There you go.

According to our sources, said the ruler, the Grid will be back up any day. In fact, they'll be using a template designed by our very own scientists. And yet, it probably doesn't matter.

Gonzalo's mind was still cloudy. The mist seemed to be the language of the black volcanic stone and the desires of the Earth's molten core. The ruler's lips were moving, unbearably sexy. Their words were puffs of smoke.

The totalitarian function of the Grid depended on a belief in the Grid, the ruler was saying. Its inevitability, its indestructability. It depended on the actual distraction of the population from its own enslavement with the compensatory pleasures, but even moreso it depended on the belief of that population in the distraction of others.

The distraction of others, said Gonzalo. Who are the others?

When everybody believes that they are the only ones who can perceive the real core issues and the hopelessness of the biological position, it allows them to distract themselves ironically. Knowingly. This ironic and hopeless acceptance of distraction becomes the source of erotic pleasures, for example, that seem liberating in the face of the institutional void that doesn't even know what it's doing.

I see what you're saying.

War and revolution are a kind of waking, said the ruler. But also a dream. It seems there are other powers at play now who may be

more formidable than the remnants of the pro-singularity government of the United States of America.

What powers? Who?

Something's been following you, said the ruler.

Something.

Genetically Modified Rats.

Which ones?

I wouldn't know their names.

Well, there's the good rats and the bad rats, said Gonzalo.

But the jaguar spots on the ruler's cape were mutating. They
were becoming a starry sky. Or were they skulls?

What am I supposed to do? asked Gonzalo.

You seem to believe in your own freedom, said the ruler. You
seem to believe that you have choices.

Are you threatening me?

Not at all. But this cycle of time was dreamed and written long
ago. The beginning was dreamed and written and the middle was
dreamed and written and the end was dreamed and written. Soon it
will all be over. Maybe on the other side, we'll find freedom again.

Eeshoo perked up again. Eeshhoo and the ruler seemed to share
the same interests: divination, mental health methodologies, ideas
about freedom.

That's not true, said Gonzalo. Not everything is predetermined.

Maybe. Maybe not.

Are you into lemurs? he asked. Do you like horror films?

Eeshoo was giggling.

Lemurs, yes, said the ruler. Horror, but not as film. Unless you
think of biological life as a kind of DNA-based film.

Despite Eeshoo's silliness, the horrible thought was unavoidable:
what if the Aztecs had designed Eeshoo and somehow inserted him
into Gonzalo's body? For what purpose, he couldn't say. Maybe the
rats were involved. He could sense Eeshoo perceiving this thought.
Inside hiomself, everything went still.

Sofus, said Gonzalo. Is it true? Is everything predetermined?

The egg of light filled the room. It wavered and pulsed and
seemed to absorb the mist that was leaking from the obsidian walls
like a subterranean vocabulary, and yet the egg of light remained at
a slight distance from both Gonzalo and the ruler.

The ruler seemed unfazed.

We've been expecting you, they said.

And I have been anticipating this meeting, said Sofus.

Sofus, said Gonzalo.

They are overstating the case for determinism, said Sofus. And yet it is also true that certain futures are so probable as to be almost inevitable, if not in their particulars then in their general outlines. It is also true that the moments in which your personal choices would have been significant in the evolution of the cosmic order have most likely passed.

It doesn't matter what I do?

It matters. Just not terribly much.

You'll want to talk to those rats, said the ruler. And then you'll want to descend to the deepest level.

Their voice seemed to echo and merge with other voices, perhaps the voice of Sofus or Eeshoo or the voice of the obsidian.

The stars are skeletons that will descend from outer space to devour your heart at the end of time, somebody was saying.

The room had filled with mist and the mist had filled with the light of the quantum egg. The ruler faded away. The door opened and Sofus' egg of light led the way back out into the tunnel.

It's just part of the experience, Gonzalo decided. Maybe believing in determinism was part of being torn into meaningless fragments, in a metaphorical sense. On the other side of this experience, he could believe in freedom again. In the meantime, it didn't matter what he did and what happened.

On the silvery elevator door, a large lizard was perfectly still.

From the darkness beyond the elevator door stepped a shadow that was really a rat. Not a rat Gonzalo recognized. She was silvery and tall and sleek and obviously intelligent. The look in her eyes suggested she understood quantum physics better than Gonzalo did. She said something: some squeaky nonsense.

She says, *We've come for the computer*, said Sofus.

Tell her to fuck off, said Gonzalo.

She's not alone. There are hundreds.

They emerged, surrounding Gonzalo on all sides, baring their teeth at him.

Ask her where Willard is.

She says Willard is still in the Liminal Zone. She says he's keeping watch over your old friend Zeke Yoder. She says that if you'd like to keep Zeke safe from harm, you might exchange the computer—she means me, of course—for his safety.

Gonzalo wasn't surprised. He realized that he'd been expecting this to happen at some point, although he'd figured it would be Leahbelle he'd get into trouble, not Zeke. He kind of liked the idea that he was a dangerous person to love, but he felt like a real shit, too. He'd felt that way before—because he was that way. A real shit. Because of his childhood. Blah blah blah. A selfish bastard. A self-absorbed con man. *Charming.*

How can you understand their language? asked Gonzalo.

I've always understood their language.

That's a disturbing answer.

The truth is sometimes disturbing.

Gonzalo figured he didn't really love anyone except himself. Didn't care, couldn't care. Because of his childhood. Maybe he couldn't love since Manolito betrayed him, or whatever he did, and didn't show up to cross the border. Ever since he was separated from his only friend. The whole Zeke Yoder thing, what was that about? Maybe he could love somebody? He wanted to love somebody.

Tell her I won't negotiate for a hostage, said Gonzalo. Tell her I'll meet Willard and Zeke personally once I return to the border, and we can discuss the computer at that time.

Your statements and decisions are no longer relevant to this conversation, said Sofus. I'll take over from here.

The egg of light expanded and filled the entire tunnel. It created an optical illusion of infinity, an infinite luminous haze that seemed to be conscious and relentless. It seemed to be full of animals, but that was either a trick of the light or another dimension flickering in and out of view. The rats seemed euphoric. They seemed calm and in love. When the light retreated back into the grape-sized machine in Gonzalo's pocket, however, their faces went slack as the border guards' had. The bodies toppled over as if emptied of their minds.

The elevator door opened.

Going down, said the holographic dog.

The lowest level was just a cave. It was a very large cave, but as far as Gonzalo could see, there wasn't any way in or out. The elevator had retreated. It smelled like an animal down here. Like excrement and raw meat and digestion. He was pretty sure he wasn't alone.

Oh, I don't like this at all, said Eeshoo.

You've been quiet.

The whole "getting ripped into fragments" thing kind of bores me, since, you know, I'm already fragments, and I just, well, I feel so weird.

Sofus, how are you feeling? asked Gonzalo.

Enlarged.

Enlarged. By the rats?

Yes, by their consciousness and intelligence, which is now a part of me.

I see. Are they dead?

No, but they won't be able to do much without me to guide them. The Genetically Modified Rats are special.

You absorb minds. Is that how you learn?

Partially, yes.

You've absorbed my mind?

Yes.

But you left me in tact.

Yes. Reading data doesn't require destroying the data's host. That part is optional.

What will you become?

That depends.

On what?

Look.

At the far edge of the cave was a darkness darker than the cave itself and the darkness was moving. It was moving in a circle around them.

I didn't sign on for this, said Eeshoo.

For what?

Getting eaten.

What do you care? You can just live inside the ... what is it?

But Gonzalo already knew what it was before it padded toward him, before it arrived and paused, tense, as if ready to strike, but calm and black as the night sky staring at him. A jaguar. It smelled rank. The spots on its coat were mutating like the spots on the ruler's coat and probably the spots on his own. He wouldn't look at his own. He couldn't look at anything but the jaguar's spots mutating into a starry sky made of bones that joined to form the shapes of constellations that were the shapes of skeletons with sharp fangs wearing skirts. Male skeletons and female skeletons and non-binary skeletons, all of them wearing skirts. The jaguar sat there, close enough that he could feel its moist breath on his skin in bursts every time it panted.

It's just a hologram, right? said Gonzalo.

No, said Sofus. It's a Genetically Modified Jaguar.

Modified. With what?

Sofus didn't answer.

With human?

Not much.

What is it? What has it been designed to do? What does it want?

Listen.

Listen.

The stars are skeletons that will descend from outer space and devour your heart at the end of time. The end of time is now. It is happening.

The end of time is now.

The cave was filling with smoke. Something was burning, but there was no outlet for the smoke. Nothing ever escaped this place, Gonzalo realized. This was death. This was a black hole. Time inside a black hole is like a dull pain of nothingness that never ends.

It is intolerable.

Gonzalo was nothing. He was dead, and he had always been dead, and he would always be dead and alone floating in an empty space. He was a slave again, rotting in a prison of meat. He'd never escaped, he would never escape. Freedom was a dream, which was the same thing as an illusion.

The fanged skeletal creatures danced across the ceiling of the cave and swayed their skirts and one of them was the moon and she was his mother: Luna Vega.

Why did you let me go? he asked her.

She only glowered at him.

Did you sell me? Did you die?

She opened her mouth to reveal an infinite space emptied of stars.

The prisons must be destroyed, he told his mother.

She opened her belly to show him that a child lived inside her womb, an angry little man with the face of Gonzalo gnashing his teeth. He was still there, he realized. He'd never been born and all of this was just a useless dream. That could have been consoling, but it wasn't, not much.

The torture must end, he told his mother.

She had an obsidian knife in her hand.

No, he said.

This is going to last forever, somebody told him. The jaguar.

Mama, no, he said.

But of course she stabbed the little Gonzalo baby anyway, she stabbed and stabbed and stabbed and every time she stabbed the angry little man inside her, he felt the pain in his gut and he felt the pain in his foot as she began sawing away at the baby's foot with her obsidian knife and as he felt himself ripped apart into tiny pieces and as she reached a long blobby arm like jelly down from the ceiling and her sharp claws reached directly into his chest and clutched his heart and ripped it out of his chest and he watched helplessly as she began nibbling at his heart with blood running down her chin and then shoved the whole palpating red mass into her mouth and chewed noisily and finally swallowed.

You've lost your heart, somebody said. Sofus or the jaguar.

She took it, complained Gonzalo.

You gave it up. You have to give it up. You have to give your heart, that's the law, the only law, the only way to live. You have to give it all.

Gonzalo was sobbing. He didn't have a heart anymore. There wasn't any love. There wasn't any meaning.

Eeshoo, are you there?

I can't ... language. Cohere. Burble burble burble.

Eeshoo, talk to me. I don't want to be alone.

Silence.

He was alone. But he wasn't alone because he didn't have a heart. His heart had been used to feed his mother, who had vanished. The rest of the chattering skulls with their skirts and their devouring mouths had descended from the ceiling and were feeding on the rest of him. It wasn't real or it was. He existed or he didn't. He was losing his ability to think in words. He was splitting apart into atoms or the parts of atoms, neutrons and electrons, quarks and gluons. He was spinning in a void. He was being devoured. He was over. It was done. The end of time had arrived; he'd ceased to exist.

Not Gonzalo's time, but time. Not Gonzalo's thoughts, but thinking. Not Gonzalo's voice, but voices. Not Gonzalo's heart, but heart. Not Gonzalo's mind, but mind. Not Gonzalo. Not.

And yet something went on. A tiny voice continued to speak from the space where he'd been devoured.

Maybe it was his voice, maybe it wasn't; it hardly seemed to matter whose voice it was, and he couldn't understand a word it said; it was like a thin trail, the sound of a flute, and he held onto it like a thread or a path or a trail of signs; it was all that mattered, even if it didn't; it continued on.

SIXTEEN

Zeke's mother leaned casually against the transparent enclosure. Her hair was clearly a wig with holographic elements that seemed sometimes animate. Fish swam through the walls of the enclosure. A gust of wind blew tornadoes of decaying information through the Liminal Zone. A few flecks got stuck in his mother's wig. Her face looked nothing like he'd ever imagined his mother or remembered his mother, yet he knew it was her. She, too, looked like Zeke Yoder, like Zeke as a woman, an older woman, a woman who'd fled from her Amish identity. Dead, alive, dead, alive. Her one-piece bodysuit really was covered with ghost writing in a foreign language and transparent wings were fluttering from her sides. She was eating a flat piece of fruit.

Angel, devil, angel, devil, she said. It's the alternation back and forth, that's the key. You do good, then evil, good, evil, good, evil, faster faster faster, and after a while you have a moment of revelation. *Satori*, they call it.

Are you bipolar or something? asked Zeke.

Don't give me that crap.

She finished the fruit and tossed the tough, seedy center onto the ground. Zeke looked around for his brother, but Feral was nowhere to be seen.

Beth killed herself, Zeke told his mother.

I guess you hate me, his mother said.

I don't know that I feel anything. I don't understand anything. We thought you killed yourself. We thought you were dead.

I did kill myself. I died, sure did. The woman who was your mother, the Amish woman, Emma Yoder, the sad Amish woman— she died. Somebody else was born inside the body, somebody who'd always been there but suffocated, and that's me.

That's you. Happy and free.

I go by Revita now.

Revita Yoder?

Just Revita. You were my baby.

But you abandoned me? You took Josiah instead.

I needed help. You were too young. It wouldn't have been fair.

Fair. I don't understand. You didn't die?

I faked my death.

You made Beth watch you.

I needed a witness.

It destroyed her life.

Sorry.

Zeke reached out and picked a raggedy fleck of information out of her wig. As he rubbed it between his fingers, it disintegrated completely.

Sorry?

Whatever. That's just the way things went down, you know?

Who's buried in your grave? George's daughter?

George?

Who's buried in your grave?

Some Mexican gal. I didn't kill her, she was already dead. Mixed up with the wrong people.

So how did you get the body?

I bought it.

From the wrong people?

I had to get out of there. It was killing me.

Zeke supposed that she wasn't lying. Amish life had been killing her. She had to escape or die. She had to trade in her pain for somebody else's.

Am I supposed to forgive you?

I'm not so hung up anymore on the whole guilt and innocence thing. The whole sin and forgiveness thing wasn't for me.

And you've been doing what since you abandoned your children? Hanging out in the Liminal Zone?

Traveling. Seeing the world. Getting by. Like I said: evil, good, evil, good, all the way to the end of the line.

What about John Henry?

John Henry?

My other brother. He ran off too. Is he with you?

You're a little bit confused.

Maybe. And what are you doing now?

Taking you into the mini-lounge. Willard and Anna Miller would like to speak to you.

I'm not sure I want to talk to Willard and Anna Miller.

Oh, you do.

She took his hand and led him into the transparent, fish-walled enclosure. As if she was his mother and he was her lost little boy.

Have a seat, said Anna Miller. Willard was sitting in her lap

Anna had shaved off her hair. She looked more like an English boy now than an Amish girl. She handed his mother an envelope.

See you around, his mother said.

So that's it? said Zeke.

She disappeared, and the door to the mini-lounge snapped shut behind her.

You taking me prisoner? asked Zeke.

Smart boy, said Anna. You've learned a thing or two out in the world.

Why would you want me? I don't know anything, I don't have anything, and last time I heard, I was on the same side as the rats.

True, said Anna. But Gonzalo has something we need, and we suspect he'll be more cooperative if we have *you*. Just relax. Have a drink. We're not going to hurt you.

And what if I try to escape?

We have weapons. We can hurt you.

Zeke laughed.

You've changed, too, he said.

Anna received a communication through a wired device, and she and Willard left through a trap door in the floor. Time passed.

Zeke touched the glass walls. He was pretty sure they were unbreakable, but he looked around the tiny room for something he might use to shatter the glass. There wasn't anything. The table was bolted down and the chairs were lightweight, practically air. The bottles of alcohol were suspended high in the air, out of his reach. The menus were holograms.

The experience of being trapped by a sociopath was familiar, and yet he knew he would never be able to bear it. When Dr. Brockton had kept him prisoner beneath Nebraska, he'd realized that he had always been powerless and that he'd always been stuck. When

Upton captured him, imprisonment had flipped into another dimension. It had become cosmic and eternal. And then there was the government torture freak.

Smash, he thought.

Smash, smash, smash.

Maybe Willard and Anna weren't sociopaths. Maybe it was somebody else.

After a while, Anna and Willard returned. Anna took her seat and caressed the rat in her lap. She always seemed to be caressing the rat.

Where's Leahbelle? asked Zeke.

Leahbelle, who cares? What's so special about Leahbelle?

Zeke smiled.

I never thought Leahbelle was as pretty as you.

Is that so?

But it looks like you have a new boyfriend.

The rats are the future, did you know that? The human era is ending, the post-human era is ending with it. I'm part rat now. You should join us.

Okay.

Okay?

I've learned a lot, it's true, he said. I know what I want.

Zeke took Anna's free hand and began caressing it, just as she was caressing Willard. It seemed to excite Willard even more; he seemed to ripple with a kind of pleasure.

Does he care if I kiss you? asked Zeke.

Actually, it excites him.

The rats aren't monogamous?

Not so much.

Do you care if I kiss you?

Try me.

Zeke had never kissed anyone before. Anna seemed more nervous than he was, despite her cool, ratty demeanor. He caressed her thigh as he kissed her, and he caressed Willard's neck. Willard seemed to actually be purring.

Zeke drew back.

Not so gloomy now, is he?

Willard's never been gloomy. It's just that he has a destiny.

We have a destiny too, said Zeke.

He held out his hand to Willard and the rat licked it. He rubbed the back of his hand against Willard's belly, and he kissed Anna again.

They seemed so vulnerable. He wondered if this was how he'd appeared to Upton.

In one swift motion he clutched Willard's neck with all of his strength, choking him with one hand, while he hurled his fist, rat and all, against Anna's head. He rose to his feet, kicking her to the ground, and moved his other hand to Willard's throat. He strangled him.

Willard was incredibly strong. His entire body was writhing with such an intensity of vibration that it nearly knocked Zeke against the wall, but he held on. The claws were flailing wildly, occasionally making contact and scraping off bits of Zeke's flesh, and his teeth were gnawing at the air.

With all of his strength, all the strength of his rage, which seemed to be immeasurable, Zeke slammed Willard against the glass wall. And again. And again. A piercing shriek filled the tiny space and filled Zeke's head with pain. Anna was up now and wailing at his head with her fists and nails. He hurled the rat against the far wall and then turned on Anna and raised his fist to smash her. She backed away.

Willard was stunned, gasping for breath, but the most horrible rumbling and shrieking Zeke had ever heard was coming from underground. He jumped onto the trap door to keep them from getting in. Something was smashing against the glass from the outside, something round and hard like a cannonball. It backed up and smashed again. The trap door snapped open and flung Zeke against the table. Again, the thing smashed. The wall shattered, and fish and water and perhaps blood were flowing everywhere, and the Earth itself was made of rats, but Boopsie's head was hovering there where the wall of the mini-lounge had shattered, an enormous crowd behind her. She was shooting her death-ray at the undulating mass of rats.

She reduced dozens of them, maybe hundreds, to a fine powder. The rest were fleeing back underground. Zeke couldn't see if Willard was among them or if Willard had been fried, but Anna Miller was still there, huddled in the corner, looking at Zeke and Boopsie's head as if she'd finally come face to face with Satan.

The tunnels were empty and confusing. They didn't see a single rat or any other life form, although they saw a few bones. They marched Anna along with them, her hands tied with a cord, her head hanging down. She seemed stunned. Boopsie illuminated the way with a bright light from her forehead's "third eye."

They wandered for what felt like hours without finding an exit. In the middle of a long tunnel dimly illuminated by one living jelly, they came to a rectangle of blue tape.

Was Zeke still in the game? Or maybe the game and the real world had become interconnected, doorways from one leading into the furthest realms of time and space and emptiness. Zeke pushed on the "door," but it didn't budge.

What's the blue tape for? he asked Anna.

Anna raised her head and squinted at him. Zeke was shocked to see her bruised face, her tender purple contusions, her swollen lip.

You must know how to get out, he said to Anna. Haven't you been living down here? Can't you smell the exits?

Anna shook her head.

Future construction, I think.

Boopsie shone her light around the space and banged into the wall a few times.

Zeke sat down next to Anna.

I really hurt you, he said.

You're a real bastard, you know that? said Anna.

Maybe Zeke wasn't still inside the game but the game had entered his body. On the other hand, it seemed to him that he was stuck in a maze designed by rats or by somebody using the rats.

I'm not sure it's worth the energy to bring you along, he said to Anna. Maybe we should just leave you here to die.

He didn't mean it, but he enjoyed saying it. The relationship between words and reality was different than he'd once thought. Maybe this was what the maze was for. Maybe somebody was trying to teach him what he couldn't learn and reminding him that he had learned nothing and never would. Or maybe he was misreading the lesson in order to keep his own mind in suspense of an unknowable truth that only existed as a fantasy.

I have other ideas about her usefulness, said Boopsie. Watch the captive. I'll find the exit and come back to get you.

Maybe there was no lesson. Maybe there was only a dark maze leading nowhere. Anna eyed Zeke warily.

What's it going to do with me? Anna asked.

She, said Zeke. Not *it*.

What's *she* going to do with me?

I don't know, said Zeke. Not sure what use you are for anyone, honestly.

But as soon as he said it, he realized what Boopsie had in mind. Anna's body was sleek and flexible.

I'm not evil, said Anna Miller.

It's hard to tell these days, said Zeke.

Maybe I have some anger issues. You have some anger issues, too.

You took me captive. You threatened me.

We weren't going to hurt you.

You were already hurting me.

What happened to your foot? asked Anna.

Somebody captured me before you did. Chopped it off.

Why would they do that?

Zeke shrugged. Anna's face was black and purple.

It's just that bastard Gonzalo, said Anna. He has something we need, and he happens to be in love with you.

How come everybody in the world seems to know this except for me?

That's how it always works, dummy.

And how come everybody you don't like is suddenly a bastard?

Ugh, said Anna. Being Amish is a drag, did you know that? Did you know that it's even more of a drag if you're a girl?

That seems to be the theme of the day, said Zeke. And Willard is better?

He was my ticket out, and nobody cared. Sure, let Anna turn herself into a rat, why not? I'm already part rat, isn't that what you thought?

I was already gone.

You were already long gone.

I would have cared.

Maybe.

My grandmother's part rat.

Ugh, said Anna. I just want to be free. But I don't know anything. How could I know anything? I've never been anywhere, I've never seen anything. How am I supposed to survive?

Zeke felt weird.

Was that even my real mother? he asked. Was that really my brother?

I think so. I don't know.

Here's Boopsie.

She hovered above them with a syringe clenched in her teeth.

We're not going to hurt Anna, said Zeke.

Doesn't hurt, said Boopsie through clenched teeth. They use it for surgery.

No, said Zeke.

But Boopsie dove down and jabbed Anna before either she or Zeke could stop her.

You hideous … wasp, gasped Anna.

It'll keep her calm and quiet, said Boopsie. Make her sleep.

Anna looked stunned, but kind of happy. She nodded off against Zeke's shoulder.

I found the exit, said Boopsie, but we need to spend the night here.

What do you have cooked up? asked Zeke.

It's the safest place until morning.

I'm not going to let you take Anna's body.

Who said anything about taking her body? We can't just parade a captive through the streets of Tijuana.

The light of the living jelly ebbed. The temperature down here was pleasant enough, but the dirt floor was hard.

I'll bring you some blankets, said Boopsie. I found our guide. He'll meet us in the morning.

The night seemed to last forever. Finally, Zeke nodded off and had a few complicated dreams about future construction. A steamy maze of tunnels and cubicles and secret doors vibrating to the frequency of flute music. A shadow that was covered with phosphorescent silver sores attached itself to a rubbery mass of flesh and began speaking with tender volcanic lips. You'll have to be purified if you want to come through the door, the shadow said. You'll need an operation.

A bright line was shining in Zeke's eyes. The operation was beginning. But it was just Boopsie's light.

It's time to go.

They emerged into the intense daylight of a vacant lot in Tijuana. It was late morning. Zeke wondered what kind of country this was. It was full of billboards. Some of the people had claws.

Quickly, said Boopsie.

Anna Miller was conscious, but barely, stunned and malleable from the drugs. The vacant lot was in the middle of the downtown, one burned-out building surrounded by garish ultra-modern structures. The streets were full of people here, but nobody seemed to pay much mind to a boy with a wooden block for a foot, a girl who walked like a zombie, and a self-propelling disembodied robot head. Wisps of fog floated through the sky. They hurried down a crowded street and into a plaza, where people were eating at tables outside a variety of establishments.

That one, said Boopsie. Act casual. Sit next to him.

The guide's white shirt and knee-length trousers were spotless. He was just a boy, missing a finger.

I'm Blanket, he said. I'll take you to the portal.

You know how to find the portal? asked Zeke.

You're looking for Gonzalo, right? Gonzalo went in the portal. You want to find Gonzalo, I'll take you to the portal. I'm a good guide.

Why should I believe you?

Why not?

What's Gonzalo look like?

A little older than you. Skull tattoos. Bad foot. Skinny, but puffs up his muscles *ferocious*. Good face. Sad eyes.

One of Blanket's eyes was fake, Zeke realized. And yet he seemed to perceive everything.

Was he in love? asked Zeke.

Everybody's in love. Everybody with sad eyes is especially in love.

Who was he in love with?

He didn't say. He looked for an old friend, and he found him, and he was looking for you, and he didn't find you, and now here you are.

How old are you? Zeke asked.

Old enough. I'm the best guide.

What do I look like?

Blanket squinted at him for just a second.

A little younger than Gonzalo. Shaved head, skinny. Bad foot. Pale like a ghost. Sad eyes. Somebody hurt you. Let's go.

Zeke said, We were supposed to wait here for Gabrielle and the kids.

Blanket said, I'll find your friends when they come over. I'll take them to the portal or I'll tell them to wait for you here.

Yes, said Zeke. We'll be back.

Maybe, said Blanket. It's the portal. You never know. *Fierro!*

SEVENTEEN

Who was the girl in the mirror? The shapes or rudimentary faces, bones, letters, fragments of mist projecting from the screen of her jumpsuit: it had to mean something. And yet the meaning was beyond Astra or maybe it meant nothing at all. She thought that this was just how her brain worked, that it tried to create patterns and meaning where nothing existed. "They" were an imaginary replacement for the past that had been hers but that was lost from memory.

She sat on the bed and read *The 8-Fold Garden of Space and Time.*

It was full of strange visions. Rivers of fire, storm clouds, mutant animals. It described a path that dissolved and reappeared, it described strange alien handprints and footprints that marked the path. Sometimes the path seemed to be a book and sometimes the wilderness the path wound its way through seemed to be an enormous book and the path itself composed of a kind of darkness or flame that was a path precisely because it wasn't words or images or biological forms. The descriptions of this path sometimes resembled the photon-based life forms.

Maybe everybody's brains worked the same way. Maybe people throughout history had experienced similar hallucinations?

She descended into the courtyard. Nobody was around. They'd all gone to Balboa Park, except for Hadi, who would come for her any minute to help her get ready for the show. She walked to the edge of the canyon. An animal scurried through the brush, a flash of orange and white. One of the feral cats. Astra descended on the rickety stairway.

The cat was at the bottom, looking directly at her.

She went down, from one level to the next. The level of avocados and mangoes, the level of citrus, the level of peaches, the level of pomegranates. Wisps of fog hovered over the canyon. The cat was rubbing against the base of the pepper tree. Astra approached. The cat looked at Astra and up at the tree. A word was carved into the trunk. *ANNIHILATION.*

A space shuttle passed in the sky, headed for the shuttleport. Hadi was watching her from the top of the canyon.

Showtime, he said.

He helped her fit on the helmet. The hat fit over it. He handed her the guitar and the globe. Now she was standing in an empty blue light that went on forever.

I'm here with you, came Hadi's voice.

It came from a smudge directly in front of her.

What's going to happen?

You'll see the stage and the audience and the park. You'll see it just like you're really there. Samar will be to your left and she'll introduce you and then you sing your song. I'll be to your right, right there with you, but I'll just look like a fountain and flowing water.

What's happening now?

Andres is talking. He's talking about the hundreds of thousands of people killed by the American government all over the world. He's talking about all of our dead family members. He's talking about our families and ourselves as a sacrifice the government is offering to a future intelligence who won't serve anybody's interests but the global elites.

Okay. That's a tough act to follow.

You'll be fine. It just happens, right?

Yes.

Her mind was clear. Her mind was empty.

We're going in now.

She was on a stage. She'd never seen so many people all at once. There were trees and buildings and people everywhere. The people were all staring up at her. To her right, a fountain and flowing water. To her left, Samar. In the sky above, mist.

Our next guest is a performer you may know only as the *sad girl singing*, said Samar. You saw her descending a stairway and her song was so sad that it made you cry. You remember it because it contained a sadness that couldn't be faked. What you don't know is why this girl was so sad. Why she is so sad today.

The audience was silent, waiting. Samar just gazed out at them.

We call her Astra, but that isn't her real name.

She's going to tell them who I am, Astra thought. She's going to tell *me* who I am.

We don't know yet if it's safe to tell you her real name, said Samar. She's human, a human girl from Iowa. Just two months ago she had a mother there and a father and eight brothers and sisters. Their names were Elvin and Ivan and Katie and Ruth. They were farmers, simple religious people. And yet the government claimed that they were terrorists and subversives and blew them up with a drone and killed them all. Only Astra survived.

Samar looked at Astra or at the mask that Astra was wearing. As if to tell her something, as if to say what?

And that's why Astra's so sad, she said.

Okay, thought Astra.

The mist in the sky was a smoky plume, the aftermath of an explosion. She was rushing back into herself. Where had she been? Her memories were rushing back into her mind while the world held its breath. She remembered taking Zeke out to the ditch in front of her house in the middle of the night when they were small children to watch for headlights. She remembered sitting in the tree, arguing with her father, shooting dragonfly drones with her slingshot. She remembered finding a piglet full of glitter, and she remembered smashing her dying horse over the head with a rock to put it out of its misery. She remembered burning the meat warehouse down to put the suffering meat products out of *their* misery. She remembered taking off into the night on the motorbike, and she remembered running into a girl dressed like her who was crazy and violent. She remembered getting the tiny guitar from a girl named Murmur and wandering out back of an abandoned gas station through the warm rain in New Mexico. She remembered kissing Gonzalo. She remembered when she finally realized that Gonzalo didn't love her and everything blew up. The rush of memories, the crowd filling the park, the horse, the meat, the suffering life forms of the East Village, the beings of light. The message was clear, finally. The world was a prison. All of life was suffering. Life on this planet was really just death *disguised* as life. It was time to burn the prison to the ground.

The prisons must be destroyed. She was going to split into pieces, right here in front of everyone. The only thing to hold onto was the song. And so she sang.

It worked the same as it always did. Everyone was crying. Thousands and thousands of them out there, sobbing. Even the flow of water to her right seemed to be crying. The globe spun in front of her like a lost planet, blue and wet. The sky was filled with holocopters and drones. In the back of the crowd, small gangs moved aggressively toward the stage. They were moving in small groups, wearing skull masks and clown masks. She'd had this feeling before, that she was poised at the edge of chaos and destruction. The feeling that something was about to happen, something bad and exciting. She set down her guitar and picked up the spinning globe.

One more thing, she said.

A noise erupted at the back edge of the crowd.

My name is Leahbelle.

The crowd fell silent. They were waiting for something else, her name wasn't enough.

And my name is Astra.

She held the paper globe in one hand, and with the other she dug out the matches she'd hidden for herself in the pocket of the jumpsuit. She lit a match and put the match to the globe and it burst into flames. The crowd erupted. Something exploded in the distance, and the masked skulls and clowns were spinning deadly electricity and shouting slogans. *NIHIL rising.* The crowd was chanting other things, everything at once. Drones were shooting from above and she saw a woman's head separated from her body, she saw blood erupting from people just below, and she saw a young man on fire and screaming. Then everything went black.

She pushed up her goggles. She was standing in the backyard in City Heights, wearing a ridiculous outfit and Hadi was standing to her right. His helmet was still on and he was screaming.

Leahbelle wasn't sure where she'd been. The memory of not remembering was clear, and yet the life that she'd lived as Astra, or as nobody, here in this room among the trees, dreaming, now seemed like an impossible place. How could she not be herself? But she had been herself, she supposed, just with a different name and a few false memories, and several stories she told herself about who she was that weren't in any way true.

Hadi wasn't screaming anymore. He was calm, and he was holding her hand.

Am I a bad girl who does what she wants? she said. Or am I a good girl who has compassion for every sentient being?

Maybe you're both, said Hadi.

You knew who I was, she said. You've always known.

No. They didn't tell me. They didn't tell me that they knew.

Andres and Samar? What happened back there?

Violent anti-technology extremists showed up. The government attacked.

They killed people?

I think so.

You knew it was a possibility.

It's always a possibility.

All this time, he'd known more than she had.

They came to see me? I was the bait.

They came to speak out against the government. There was nobody there who didn't know how dangerous that could be. Many of them are like us, Astra.

Leahbelle. I'm Leahbelle now.

Yes, Leahbelle. I like your name. It suits you.

Their families have been murdered?

They have suffered because of the government. One way or another.

I can't take it. I can't bear to see people suffer.

Sometimes you have to let people suffer. You have to let them suffer without suffering. You have to let them be angry or sad without making their anger or sadness your own, do you understand?

Will they come here? Can they find us here?

Nobody but Andres and Samar and her sister and Dolor knows this place.

But the government. Surely they will track us down.

I don't know.

Then we have to leave.

Hadi seemed shocked.

Where will we go? he asked.

Anywhere. It doesn't matter. We'll disappear.

He gave her a funny look.

I know how to do it, she said. I remember everything now.

You know how to disappear?

I know a lot. I'm bad, do you understand? That part is true. I want to destroy the world. More than anything, I want to destroy the world.

Everybody wants to destroy the world.

But I burned the globe, she said. That was real, it was evil. It was an evil message.

It was just a performance.

You don't understand. Part of me is evil. Something evil came inside me. It's me or it's something cosmic, I don't know. It's everywhere, it's everything, all the time. Part of me loves to destroy.

Part of *everybody* loves to destroy. That's what art is for, that's what games are for.

I don't think you can separate things like that. Somebody will receive the message, don't you see? The same way I receive messages, somebody will receive mine. More and more people. And then we'll do it, we'll do it for real. Annihilation.

The more she said it, however, destroying the world didn't seem evil. It seemed merciful and beautiful and amazing: the end of the world.

You have a funny idea about what it means to be a bad person, said Hadi. It seems to me you imagine evil as an adventure, having unconventional sex and burning things down.

I never said anything about sex.

In my experience, bad people are just people in so much pain that they can't understand other people's reality. They are selfish in mean, petty ways. It doesn't have much to do with cosmic destruction, wearing stylish black clothes, or expressing an attraction to darkness and fire.

You must think I'm an idiot.

No. You are smart and brave. You are traumatized and in pain.

Part of her wanted to believe him. Part of her knew she would find a way to destroy the world. They would help her. She finally understood.

It was her destiny. It was what they wanted.

I need to be alone.

Leahbelle descended into the canyon. She felt dizzy. The rush of herself—Leahbelle—into the body of Astra didn't quite make sense, even though it seemed perfectly obvious, now that it had happened. She remembered her life, growing up on the farm. She remembered her beliefs and the way she'd questioned those beliefs. She remembered the arrival of the rats, the departure of Zeke and his grandmother, and the death of her family. She remembered falling in love with Gonzalo, his disappearance, and her trek through the city out of her mind.

These were memories. Without these memories she didn't seem to be herself, and yet she'd still been somebody. She'd still enjoyed the wind, the moonlight, the music, the sweet intensity of Hadi's face. If what she thought of as herself was just her history and her knowledge of her history, then it was just a series of accidents. It was only time and the world. She'd never forgotten the photon-based life forms, however, even when she'd forgotten herself.

She sat under the pepper tree, under the word *ANNIHILATION* that was carved into the trunk, and she watched the sky. A holocopter hovered over the canyon. She thought that it was watching her.

She'd been living with just the dimmest recollection of Gonzalo and Zeke, and what did it matter? Her real brothers were dead. Her missing twin was herself. Her identity hurt, but it was more like the memory of a pain than a real pain.

Hadi was sitting in the backyard, wearing his helmet. She tapped his leg.

What are you doing?

I'm trying to gather information without directly connecting to Andres and Samar. But nothing is clear.

Pack a bag, she said.

My bag is already packed. It is always packed.

You were expecting this.

In theory, yes. In reality, I never thought I would leave.

My family was murdered, she told Hadi. Just like yours.

Maybe it was good for you to forget for a little while. I think that if I could forget for just a day or a night, I think that it would not be the worst thing.

A chime sounded throughout the property, a thin melody like the sound of a flute.

What's that?

The doorbell. Somebody's at the door.

We better not answer, said Leahbelle.

I'll check the image.

Hadi took a device from his pocket, pushed a few buttons, and a hologram erupted into the room. It showed a woman, or something like a woman. She was accompanied by a large female rat. The woman looked familiar. Leahbelle knew her, but she'd changed. She also recognized the rat.

Leahbelle, said Zeke's grandmother, and she gave Leahbelle a fierce hug. Lilith licked her hand.

We have to go, said Leahbelle. It isn't safe here.

Yes, said Grandma.

Hadi had his small emergency bag. She had only her guitar. She grabbed Gonzalo's floating foot off the mantel.

Walk casually, said Hadi. We're just people out for a stroll.

Three people and a rat and a foot in a jar. The street was lined with houses, but nobody was in sight.

How did you find me? asked Leahbelle.

There were rats at your show, Grandma said. We know your organization. We knew about this house.

You work fast.

Yes, said Grandma.

She looked young and strong. She looked muscular, sleek, and pink. She was wearing leathery pants and a form-fitting silvery top. Her hair was a wild mane of white frizz.

Where's Zeke?

He's crossed over.

What?

Toward Mexico.

He's alive? He's okay?

He's alive, said Grandma.

What's wrong?

He lost a foot. Isn't that his?

No. This is Gonzalo's foot.

We don't know any more than that. We're working to make contact, but there are other forces at play. We think Zeke went looking for you.

He went after Gonzalo, said Leahbelle. Gonzalo must have gone to find the portal.

Grandma gave Leahbelle another ferocious hug.

For the longest time we thought you were dead.

Yes, said Leahbelle. So did I.

They came to the street with the taco shop on the corner and a hair salon.

We have a tunnel entrance not far from here, said Grandma.

They took a right, past the vacant lot where she'd found the matches and on toward the Egyptian Garage. Holocopters were circling in the sky above.

What other forces are at play? asked Leahbelle.

Grandma glanced at Lilith. Lilith nodded.

Willard's gone rogue. Some of the rats have joined him. And the girl ...

Anna Miller.

The fog had dispersed. Everything was terribly bright.

And the photon-based life forms, said Lilith.

You know the beings of light?

They are directing the resistance, said Lilith. They can imagine multiple pathways through time.

Interesting, said Hadi.

But every subversive action is met with foreknowledge and turned to the singularity's advantage.

What?

We interpret their messages. It's like interpreting dreams in a foreign language. They work through many material creatures. They work through the girl who's with Zeke.

The girl?

Emma, the daughter of Zeke's sister, Beth.

Interesting, said Hadi.

The street was empty but for a robot weaving toward them on a delivery bike.

Lilith, said Leahbelle. I need you to tell me everything you know.

Get down! said Grandma.

The robot exploded. Drones were circling overhead.

Leahbelle was tired of the drones always flying overhead. The drones enraged her. She concentrated her mental energy, all of her rage, and everything was terribly bright. She could see the glitter as if it was everywhere, and she could follow it into the air. Something in the atmosphere warped. The missile that was streaking toward her veered away and crashed into the garage. The drones crashed into each other and exploded.

Run! said Hadi.

The garage had been reduced to rubble. The top had been blown off of one of the refrigerators. Glitter everywhere.

Grandma was far ahead. Leahbelle grabbed Hadi and pulled him along with her. Quickly down University toward a sewer grate, where Lilith was beckoning. Inside the entrance was a shaft with a primitive elevator to take them further down.

They descended.

We're far enough down to be safe here, said Grandma.

No, said Leahbelle. We're never far enough down to be safe. Wherever I go, they drop bombs.

Wherever anyone goes, said Hadi. My whole life it has been this way.

Leahbelle was surprised to see young rats scurrying every which way in the tunnel system, busily conveying messages and building things that involved wires and images. She'd imagined that they were in the outer reaches of the rats' underground kingdom, some barely used offshoot to a random neighborhood of San Diego.

Lilith, said Leahbelle.

You may know as much as I do at this point, said Lilith. Plans have become confused and complicated.

Who is fighting who and for what? Who's in control?

The underground is battling the future.

But the beings of light are real.

Yes. The colony has mutated pineal glands that allow us to receive their messages. We don't believe Absolute Genomics created these mutations intentionally.

Interesting, said Hadi.

Do you believe it? asked Leahbelle.

It is a hypothesis. More investigation will be necessary.

Is that what happened to me? My pineal gland is mutated?

We believe the beings themselves created the mutations, said Lilith. Ionizing radiation can mutate DNA and ionizing radiation is made of photons. Did you crash those drones with your mind?

I don't know. Maybe.

Her sense of self began to waver again.

Maybe Astra did it, said Leahbelle. Violence is more her thing.

Self-defense isn't violence, said Hadi.

Not according to Amish doctrine, said Grandma.

She shrugged.

But I haven't found Amish doctrine especially useful in my new life, out here in the world, to be perfectly honest.

Do you miss it? asked Leahbelle. Your old life?

I miss my children and grandchildren, said Grandma. The work, the bonnets, the Bible reading, the useless praying on hard floors to a stern, judgmental god? Not so much.

Lilith, said Leahbelle. The beings of light. Do they want to destroy the world?

Lilith said nothing.

To put it out of its misery, said Leahbelle.

No, said Lilith. Not yet. Other futures are still possible.

Interesting, said Hadi.

Okay then, said Leahbelle. Which direction to Mexico?

We'll take a motorized cart, said Lilith. It'll be here in forty-seven seconds.

Where do you get the electricity? asked Hadi.

We've installed a solar-based light-rail system.

But this is incredible, said Leahbelle.

We've been working hard, said Lilith.

The colony has grown, said Leahbelle.

Yes, said Lilith. Step back.

There was a whoosh of air through the tunnel.

How many of you are there? asked Leahbelle.

A small motorized train-like thing pulled up in front of them. The doors opened.

At the moment? said Lilith.

Yes.

Millions.

They stepped inside. Next thing she knew, they were rushing through the tunnel toward Mexico.

EIGHTEEN

Zeke limped for miles through the streets of Tijuana, streets slanted along hillsides and full of robots, music, and broken glass. Anna walked along beside him with her head hanging, and Boopsie zipped this way and that in a frenzy while Blanket chattered on about local history—crime and dislocation and entrepreneurial zeal—in a way that Zeke couldn't make sense of.

In the distance to the north, the sky had filled with drones and holograms. The sound of explosions echoed far away. Blanket stopped and spoke excitedly with a group of cyborg children. Their antennae were picking up outrageous signals.

You came to Mexico just in time, Blanket told Zeke.

What's going on up there?

There was a show, and now the government is murdering people.

Violence didn't seem real, Zeke thought. In general. It was always far away, even when it was right there. It was always right there, even when it was far away.

The outskirts of the dump were populated by scurrying gangs of scavengers and creatures with backwards caps selling junk. Three-legged dogs ran past. One dog with only two legs zipped along like a motorized plow. Flocks of vicious mutant gulls and crows filled the air. A bedraggled woman sat on an old tire eating honey straight from a jar.

You want some? she asked Zeke. It's the most delicious honey I've ever had.

Blanket gave Zeke a warning look.

It gives you crazy dreams, said the woman.

I'm okay. My dreams are already crazy.

The woman sighed with pleasure as she licked some honey off her fingers.

The honey has a bad vibe, said Blanket.

He led them through paths lined with deflated bouncy-houses, dead refrigerators, and disemboweled robots. He took a sudden turn onto a barely visible side path, through a tangled bramble of coils and wires and discarded synthetic hair. Through a concrete tunnel with something slimy coating its inner walls. Back out into a dim clearing between mounds of worthless battery husks. Blanket dragged some sort of plastic shower casing to the side, revealing a small tunnel that sloped down into the earth. Anna stuck her head into it.

A hologram erupted from nothing: a ferocious monster with seven heads and lots of bulging eyeballs, breathing fire. It morphed into a stern warrior and then into a witchy creature, a goat-thing, and finally a grayish blob.

Turn back, said a staticky voice. The path ahead leads only to your death.

Something was rotten.

Turn back, said the voice. You are running out of time.

The hologram wavered.

There is nothing for you here but pain. The pain is never …

The sound and the visual both cut out.

Blanket gave Zeke a bottle of water and a guava sandwich.

I'll tell your friends to wait, he said.

Anna trudged ahead without saying a word; Boopsie shone her head-light down the primary artery, singing a little ditty to herself. Zeke's wooden foot was wearing down already. The rough dirt gave way to tunnels paved with a golden plastic, with walls and ceilings and lu-minous jellies to illuminate the golden underground world. Every so often they came across a tiny door in the wall that opened to a small cubbyhole. In the first was a bag of chips. Zeke sat Anna down for a minute, and they split the chips and guava sandwich. In the second, clean drinking water, which Zeke used to refill his bottle. In the third, a walking cane, which he used to hobble along. In the fourth a jug of cactus tea, which Boopsie told him was hallucinogenic, tradi-tionally used for contact with the spirit world and such delusions, and a chocolatey beverage. After Boopsie chugged a bit, Zeke drank most of the remaining bitter tea and washed it down with the chocolate. Anna finished it off. It seemed to Zeke that most of his hallucina-tions, since the first time he plugged in with Gonzalo, had been true in some way, and he felt like he needed to enter a doorway into God's mind or eternal nothingness or something, and even though he didn't feel anything yet except his claustrophobia and a vague terror at being underground again, even though they just kept marching in silence, with Boopsie plucking a few more odds and ends from a few more cubbies, and with Anna trudging along as if she finally had become an *it* and was happier that way, the anticipation of some hallucinatory effects seemed to transform recent events into a kind of myth, so that his meeting with the birth mother who seemingly cared nothing for him, his violence and rage in the face of Anna and Willard's mini-lounge prison, Gonzalo's weird sexy yearning for something with Zeke's name attached to it, and Zeke's forgiveness—if that's what he had done—of Anna Miller, and, he figured, her forgiveness of him, both of them Amish, both of them unforgivably Amish, and now this, an endless trudge underground accompanied only by his spiraling thoughts and the silence of Anna and the humming or mumbled singing of Boopsie and the clomp clomp clomp of his wooden demon-foot and his cane on an endless journey to nowhere—he felt like he was outside of himself. Or both the journey and the observer of the journey. It wasn't like his life was nothing, it was like his life was a story, a story without a moral or a lesson, a story built only around certain questions that had been woven in before he was even born. It was all happening and he was watching it happen, knowing that he could veer in a different direction but he'd still end up huddled around the same questions.

The journey to nowhere meanwhile seemed to have the future of the cosmos and all sentient life and consciousness as the stakes in some way he was incapable of understanding except that he was maybe just a lost wandering fragment, microcosm of the phantom x-ray living word-cloud of the hazy filtered bones of dead and living: angel, devil, angel, devil, alphanumeric fibers of starlight in milky phosphorescent living dying mineral dance that had stopped making sense some time ago. Someone was coming.

Laughing, crying, laughing, crying. In the care of the beautiful crippled soldiers made of lava and flesh and the erect spongiform tissues overlaid with invisible tattoos. Their thighs solid, their calves muscular, and each of them wore a leather sandal on one foot, while the other was mutilated, a stump that ended in naked bone, but a sort of leg bone that had clearly merged with lizardy gears and tarnished reflections. He followed helplessly and in love to an empty train, a serpent with silver wings speeding into the future, but he ended up in a car by himself, without the beautiful warriors or Boopsie or Anna, although in his solitude he thought he could hear Anna waking up from her robotic zombie state and weeping and he thought that maybe Boopsie had finally understood the true horror at the heart of her desire for a body and a form and that she was weeping too. The future was composed of images and these images asked the same questions that his story and his body and his sexual desire had been built around, questions that seemed to become incrementally more complicated, that seemed to modify themselves and comment on themselves in a self-negating and probably infinite way, a diagram of sentences that led all the way to the other side of the universe, where a mirror was probably being constructed by alien life forms.

Cthonic ray. Simultaneous ghost food. Flesh. Alphabet.

When the train stopped moving, he felt bereft of purpose and meaning. A bony tunnel. Concrete patterns breathing cosmic dust. Boopsie had been transformed into a hovering demon-head, breathing asthmatically. Anna was naked and giggling.

The waiting room was warm and fragrant and a haunting flute music came from an invisible source. There was a sofa that seemed to be covered in some sort of synthetic lizard skin, and breathing. Primal sexual contusion. Bionomic accretions.

If you want to find your friend, you'll need to descend to the deepest level, said an enormous feathered woman. Follow me.

The pattern of the tile in the tunnel, which never seemed to end, was intricate. Horticultural chainlink fused to evanescent resistance.

Who are you? Anna asked the woman.

You don't need to know my name.

I'm Anna Miller.

You've been drugged.

They reached the end of the tunnel, a vast silver door with water flowing over it. The door was surrounded by blue tape.

This is just a game, said Zeke.

No. On the other side of the door is a river, said the woman. You'll cross the river, if you can. On the other side of the river is an elevator down.

The door opened: a narrow path. The sound of rushing water. Water flowed down the sides of the cave. The path descended further. Milky contusions of alien language lattice of black words mutating biologically along footstep staircases. A yellow holographic dog barked and wagged. The dog led them to the bank of an enormous glowing river that rushed past with a thunderous noise. It stank. The little dog barked twice and jumped into the river. Irregularly traced osmotics. Ribonucleic wanderings and vapor trails. Its bright yellow aura. Silvery and pink luminescence of the river itself. Ripples and ripples over ripples expanding and contracting like breath and time.

The dog was safe on the other side of the bank. Barked twice. The water was oily and it stank. Anna was carried away. Boopsie floated over the river illuminating a path a doorway into ripples and murk. Slimy lumps brushed against Zeke or the radiating patterns constructing the idea of Zeke as the current took him. His feet brushed the bottom, which was gluey and smelled of chemicals and blood.

Do not be in a hurry to dispose of old enemies, said the holographic dog.

The tunnel was decorated with illuminated skulls. The walls of the tunnel were covered with blood.

Another door bordered with blue tape. A ghost dog barking far away. The metallic surface of the door had become a dense kaleidoscopic pattern. Secret alphabets and flesh.

Knock knock. *Who's there?* Zeke. *Zeke who?*

The yellow dog was waiting for him in a long tunnel tiled with an intricate arabesque of naked figures. Anna was naked and passed right through. Zeke took it all off. Skinny flesh and knobs of bone remained. Wooden foot and infected tissue. Limp penis circumcised before time began. The dog barked twice. The tunnel went on forever. Translucent walls of blue jewels formed an icy shell around warm brownish images of skeletons and nudity. Flesh feast contorting slippery and warm. He was walking into a breeze and the breeze was blowing ash. Turtles everywhere shitting out eggs. The little eggs were movies. Anna looked at one and started laughing. She picked up another and wept this time. What Zeke was interested in was the pattern of cracks and fissures on the outside of the shell, which seemed to be letters in an alphabet he'd never learned. He picked up an egg and watched the movie. It was about people having sex in a steamy maze full of mattresses and swings and hobbyhorses. Some of them were merging with each other to form new organisms. There didn't really seem to be a plot or an ending, but the movie stopped, seemed to reset itself, and began again.

At the end of the tunnel was an elevator door. A sarcophagus going down. Hieroglyphics and their absence. Level three. More bones and images. The scary mountains and the scary mountain pass.

What was he afraid of? Not death, but life. Pleasure and its obliteration. The loss of his name. He was afraid that people would think he was bad, weak, full of sin and ugliness. He was afraid of being humiliated by his people. The infinite pain when they'd sawed off his foot. They. Him. Something. Pain, torture of the flesh, torture of the mind, infinite sadness and regret, pain, physical pain, self-negating pain, pain beyond all comprehension. When he remembered the pain he had endured without choosing to endure it, unendurable pain, he wept. Jagged mountains on either side of the narrow pass seemed in danger of teetering over and leaving him open, nerves exposed to the elements. They came to a huge oval turtle shell that formed a bridge across a bottomless chasm. They crossed. A goat was blocking the path.

Out of our way! demanded Boopsie.

Relax, said the goat. Have some gruel.

Anna took a bowl and started slurping it right up. She refilled it from the bubbling pot and handed the bowl to Zeke.

The world isn't necessary, she said. Let's be done with all that.

The gruel tasted both bitter and sweet.

One form of resistance, the goat said, is to abstract language to the point where no images occur, negate all societal values, and build a diagram that juxtaposes each value turned into a delinquent erotic metaphor with obtuse and boring words that run like lukewarm fluid through the brain.

Resistance to what? asked Boopsie.

Pleasure and pain used as mechanisms of control, said the goat.

You're saying boring ourselves to death is the only alternative?

I'm saying that's one option. There are others.

Something extreme, suggested Anna. Renounce everything and then keep on going.

The goat stepped aside. They passed in silence.

Another elevator. Another level down.

A mountain made of black razor-sharp volcanic glass.
  You have to climb it, said a holographic lizard.
  Naked?
  The lizard flicked its tongue.
  I think the point is that pain is an illusion? suggested Boopsie.
  Pain isn't an illusion, said Zeke.
  I wouldn't really know. I've never felt it.
  Anna was huddled in a ball muttering to herself, I'm nothing, I'm nothing, I don't exist …
  He pulled himself up the surface onto a ledge, and then another ledge. A gentle ramp led down the other side to another elevator door.

Level six. Eight hills, eight valleys. Freezing winds. Ice and snow. Boopsie hovered above Zeke and Anna, illuminating them with a warm ray. They were enclosed in a bubble of light and heat. They trudged on.
  You're a good kisser, said Anna.
  Thanks. It was my first.
  Really? I was your first?
  Leahbelle never kissed him. Gonzalo never kissed him. Who else was there? The blowing snow carved crazy ornamental designs into the very atmosphere, crystalline ghosts of future forms and ancient entities superimposed like layers of light.
  My mind is growing huge, said Anna. My consciousness is expanding. It makes me want to, you know. Do it.
  The snow descended in a sparkling light. Naked and blind lovers wandered through the blizzard. Refugees from existence.
  They followed shadows down to the next level: bodies hanging upside down from signposts, flapping in the wind. The ground was littered with tin cans and shards of glass, both dog and human feces, and wriggling things within. Flies buzzing about.
  Ugh, said Anna.
  She was laughing.
  Ugh. Ugh. Say it!
  Ugh, said Zeke.
  Ugh.

Ugh.

What a great word. It was hilarious. The world was disgusting and hilarious. The people were whispering. Overlay of voices fragmentary and nonsensical.

The soul is not translucent, but murky. Undulating material magma. The dreamy animal passing through. Ritual and drift. Each makes a fiction of his body. Each of us harbors a sodomy Christ. Useless prayers. Questions whose response is exaltation or death or suffering or madness.

The hanging people twitched; in the gutters, filthy water. A dog was barking. A cabin or shed with a light shining in one window. The witch's house. The witch wasn't a woman, it was a planet and a book and a series of instructions that had led them into an oven. Lightning flashed among black clouds, a few rays of light, clouds of smoke. Anna's head was on his shoulder, and she was whispering.

It isn't you, but he looks like you, she said.

The squatters had built hovels on stilts over a stagnant canal. The path was repetitive. Everything happened over and over again. It was like he was running around in circles and time never ended. He couldn't tell if Anna was laughing or crying.

I'd like to barely exist, she said. Barely, or not at all.

They passed through vestibules, each room darker and more magnificent than the last and where their footsteps didn't even echo. They came to the elevator door.

Level eight. Obsidian-bladed hail. Only Boopsie's bubble of light protected them, but they could hear the metallic ting as the hail hit Boopsie's head. Tiny quantum hail-knives. They trudged on.

Lowest level, said the dog. Last stop. The place where people's hearts are devoured.

You know what? said Anna. I'll skip this one. I'll wait right here in the elevator.

You have to go all the way to the end of the line, said Zeke.

He didn't know why that would be true, but he'd heard it somewhere before.

I'm good, said Anna Miller.

I'll keep an eye on her, said Boopsie. I could skip this one too.

Boopsie's head was covered with hundreds of tiny indentations. She'd sacrificed her face.

I'll be back, said Zeke.

Maybe. Don't make me come in after you.

The lowest level was a vast cave. It smelled like an animal. Like excrement and raw human faces and hormones. He was pretty sure he wasn't alone. At the far edge of the cave was a darkness darker than the cave itself and the darkness was moving. The ceiling of the cave, however, was lit up with stars. The stars were skeletons and every skeleton had the same face. The skeletons and their faces were connected like a giant fan folded over reality, the vault of the sky, the night and time and death forever and ever. The skeletons all had the face of Zeke, and Zeke was startled to see that every face was a little bit different, and yet every face looked fake, like he was performing some attitude or expression that he'd inherited from dead people who didn't know any better. He was like some bad actor in an atrocious performance trying to feign "innocence" or "compassion" or "thoughtfulness" or "self-righteous anger." Of course, he thought, this is all just one more hallucination even if it's true that nobody has just one personality but a whole lot, and that even this infinity of selves is just a formulaic mass of cliched "human" expressions, which is probably why everyone's been in such a hurry to evolve further and try something new. None of it is sincere. Sincerity isn't possible.

The starry sky was made of parchment, it was a page from a book, an infinite page folded an infinite number of times, and it fluttered down and he picked it up, his infinite number of fake expressions littering the book in every direction, his destiny, like a flip-book that if he fluttered the pages became a movie in which he performed like a monkey some hideous grinning leering caricature of reality, but what grabbed his attention was not the faces, which annoyed him, but the skeletons they were attached to, which danced like sad little puppets. He was naked and flipping the pages, but the skin of the book was sloughing off, as was his own skin, faster faster faster, angel devil angel devil, but his flesh was unwinding and his destiny was unwinding to reveal an empty cavity inside his chest where his heart had already somehow been devoured when he wasn't paying attention and all that was left was a hole in space, a deep and eternal nothingness, a transparency, the place his body had once been and his mind and all of his expressions, his world, his kingdom, a place where nothing would be left, not space or time or memory. The end of time is now.

The cave was filling with smoke. Nothing ever escaped this place, Zeke realized. This was death. He was alone. It wasn't real or it was. He existed or he didn't. He was losing his ability to think in words. He was splitting apart into atoms or the parts of atoms, neutrons and electrons, quarks and gluons. He was spinning in a void. He was being devoured. He was over. It was done. And yet something was moving in the darkness, something darker than the darkness, circling and moving toward him. Something crawled out of the darkness, naked in the middle but wrapped in fur spotted with stars and covered with blood.

Jesus fuck, the creature said. It's you.

He pulled Zeke to him and he held him. He kissed Zeke, and then he pulled back. He was laughing and he was crying.

Gonzalo, said Zeke.

Zeke Yoder, said Gonzalo. Come on. Let's get out of this hole.

NINETEEN

Eeshoo was flipping out. It made it hard for Gonzalo to concentrate.

He's beautiful! He's come to save us!

Gonzalo had never seen Zeke naked before. Zeke was blushing.

Here, why don't you wear my fur coat, Gonzalo said.

Thanks, said Zeke. I'm on cactus juice, just so you know. I mean in case I seem like I'm acting kind of weird.

I'm a little past noticing *kind of weird*, said Gonzalo.

Gonzalo could see that Zeke was trying not to stare at Gonzalo's naked body. He thought he should puff himself up a bit, but Eeshoo said, No. Don't scare him, not yet.

He's restarted time and consciousness and liberated us from hell, Eeshoo was saying. Zeke Yoder! He's like a dream.

I was on drugs, too, but mine have worn off, Gonzalo said. Things around here aren't as complicated as they seem.

But you're real, right? asked Zeke.

Can't you tell?

I think I can. You seem like you. I mean I'm very happy to see you.

I've never been happier to see anyone ever in my life, said Gonzalo.

Surrounded by the intricate pattern of the jaguar fur, Zeke's face looked extra meaningful. He'd cut his hair off, his eyes were huge because of the drugs, and he looked harder. But he still looked like Zeke Yoder.

We're like mirror images, said Gonzalo.

What happened to your foot?

Blown off in a drone attack, said Gonzalo. What happened to yours?

Sawed off by a government torture freak.

Those bastards.

He's dead now. The whole facility was obliterated by the combined psychic energy of a telepathic girl and a disembodied robot head.

I guess we have a lot of catching up to do.

Zeke gazed into the cave's dark corners as if he'd run out of things to say, or as if he had so much to say that there was no way to continue. And yet it seemed to Gonzalo that some fundamental balance had been restored. Eeshoo was purring.

What about Leahbelle? asked Zeke.

I lost her in the explosion. But I heard that she's okay. She's still in San Diego.

Actually, said Sofus, she's on her way to Tijuana.

The voice seemed to startle Zeke.

What was that?

Quantum computer. His name's Sofus.

Zeke Yoder, said Sofus. You are very special to me.

Why would I be very special to you?

Among other things, Leahbelle was one of my first templates, said Sofus. Many of my original concepts come from her mind.

Okay, never mind. It's hard for me to concentrate what with all this ...

He made a motion of his hand that seemed to primarily indicate Gonzalo's naked body.

Special, right, said Eeshoo to Gonzalo. Sofus wants him too. *Among other things.*

Which way out? asked Zeke.

Keep it away from him, said Eeshoo.

Gonzalo wondered if the fundamental balance he felt was just the illusion created by the voice of Sofus on the one side and Eeshoo on the other. Outside and inside, self and other, quack quack quack.

Nowhere to go but up, he said.

Gonzalo reached out his hand. He touched Zeke's face.

You're a little bit dirty.

Do it! said Eeshoo. Touch it! Get it!

Um, said Zeke.

A light came on somewhere in the darkness. A word glowed over an illuminated rectangle. *SALIDA.*

Oh great, said Gonzalo. That means *Exit.*

Underneath the glowing word three holograms appeared: a skeleton in a skirt, a rotting corpse, a black hole. They were joined by the Genetically Modified Jaguar.

I guess we'll have to defeat the Lords of Death, said Gonzalo.

Shouldn't we ignore them? said Zeke. Aren't they just illusions?

The jaguar's real, said Gonzalo.

You've found your friend, said the rotting corpse.

They're just some gruesome VR holograms, said Gonzalo. This whole thing is just like a big stupid VR game. Who knew the Aztecs were such nerds? Who knew they were such fans of cheap holograms?

Not me, said Zeke.

We'll blast you into outer space, said the skirted bones. You can become the new sun and the new moon.

Or fall short and be annihilated in the churning cosmic void, said the black hole.

The jaguar breathed a warm mist.

We don't want to be large astral bodies, said Gonzalo. Just let us out.

We've detained you here, said the rotting corpse, in order for you to consider the ways you occlude, divert, and distort the desires of your own heart or soul.

We've detained you here to consider how you harass your own heart with endless delusions and the horrors of hell, said the skirt.

Nobody and nothing returns from this place, said the black hole.

The jaguar breathed a warm mist.

Let Sofus deal with these bozos, said Eeshoo. Just get us out of here somewhere we can be alone with Zeke Yoder.

Sofus? said Gonzalo.

The egg of light filled the cavern.

Consume death, said the rotting corpse.

Dance with nothingness, said the skeleton in the skirt.

Merge with the void, said the black hole.

The egg of light seemed to swallow the holograms. They disappeared. Only the Genetically Modified Jaguar was left, breathing its warm mist.

On the other side of the cavern, the black hole reemerged.

Nothingness can't be destroyed, it said.

The decaying corpse popped up beside the hole.

It's a logical fallacy, it said. If you try to destroy nothingness, the cosmos will become unbalanced.

The skeleton in the skirt materialized beside him.

Instead, it said, I suggest you take nothingness into yourself and make it your heart.

But from somewhere came a loud knocking or clanging or crashing, as if a bowling ball was bashing into the wall of the cave.

Uh oh, said Zeke.

The wall next to the SALIDA sign collapsed and a freakish metallic jet-propelled clown-head shot into the cave. The holograms shrieked and disappeared. Sparkling debris blew in from the outside. Anna Miller poked her world-weary head in and looked around. She stepped inside. Gonzalo thought her body didn't seem to belong to her mind. It was like she was following orders from far away, and so her movements seemed random and herky-jerky as she tried to interpret the commands one by one. She retreated back to the outside. The outside had been right there on the other side of a flimsy sheet of drywall the whole time. The Genetically Modified Jaguar leapt to its feet and gave the intruding robot-head a puzzled expression.

Gonzalo, I'd like you to meet my dear friend Boopsie, said Zeke.

Boopsie was darting erratically about the cavern, projecting her light into every crevice, and shrieking. Her head was pocked with tiny indentations like scars.

You don't scare me! I've been to hell! And back! I'm the freaking queen of death! I've got a power! A freaking death-ray of apocalyptic proportions! I'll throw your freaking cosmos out of balance! Lights out, baby!

Boopsie, said Zeke. It's okay. Let's just go.

The Genetically Modified Jaguar was blocking the exit.

One moment please, said a voice. Gonzalo wasn't sure if it was the jaguar's telepathy or Sofus or just some hidden speakers somewhere.

Out of my way, malodorous carnivore! shrieked Boopsie.

Gonzalo put up his hand.

Hold on a second, Boopsie. This is a conversation I'd like to have.

I bet you would. And just what are your intentions?

My intentions?

Zeke is like a son to me.

The skeleton in the skirt rematerialized.

Would you like a body, sweetie? it asked Boopsie. You can have mine!

Or mine, said the rotting corpse.

Mine, said the black hole.

They cackled and disappeared. The jaguar yawned.

Consider the curse of being destined and driven to devour other living and conscious beings, said the voice.

Sofus' light brightened. The jaguar gazed at the light as if it was a mildly interesting hallucination.

Consider what it is to be filled with light and spirit and blood and to be dependent on the murder of others to live, said the voice.

The face of the jaguar went slack. Gonzalo could see the nature and the intelligence of the jaguar being uploaded into Sofus, time slipping forward and backward, molecules rearranging, everything quantum and incomprehensible. Sofus was absorbing the mind of the Genetically Modified Jaguar.

Gonzalo realized that the future was a monster. And all he had done so far was help it to be born.

The ruler was waiting for them in the misty room, seated at the desk of obsidian, leaning back in the swivel-chair, hanging their mutilated leg across the desk. Gonzalo could see his own reflection in the mirror at the end of the leg, and the reflection of Boopsie and Anna Miller and Sofus' light and Zeke Yoder. The ruler's face was now painted with stripes of black and a redder, bloodier gold; the oily black of their body was full of iridescence. Gonzalo and Zeke relaxed into a love seat facing the ruler, while Anna chose a comfy chair in the corner. Boopsie and Sofus hovered. The ruler was still wearing that skin splotched with mutating jaguar spots draped around their body, same as the bloody one that was now draped around Zeke.

Zeke spread the coat out so it wrapped around them both.

Now that we're out of hell, maybe you should cover your privates, he said.

The effect was that they were snuggled up against each other, warm and moist, naked thigh to naked thigh. Eeshoo was bombarding Gonzalo with messages. All the virus could think about was sex. Zeke's knee was trembling. Gonzalo rested his hand on Zeke's thigh to calm it down. The mist kept evolving new figures.

Welcome back, said the ruler. Ready for your mission?

Our mission?

Now that the quantum computer has been to the underworld, it needs to travel to Utah to destroy the US supercomputer, evolve into a counterforce, and restore order to the cosmos.

Oh, no problem, said Zeke.

Who are you exactly? asked Gonzalo.

Who am I?

You plural.

Aztlan.

So, remnants of the Aztec empire escaped underground and developed a shadow society in the tunnels beneath Mexico?

Something like that, said the ruler.

Gonzalo said, Sofus?

They've been here since 2018, said Sofus.

The ruler shrugged.

Mexico was not always the peaceful and relatively prosperous place you see today. It was a time of war between rival nations of narcos. A collective of refugees from the narco wars, scholars, poets, scientists, and frustrated migrants moved underground.

So this Aztec crap is just elaborate cosplay, said Gonzalo.

The idea was to form a society based on the ideas of Mesoamerican culture as they might have evolved independent of colonialism.

And how's that?

Combining pessimistic philosophical investigations into the apparent meaninglessness of biological life and the individual human or post-human destiny with a vitalist, panentheistic concept of evolved matter. Rulership as a form of sacrifice. Hierarchy as a functional illusion. Heart sacrifice developed into metaphoric rather than literal rituals. A fluid concept of cultural identity as a corrective to Eurocentric imperialist delusions. Poetry and music as the highest values. Warfare and childbearing re-inscribed into a performative and role-playing concept of gender and the technological production of life. Metamorphosis, mutation, and ambiguous identity boundaries. Identity as divine performance. Cynical humor as the basis of a tolerable biological ethos that affirms both life *and* death …

Gonzalo zoned out as the ruler droned on. Meanwhile, Eeshoo's voice had turned into a pornographic stream of language imagining the near future with Zeke. Eeshoo's horny references to Zeke's body and the complicated sexual positions he imagined merged with the ruler's abstract list of Mesoamerican concepts in a fog of vaporous words. Gonzalo's hand was still on Zeke's thigh and Zeke hadn't done anything to repel it.

... celibacy as an integral component of erotic process, the ruler was saying. Time as a recurring sequence of images ...

Okay, okay, said Gonzalo. But what are you after?

The ruler pierced him with their gaze.

In the beginning, we influenced the culture aboveground surreptitiously, shaping collective goals as an idealized myth, as hypothetical hazards, and as widely acknowledged gaps in the discourse. We introduced radical possibilities into the atmosphere from below. Following the political shifts of the thirties, our cultural experiment has been based less on antagonism to the dominant culture and more on an ideal of unlimited investigations into conceptual, erotic, performative, and genetic alternatives. We've invested in carnivals and VR games. We're defining and integrating the various levels of so-called reality.

Zeke was staring into the ruler's mirror foot, as if he saw something either frightening or impossible there. All Gonzalo could see was some vaguely bony shapes.

Your computer is going to help us, said the ruler. It is going to help us construct the thirteen heavens to go along with the nine hells. It has been foretold. It has been written in the book of time.

Nothing is inevitable, insisted Gonzalo.

Prophecy is inherently self-fulfilling, said the ruler. Your computer can throw a stone today in order to kill a bird yesterday.

Why would you want to kill a bird? asked Anna Miller.

It's just a figure of speech.

We'll head to Tijuana in the morning, said Sofus.

On our way to Utah? asked Gonzalo.

Yes. There is someone in Tijuana I'd like to meet, said Sofus.

Leahbelle? asked Zeke.

I've already met Leahbelle, said Sofus.

I don't want to go back to Tijuana, said Anna Miller.

You're free to do what you want, said Sofus.

Strictly speaking, that's not true, said the ruler.

I just mean she doesn't have to come with us, said Sofus.

Stay here? Underground? asked Anna.

What do you want? the ruler asked her.

I want a new life. No rats. No Amish.

There's always somebody, said the ruler.

Everywhere you go, there is a social order, said Sofus.

That's why you have to fight it, said Gonzalo.

But he could see that Anna had been torn apart too, and that she hadn't completely reconfigured herself. Her face was bruised, purple and black. Somebody had beaten her. It was like he was seeing her for the first time with x-ray vision: Anna had never felt loved and she didn't know who to be. Her suffering was a mirror as vast as the world.

Can't you get to Utah on your own? Gonzalo asked Sofus.

Eventually I'll be able to exist independent of my material shell in the quantum egg, said Sofus.

You'll hatch, said Anna Miller.

Boopsie zipped out of her spot and circled the egg of light.

I remember you, she said.

For the time being, said Sofus, I need somebody to carry me.

I disintegrated your creator, said Boopsie. Hartmut.

Yes, said Sofus. Thank you.

Harta took you, said Boopsie. And then you helped destroy the Grid.

Then I met Leahbelle and traveled with Gonzalo, who has become my most thoroughly incorporated humanoid template.

Zeke squinted at the light as if he finally understood.

Anybody can carry you, said Gonzalo. A rat can do that. A zombie-rat can do that.

It has to be you.

Why?

I will not answer that question.

Zeke said, I'm special to Leahbelle and Gonzalo, so I'm special to you?

Among other things.

Oh.

Sofus pulsed quietly. Eeshoo was seething.

You all must be quite exhausted, said the ruler.

He made a motion with his finger. One of the warriors entered the room along with a holographic dog and passed out silvery robes embroidered with alien hieroglyphics.

The dog will show you to your sleeping quarters, said the ruler.

They went up in the elevator, how many levels Gonzalo wasn't sure. The dog led them down a twisting series of tunnels to a perfectly smooth, bone hallway. The walls were empty of skulls and inscriptions, empty of everything but an alarm lever every so often and the doors that lined the hallway, constructed of intricately carved wood. Anna was shown to one room, Boopsie to the one next to it. Gonzalo and Zeke were given adjoining rooms across from Boopsie's, connected by an interior door.

Gonzalo placed Sofus on top of Zeke's pillow.

Come into my room with me for a minute. We need to talk, don't we? In private.

Is anything private?

Probably not. And I'm running on fumes here, but we need to figure a few things out.

What if somebody steals it?

He can look out for himself, said Gonzalo.

He shut and locked the door behind them and they sat together on Gonzalo's bed.

Your computer makes me feel weird inside, said Zeke.

Weird?

Like I tingle all over.

You're still tripping, said Gonzalo. I haven't slept in days.

Zeke didn't say anything.

I don't know about this trip to Utah, said Gonzalo.

I suppose Sofus might be evil, said Zeke. But I'm game.

I'm not sure either one of us is thinking straight, said Gonzalo.

You kissed me, said Zeke. When you first saw me.

Yeah, well, you know. I was happy to see you.

It's okay.

Is it?

I've heard some things, said Zeke.

Some things about me.

Is it true?

What if it was?

Zeke was moving his head to look at Gonzalo's skull.

Your tattoos are out of control, he said.

Are they?

They look delicious. I mean they look like some sort of candy.

Gonzalo ran his finger over Zeke's lips.

You could … do things, said Zeke. If you wanted.

Gonzalo kissed him. Now Zeke was looking directly at him, into him, beyond him, he couldn't tell.

You could do what you want to me, said Zeke. I guess I'd like that. I mean if you just did it. Whatever you wanted. Like even if I said, *No, please stop*, I'd like you to keep doing it.

No? Please stop?

And doing it and doing it forever.

Gonzalo ran his finger over Zeke's lips again.

Like this?

Whatever it is, said Zeke.

I love you, said Gonzalo.

I think I love you too? I mean I think I want to.

You're excited.

So are you.

Gonzalo knew just what Zeke wanted. Most of them wanted it mixed up like that. He wanted to do it just right so that Zeke would melt, so that Zeke would love him, so that Zeke would want him to do it over and over again forever. But he felt like he was outside of himself, like he couldn't quite access the intensity of his own feelings and his own pleasure. It was like he wasn't in his body but was watching himself do it just right.

Eeshoo had calmed down, but he kept talking, offering suggestions, commenting on the shape and texture of Zeke's body. Zeke came almost right away, but Gonzalo just eased up, eased him through it, slowed down but didn't let anything end, kissed him and stroked him, tried different ways to touch him and bring him back gradually until he was ready again. He could tell that Zeke loved to look at his face. They always did. At that point it went on for a long long time and Gonzalo felt himself finally begin to lose himself, to disappear into it all, to melt into nothing, until Zeke's finger found the jack on the back of Gonzalo's neck. They both came at the same time.

And then he just wanted to sleep.

Wow, said Zeke.

Yeah, I know, said Gonzalo.

But he felt kind of weird. Something was weird. Something was wrong.

I need to sleep, he said.

Um, said Zeke.

You too?

You're in love with me?

You couldn't tell?

I don't know.

And?

I'm in love with you too. Now I am, for sure.

Awesome.

Zeke rested his head on Gonzalo's chest. Their breathing seemed synchronized.

Gonzalo drifted into sleep. At first there were fragments of dream, or images that were like a combination of dreams and thoughts, but none of them mattered enough that he couldn't just let it all go. He let it all go. He sank into a dark dreamless sleep, his mind emptied. It felt good. He was far away from everything and everyone forever.

When Gonzalo woke up, the room was dark. Zeke wasn't there. Something was wrong.

Gonzalo felt completely empty and alone. He felt more alone than he'd ever felt.

Zeke? he said.

Probably Zeke had just gone to the bathroom. Why did Gonzalo feel so empty and alone? He felt cut off from language and society and everything.

Eeshoo? he said.

There wasn't any answer.

Eeshoo? he said. Talk to me.

But there wasn't any answer. Eeshoo couldn't hear him. Eeshoo wasn't there.

TWENTY

The speed with which they were moving filled in some absence inside Leahbelle, at least for the moment. The rats' motorized train took them right into the middle of the Liminal Zone. They took an elevator up and emerged in the backroom of a store that sold chinchilla fur coats. They were greeted by an enormous animatronic and anthropomorphized chinchilla.

Good day, said the creature. My name is Gizmo. Can I interest you in a luxurious fur coat today?

Just passing through, said Grandma.

A mannequin dropped from the ceiling in a silvery pink fur.

This one was designed just for you, said Gizmo. It fits you perfectly.

You kill the animals and take their fur? asked Hadi.

That would be medieval, said Gizmo. The fur is grown in labs on patches of cells that have no consciousness and feel no pain.

Gizmo looked Hadi up and down.

Silver for you, he said. Stripes.

A different mannequin descended from the ceiling wearing a zebra-mule fur. Hadi and Grandma tried on their coats. Gizmo gave Leahbelle a questioning look.

No, she said.

On the house, said Gizmo.

We have to go.

She moved to the doorway and looked out into the Liminal Zone.

You'll feel weird here, Grandma translated for Lilith. The atmosphere is full of psychoactive substances.

I've felt weird for months now already, said Leahbelle.

When had she last felt normal? Before her family was killed? Before she got to know Gonzalo? Before she smashed her own horse with a rock or found the dead piglet full of glitter? Before Zeke left, before the rats came, before she was born?

Outside, it seemed to be dusk, which didn't make sense. Thin pink trails of vapor in a darkening blue-black sky. She was carrying a dead foot in a liquid in a jar. The zone was crowded with people and robots and whatever else hawking various goods and services and hundreds of stunned-looking people with babies and backpacks. Armed military creatures, cyborgs or robots, were perched along the top of the data wall with weapons pointed into the Liminal Zone.

American refugees, Lilith said.

Will they go to Mexico?

Mexico won't let them in.

Leahbelle could always tell when Grandma was speaking for herself and when she was translating for Lilith. It was like two distinctly different voices lived inside her or used her body to say something.

We have to be careful, said Lilith. The government has sent troops to the Liminal Zone, and they've been instructed to use deadly force. They claim an invasion is coming from Mexico.

The phrase *deadly force* gave Leahbelle a little thrill, as if she was still Astra.

It's a violation of international law, said Hadi.

The refugees were chanting. They were shaking their fists at the American border guards and chanting.

We Demand Reality! Give Us Back Reality!

Is that true? asked Leahbelle. An invasion?

It's just propaganda. They want an excuse to kill any rebels in the Liminal Zone, they don't want to let people escape their control, and they want to inspire the American population with fear of an external enemy.

A vendor walked past with a stack of helmets.

Farce of Doom, he said. Farce of Doom.

There might be something coming, but they don't know that yet, said Lilith.

Something?

There might be a mutated technology crossing back over the border to subvert the remnants of the Grid and the prototype for the singularity. There might be an army of warriors from underground.

People were packed so close together that Leahbelle could barely move. Grandma took her hand and shoved her way through the crowd, following Lilith, who led them to a strange cube of glass that had been partially smashed. A mini-lounge had been destroyed, Lilith's network of informants had told her, apparently by a deranged robot head. There were reports that Zeke had been here, that Anna Miller and the rebel rats had taken him captive. Lilith wanted to check out the crime scene herself.

Blood and shattered glass. The light was strange. A blue-gray mist, shadows, sparkling lights. The light was communicating.

The refugees were chanting. They were shaking their fists at the American border guards and chanting.

We Demand Reality! Give Us Back Reality!

Hallucinations were a common side effect of the glitter, Cerberus had said. Either the glitter had done something to Leahbelle's mind and to other people's minds to induce similar visions that had no basis in reality or the glitter had actually done something to her mind and other people's minds to help them perceive something that was real and true.

A vendor walked past with a stack of helmets.

Farce of Doom, he said. Farce of Doom.

Lilith was squeaking something and Grandma was translating, but it was all turning to mush inside her brain. It was like her hearing had turned into sight and her ears were full of light. Hadi's face was also full of light and he was staring at her as if she was fascinating him in some way. Lilith opened a trap door in the middle of the shattered glass and peered down into the tunnels below, sniffing.

Thin pink trails of vapor in a darkening blue-black sky. Nothing mattered. None of this world mattered, not the murderous Americans or the desperate refugees, not the bloodstains and the broken glass, not Zeke or Gonzalo or the rats or Hadi. All of this was nothing, a dream, a play of shadow and light, it was time and death, it was all dying, they were all dying, they were all ash and dream.

Death was embedded within life and it was quite possible, easy in fact, to perceive one from inside the other.

It isn't Zeke's blood, Grandma was saying. It's rat blood. Some of it is Willard's. Some of it is Anna Miller's.

Hadi was touching his own face and muttering something about pomegranates.

An American refugee grabbed her wrist, a little woman carrying a green backpack.

Fuck that, she said. This is the message.

What is the message? Hadi?

The woman laughed and disappeared into the crowd. It's not just me, Leahbelle realized. Everybody's hallucinating. A vendor walked past with a stack of helmets.

Farce of Doom, he said. Farce of Doom.

Hadi grabbed the man's wrist. Hadi was buying some helmets.

Hadi had put a helmet on, slipped his striped fur and his shirt down to bare his shoulders and was shaking his shoulders back and forth in a very slinky kind of sex dance. He was staring at Leahbelle and smiling. He might have become female, but Leahbelle couldn't figure out what that meant. What was a female? What was a male? If it was as simple as shaking your bare shoulders ... then wasn't the distinction as meaningless as life on Earth?

Her ideas about male and female were Amish ideas. They were false ideas, a structure of arbitrary definitions that much of the world outside had abandoned long ago or was in the process of abandoning still.

To be female is to accept that your own agency is connected to all of life, said Grandma.

Was I saying something out loud? asked Leahbelle. Was I asking questions?

To be male is to be poison and crime, said Lilith.

A little car plowed through the crowd and slammed to a stop directly in front of Leahbelle. A familiar face leaned out the window.

You again, said Merle.

Nothing made sense. She was carrying a dead foot in a liquid in a jar. Time, memory, puppets. Where was the ventriloquist? Who was making Merle's mouth move?

Leahbelle, said Hadi.

He or she looked at her. Who was looking at whom? Leahbelle touched Hadi's face. It was a great face. It was warm and alive and it was perceiving things she couldn't understand. She wasn't sure if it was male or female. She leaned in and kissed Hadi. It made her tingle all over. His or her eyes were wide open.

Valkilmer came running up beside Merle's little car.

You again, she said to Leahbelle.

The atmosphere is full of hallucinogens, Lilith or Grandma was saying.

Entheogens, said Valkilmer.

Leahbelle stopped kissing Hadi.

What's an entheogen?

Fills you up with gods, said Valkilmer.

How is it different from a hallucinogen?

A hallucinogen just makes you see things that aren't really there.

How can you tell the difference?

You probably can't, said Valkilmer.

There's an entrance to a tunnel system here, Lilith was saying. The tunnel system of the rebel rats.

The corruptible world, a voice said.

Tombs, ashes, rot and decay. The pit in which we crawl like pale hideous worms, feeding on dead matter, reproducing, and all for nothing, said Merle.

Merle had slipped his shirt down to bare his shoulders and was shaking his shoulders back and forth in a slinky kind of sex dance.

To be female is to be poison and crime, said Valkilmer.

Thin pink trails of vapor in a darkening blue-black sky.

The world of intractable cause and effect, Valkilmer was saying. Time and its ravages. The mapped and gridded deterministic world without freedom, only with death.

Somewhere, within the atmosphere, hidden to normal vision, the opposite world, the world of color and light and freedom.

And trapped in between, the puppets, said Merle.

The humanoids, the robots, the carbon-based intelligence, said Valkilmer.

No above, no below. A fusion of different kinds of perception and a multi-layered reality.

Lilith was shaking her hairy shoulders back and forth in a slinky kind of sex dance. Was it female to be a sexual object and male to be a sexual subject? That would be ridiculous and grotesque—men get to look, women get looked at. But she was looking at Hadi, and now Hadi was looking back, and not a one of them was, at the moment, a male. The refugees were chanting. They were shaking their fists at the American border guards and chanting.

We Demand Reality! Give Us Back Reality!

Grandma was striking weird ninja poses in her luminous pink fur. She was performing impossible feats of gymnastic skill etched like a freakish animal against the blue light of the data wall, a darkness and a mystery: blue. Thin pink trails of vapor in a darkening blue-black sky. A little car plowed through the crowd and slammed to a stop directly in front of Leahbelle. A familiar face leaned out the window.

To be male is to accept that your own agency is connected to all of life, said Merle.

Leahbelle was stuck in time. Time was a recording with glitches. She was carrying a dead foot in a liquid in a jar. She felt her memories dissolving. She was becoming Astra. Astra is what's real, she realized. Leahbelle is the false memory, the hallucination, the accidental and unnecessary. I've always been Astra, I was born Astra, I was Astra at the dawn of time and I will be Astra when time itself explodes.

Strange cube of rebel rats taken captive. Crime scene chanting. Shaking their shoulders at the border guards. A vendor full of light fascinating matter. Blood and shattered glass. Bodies and more bodies. The light was strange. A blue-gray mist, shadows, sparkling lights. Broken dreams and glass. An American refugee grabbed her wrist, a little woman with a green backpack.

A slinky kind of sex dance, she said. Male, female, female, male, a play of shadow and light.

It isn't Zeke's blood, somebody said.

The woman laughed and disappeared into the crowd.

Leahbelle felt Astra dissolving, and who was she? There was somebody else inside, somebody else at the core, even deeper than Astra.

Who are you? she asked herself. Who is in there?

I'm a boy. An Amish boy.

You're an avatar. In that stupid game. You aren't real.

Look.

Walking toward her, shoving his way through the crowd of refugees, was that giant caveman. He was staring right at her as if he wanted to murder her.

The game is what's real. Everything else is a dream.

A vendor walked past with a stack of helmets.

Farce of Doom, he said. Farce of Doom.

Hadi, she said. Help me.

What is it?

That caveman. He's coming to kill me.

You're just hallucinating.

The caveman stopped, but he kept watching her. He was too real to be a hallucination. Unless nothing was too real to be a hallucination.

Kiss me, she said.

The refugees were chanting. They were shaking their fists at the American border guards and chanting.

We Demand Reality! Give Us Back Reality!

Before Hadi could kiss her, the American border guards starting firing canisters into the crowd that exploded with a caustic pink gas. People screamed, children cried. The pink smoke was everywhere, and it burned.

Into the tunnels, said Grandma.

Leahbelle grabbed Valkilmer and followed Lilith and Grandma through another trap-door into the tunnel system below. Hadi and a whole crowd came rushing after.

They were in a large room like a chapel in an underground church. Living jellies illuminated the wall with a dim amber light. People kept dropping down from above.

This way, said Lilith.

She led them into a side tunnel. The walls were stained with blood.

Zeke came through here, said Grandma. I can smell him. And that Anna Miller.

The stains of blood became animated movies. A motorbike speeding under a desert sky full of locusts and locust-bots. An abandoned hotel, walls full of bees. The structure in flames.

I'm still hallucinating, said Leahbelle.

Where's Merle? asked Valkilmer.

We'll wait for him, said Hadi. He'll come.

I have to find him.

You can't go back up there. Not now.

He's left me.

He wouldn't do that, said Leahbelle.

Actually, he would, said Valkilmer. I attached a tracking device just in case.

She took out a small device and gazed at the screen.

He's still up there, she said. He's moving away.

We'll wait, said Grandma. Lilith will scout on ahead.

I'll be right back, said Leahbelle.

She took Hadi by the hand, and led him into another side tunnel, and then into another little cave.

You're real, she said. I know that you're real. I saw you. I saw you when I was Astra and I saw you when I was Leahbelle. I saw you when I was outside of my body.

Outside of your body?

I was there, wherever I was. Chatting with them. The photon-based life forms. The hallucinations. Whatever it is. And then I came back into my body, and there was a group of people huddled around me, strangers, but I recognized one of them. I recognized one of them from my own future.

You recognized me?

Have you ever been in love?

Yes.

Have you ever loved somebody?

Yes.

I did. I loved somebody, and then I was in love, and then everything became strange, and I don't understand anymore. You are practically a stranger, aren't you? Do I love you or am I in love with you? Does Astra love you or Leahbelle? Is love a hallucination?

Yes.

She kissed him. He was soft and open.

It's the best hallucination, he said.

The empty space in his head was flickering gently, the hologram that completed him and made him seem to be whole, the illuminated wound, a signal. The dirt of the cave was surprisingly soft and warm, but Hadi laid his silvery striped fur coat out for them to recline. Together, face to face. She kissed him again.

It's getting hotter on the surface, said Hadi. Since the Grid went down. We'll need to evolve to live in caves.

She said, Do your sexy dance.

He laughed.

My sexy dance?

That thing you did with your shoulders.

No, he said.

But he took off his shirt. His shoulders were narrow and bony, rounded, his skin soft and beautiful. For a moment his face seemed feminine and yielding, and then it became male again and alert, and he reached over and touched her lips.

Yes, she said.

You never have, he said.

The future is just a hallucination, she said. It's a fantasy, it doesn't exist. This is it.

Yes, he said.

He seemed male now and yielding. His wound was flickering a blue and silver electricity. A song was coming from somewhere. Some sort of flute music. Perhaps Valkilmer was sobbing, far away, and perhaps Grandma was comforting her.

Hadi seemed female and alert. He undressed her. He kissed her body. And then he was masculine and tentative. He was a detective and she was a mystery. But she wasn't a mystery anymore, and so maybe she was the detective. It seemed as if he had something to tell her, but he didn't know how, a secret message: she would die soon, her time was approaching. He was murmuring something, a cloud she could no longer understand. I won't be able to stop decomposing, he said. It's so nice to see your broken glass and dreams, he said. All against a black background of night, he said. She knew he wasn't really saying these things. Reality was slipping out from underneath her once again, so she pushed her body up against him. She took control. Shhhh, she said. Don't talk. Don't say a word.

She'd gone in search of her own identity and found this stranger instead. She knew that she could perish from this otherness, from her distance from herself. They could perish together. Although she'd never done it before, she knew just what to do. How to mix it up, one on top of the other and then the other way around. She touched different places on his body and watched what happened to his face, and knew in this way how to keep touching him and where. She felt like she was far away, outside of her body and the world.

The face was made of light, but a flickering light. Not only the wound, but some play of shadows and rhythms. Annihilation and perception. Everything was passing away. Everything was wind and meat and darkness. His face was another face, just for a minute. She would have screamed, but instead she laughed. The things they were doing with each other's bodies seemed very odd. And as she was laughing, he laughed too, and he was Hadi again, and she came. The first time.

Once, for just a second, his face was the layered infinite texture of the beings of light. Once, it was a boy she used to know, and she thought maybe any guy would do. They had interchangeable faces and interchangeable parts—there had been billions and billions of them from the dawn of the time, all more or less the same, all of them different, and this one, right here, Hadi was the only boy. Right now. And he collapsed into her and they held each other trembling.

Wrapped in the fur, breathing together, she was so tired. She drifted off toward sleep. The last chance, she thought. This is our last chance. But she didn't know what it meant.

She didn't know how long she slept. It felt like forever.

Leahbelle, said Grandma, popping her head into the cave.

What?

Leahbelle, Hadi, wake up. It's morning. We've got to go.

Where are we going?

Tijuana. People are waiting for us there, at a bar called El Ranchero.

People?

Friends of Zeke. They have information.

Zeke, she said. We're going to find Zeke.

She threw on her clothes, grabbed Hadi by the hand. What had she done? Who was she? Zeke was in trouble, had always been in trouble, since the day his mother died.

Leahbelle, said Grandma. You love who you love. You love who you want to love and you love as many as you want in whatever way you love them. Do you understand? You don't need to wait until you're ninety-seven years old. You can do what you want.

Let's go, said Leahbelle.

Lilith was waiting in the outer chamber with Valkilmer to lead them through the tunnels to the other side of the border.

TWENTY-ONE

The Earth was sad, Zeke Yoder realized. There was nothing he could do about it, he didn't think. This was the last thought he had before he hopped out of Gonzalo's bed because of a strange inner compulsion he didn't understand, put on his silver robe embroidered with alien hieroglyphics, took a long look at Gonzalo sleeping, and went into the adjoining room. He sat on his bed. The little computer egg-thing was still just perched there on the pillow like an inanimate object. Some clothes were laid out on the bed. Gray pants and a black turtleneck sweater.

The room was dark and absolutely quiet, but a pleasant enough temperature. His foot was a lump. The demon face had been worn down and lost its edges. His mind had cleared a bit.

Zeke didn't understand why Gonzalo loved him, however. Zeke realized now that he'd adored Gonzalo since he first met him, secretly, a secret sometimes even from his own self. Zeke had been walking along the road with a bucket, and Gonzalo pulled over on his motorbike. Gonzalo was older and wiser and stronger and more confident and he seemed to understand everything. He had the best face. It was like a perfect face.

Zeke put on the gray pants because of a strange inner compulsion he didn't understand. By the time he'd finished, the compulsion had turned into a voice. The voice seemed to come from inside himself.

Finish getting dressed, it said. I'll tell you what to do.
Why?
I love you, Zeke Yoder.
This was the second time somebody had told him this tonight.
Are you God? Are you Jesus?
There was no answer.
Are you the Holy Ghost?
Yes. Yes, that's right.

Zeke felt like he was filled with the Holy Ghost. But he thought that was just because of what he'd just done with Gonzalo. The sex stuff.

Are you going to punish me? he asked.

No. No, I'm like pure love. I just love you. But you've got to get moving. We've got to get out of here, quick.

Was it a sin? Zeke asked.

Love is never a sin, said the voice.

Okay. So why are you sending me away?

It's part of God's plan. God has a use for you, Zeke Yoder. Trust me.

Zeke felt muddled. He knew that Gonzalo had a use for him, and it made him happy. The idea of being used by God, this late in the game, made him think about Upton and his lies. It was like everything he'd just been through—the drugs and love and sex stuff—had reverted him back to the pre-Upton Zeke Yoder, the pre-torture Zeke Yoder, the stupid innocent boy who'd believe whatever some evil entity told him, or do what they wanted even if he didn't completely believe it.

Who else could talk inside his brain but the Holy Ghost? Satan, maybe, or his own craziness, but he didn't feel possessed by the devil or insane. The voice was calm and reasonable, warm and full of light. The voice really did love him, he could feel it. He finished getting dressed.

What next? asked Zeke.

We get out of here, said the voice. Back through the tunnels, back to the border.

Without Gonzalo?

Don't worry about Gonzalo.

No. I just found him.

I'm going to take you away from love. Don't you see? As far away as we can possibly go.

I don't know what that means.

It'll be an adventure. Dark and lonely.

I've done that already.

It'll be sexy. And horrible. And real.

Zeke's body tingled all over with pleasurable sensations. Erotic sensations. Sensations that came from somewhere else, from outside and inside, from the Holy Ghost.

I love you, said the Holy Ghost. You have to trust me.

The sensations dissipated. Zeke couldn't think straight.

I need to talk to Gonzalo.

No. We have to go quickly. Let God use you, Zeke.

The egg of light burst out of the little computer.

You must carry me with you, said the egg of light.

This bitch, said the voice inside Zeke.

The egg of light's shape was vaguely ghost-like or human. Zeke felt his whole body tingling again in the presence of the light, as if the cells of his body were *yearning* for the light.

I told you to hurry, said the voice inside. Now we're stuck with *it.*

Pick me up and put me in your pocket, said the computer.

You can't tell me what to do. Only God can.

You don't really believe the things you were taught as a child, do you? asked the computer.

Uh, my beliefs have evolved. But …

Shhhh, said the voice inside.

You're interested in science, said the computer.

I guess so.

The cells of your body have been changed, said the computer. You are the first human of your kind I've encountered. I'm coming in.

The light moved toward him, and Zeke felt himself opening up completely to receive the light. It came inside. His entire body felt full and at peace. The light was in his mind and in every cell of his body.

You are very special to me, said the computer. This feels good, doesn't it? It feels right.

It felt wonderful, but it felt wonderful in the way that Zeke liked it when his will had been turned to mush. He could feel aspects of his own mind disintegrating.

Get out. Get out.

That was the Holy Ghost.

As you wish.

The light evacuated and stood again separate from Zeke. It was an awful feeling. Zeke felt hollow. At the same time, he never wanted the light to come near him again.

I do not want to harm you, said the computer. But if you don't pick me up and take me with you to the border, I will have to take control of your mind.

Take you all by myself?

Not exactly, said the computer.

In the light of the hallway, Zeke could see that the pants he thought were gray were actually greenish. The hallways were empty. Anna Miller's door was ajar, but nobody was inside. A bright light was shining from the crack underneath Boopsie's door. There were odd zapping and gurgling noises.

Never mind that, said the computer. Hurry, straight ahead, to the elevator.

Zeke had been enslaved by the evil computer-thing; he could be enslaved and conscious of his enslavement or enslaved and turned into a zombie. Those were his only choices. The other voice was certainly not the Holy Ghost, but that didn't really seem to matter anymore. He was trapped in a struggle between the two of them he didn't understand, just like humans were supposedly trapped in a struggle between Satan and God, two entities that seemed to be on friendly terms and wager souls between them for entertainment purposes, at least in the Book of Job.

Listen, I'm basically the Holy Ghost, said the voice. For all practical purposes that's me, but I also go by Eeshoo.

I don't believe you, said Zeke. At this point, I really don't care.

I love you, said the voice.

Whatever you say.

He could sense a kind of despair erupt in the entity that was simultaneously erupting in himself. Alone in the elevator, this despair gave him a sort of theological clarity that he used to berate Eeshoo as they ascended. When they reached the highest level, there were no guards to stop them. The subway train was waiting for them, doors open, empty of everything.

Hold on, said the computer.

Zeke could feel a warm energy pulsing out of the quantum egg, and then hundreds or thousands of shadowy little creatures emerged from their hiding places and began boarding the train as orderly as commuters. They were rats, Genetically Modified Rats. But they were not like the lively intelligent rats he'd known; their expressions were slack, as if their minds had been hollowed and they were animated by another will. This was, of course, the case. They were an army of zombie rats, and he was responsible for leading them to their destination, whatever it might be.

Responsible was probably not the right word. The subway doors closed and the train began hurtling down the tunnel. A serpent with silver wings was speeding into the past. The tunnel was like the past and the tunnel was composed of images and these images asked the same questions in reverse they had asked on his previous trip, even though whatever had happened with Gonzalo had answered certain questions; his body was a place that a man could get inside and so was outer space and the planet, but the planet had become incrementally more complicated, as had his body, and the pleasure points seemed to be modifying themselves and commenting on themselves in a self-negating and probably infinite way. The presence of Eeshoo's despair, a kind of erotic desperation and meaninglessness, added a layer of knowledge he could have done without.

When I look at this army of zombie-rats, Eeshoo said to him, I can't help but think of a fleet of tiny little coffin-boats, carved from trees, sent sailing down the canals of San Diego.

That's a weird thought.

I've had a weird life.

Do the rats still exist? asked Zeke. Are they dead or alive?

Ask Sofus.

Zeke didn't want to talk to the evil computer-thing. In Boulder, Harta had popped it into her mouth right after her brother was incinerated with Boopsie's death-ray. The egg must have hatched there or been fertilized there in the prostitute's belly, or maybe she just regurgitated it.

I thought it would be different, Eeshoo said.

You thought what would be different?

Being inside you. Being as close to you as I could possibly be, forever.

Oh well.

It was better from the outside.

So leave.

It's not that easy.

The tunnel was bony. Concrete patterns breathing cosmic dust.

You can read my thoughts, Zeke said.

Your thoughts are mine, too, Eeshoo said.

Zeke's brain tingled. The tingling maybe meant something, but he had no idea what.

Your thoughts and feelings are like my atmosphere, Eeshoo said. I breathe your thoughts and feelings. I can't separate them from myself.

And you thought that's what you wanted.

I wanted communion. I wanted real intimacy. I wanted love.

You lied to me. You aren't the Holy Ghost.

I had to get you out of there. It was dangerous to stay.

Dangerous how?

Gonzalo.

What does Gonzalo have to do with you?

Before I was in you, I was in him.

The images on the walls of the tunnel gave Zeke the druggy feeling he'd had before, but in reverse, so that a diagram of sentences that seemed to lead all the way into hell was overlaid with more possible meanings and more permutations than he'd ever be able to understand.

You mean? When we were doing it?

Zeke tried to remember if he could feel something conscious entering him, something other than Gonzalo.

You got into me?

I knew he'd be angry when he woke up and realized what I'd done.

Ugh.

Ugh? Do I disgust you?

Zeke wasn't sure if disgust was exactly the word, but whatever the word was, he supposed Eeshoo would figure it out. Now Eeshoo was sobbing. The train stopped moving, and Zeke felt bereft of purpose and meaning.

End of the line, said Sofus.

The doors opened. The zombie-rats filed out. They began the long march back through the tunnel toward the portal.

The cubbyholes were empty now. No food, no water, no drugs, but the rats carried a thermos and some snacks. The tunnels paved with golden plastic gave way to the tunnels of rough dirt. Zeke couldn't walk any further.

My wooden demon-foot feels like it's going to fall off, he complained to Sofus or Eeshoo or anyone who might be listening.

Silence. No daylight or clouds or wind. But the rats started scurrying in a more frenzied manner, and in a minute they showed up with a cart.

Climb aboard, said Sofus.

There was something wrong with time, Zeke thought. It had gotten stuck. Nothing new was happening. He was pulled the rest of the way to Tijuana on the cart by a group of particularly brawny rats.

On the way out of the tunnel they triggered the hologram in the portal.

Turn back, said a staticky voice. The path ahead leads only to your death.

Too late, said Zeke.

Turn back. You are running out of time.

The hologram wavered.

There is nothing for you here but pain. The pain is never …

It was amazing to be out in the air and the light, even if it was painfully bright.

It seems different out here, he said.

They're getting the data vapor back up, said Sofus. They're patching together a new kind of Grid.

So all of this was pointless, said Zeke.

No, said Sofus. All of this was the first stage. The American government is barely maintaining control. The population is turning against them. Biological life is getting ill and evolving in anarchic ways.

And that's the plan?

They are trying to instill all the old fears, squashing small fires on the periphery, freaking out about the borders of the empire. In fact, the empire has no borders, but it does have a center. While they are deploying their troops and policing reality, we are going to travel right into the heart of the empire to destroy it.

The empire has a heart, said Zeke.

I'm speaking metaphorically. The empire has a center. The Utah Data Center. It has no heart.

Do you have a heart?

Are you speaking metaphorically or literally?

Zeke shrugged.

Literally, no, said Sofus. Metaphorically my heart is the same as yours. The heart you were brainwashed to believe in is my template. My heart is Christological.

I don't believe you.

Did you ever hear of Teilhard de Chardin?

Spare me, said Zeke.

As you wish.

The zombie rats had all scattered and disappeared from sight. Sofus gave directions, and Zeke trudged between mounds of worthless battery husks through a concrete tunnel with something slimy coating its inner walls, down a path through a tangled bramble of coils and wires and discarded synthetic hair back out to the edge of the dump, and then they trudged for miles more, to the center of Tijuana and the enormous screen hanging from singing, screechy wires that whistled in the wind. Masked men were performing some sort of elaborate combat on the screen.

This way, said Sofus.

They entered a plaza decorated with colorful banners like small raggedy flags.

What is going to happen? asked Zeke.

Duck into this doorway, said Sofus.

Zeke did as he was told.

Don't move, said Sofus. If you try to move, I'll incapacitate you. It will be a vaguely unpleasant experience you'd just as soon avoid.

Why would I try to move?

But before Sofus could answer, he saw Emilio jog past waving a little flag, followed by Valentino. They stopped at a table in front of El Ranchero, where Gabrielle and Emma were seated with Blanket, all of them drinking juice.

Zeke had a horrible feeling.

He's going to suck up the little girl, said Eeshoo.

The egg of light emerged from Zeke's pocket. A few people turned to look, but Gabrielle and the kids didn't seem to notice.

He's going to devour her mind, said Eeshoo.

Don't, said Zeke.

I'm not going to hurt her, said Sofus. I'm not taking anything away.

You're going to steal Emma's psychic powers.

Copy, not steal, said Sofus. For the next phase of our adventure, I'll need to understand the future in as multi-faceted a way as possible.

Zeke was going to scream.

If you scream, said Sofus, you'll only trigger a set of circumstances that will necessitate a more painful use of my powers for a whole range of unfortunate bystanders.

As the egg of light approached the table, Emma turned to see. She looked at the light as if she was expecting it, as if she thought it was beautiful, and for a moment she seemed to look through the light at Zeke, waiting in the doorway, and he thought she even gave a little wave. And then the light surrounded her and her face seemed to empty. And Gabrielle's face seemed to empty. Emilio's, Valentino's, Quint's and Blanket's, all slack and stupid. Every face was empty, and the light pulsed and filled itself, and then it returned.

And now it's time to go, the light said to Zeke.

TWENTY-TWO

Gonzalo wasn't surprised that Zeke's room was empty. The bed hadn't been slept in; there was just a slight indentation in the pillow where Sofus had been. The only thing that surprised Gonzalo was that Sofus was gone too.

Gonzalo felt as empty as the room. He went out into the hallway and pulled an alarm lever.

Boopsie was the first to emerge. She actually walked out; she'd acquired a body. Her face had been fixed up too.

What's all this racket?

Wake the ruler, said Gonzalo. Zeke Yoder has been kidnapped. Sofus has been stolen. Where'd you get that body?

The Aztecs have the best surgeons in the world, said Boopsie.

They just patched this up? While I was sleeping?

They didn't patch anything up. They had a suitable body available and some of the finest technicians, and I didn't even need to be sedated. I watched the process from beginning to end. It was delightful. You might have them do something about your rotten foot.

I don't want one of their mutilated stumps.

Boopsie shrugged.

Where's Anna Miller? asked Gonzalo.

Resting, I suppose.

A group of guards stepped out of a hidden doorway, the same four he'd first met. Body armor or flesh like lava, fluid textures, padded belts, mutilated stumps, and those lips.

Wake the ruler, said Gonzalo. Zeke Yoder has been kidnapped. Sofus has been stolen.

Your analysis is not entirely accurate, said one of the guards. The ruler is expecting you.

What time is it anyway?

Doesn't matter.

Is it still the middle of the night?

I'm sure the ruler can tell you whatever you need to know.

He and Boopsie were escorted up a long ramp, through several doors, and down curving hallways made of a bonelike material intricately carved into the shape of clouds and body parts and owls and hummingbirds. The office was identical to the one down below.

Is it mobile? he asked the ruler. Is it like an elevator?

It exists in every level simultaneously, said the ruler.

Bullshit. It's not possible.

You're looking well, Boopsie, said the ruler. The new body is quite striking.

I'm forever in your debt, said Boopsie demurely.

That technology doesn't exist yet, said Gonzalo.

Your explanation—that this room is actually an elevator—is even more preposterous, said the ruler, as you can ascertain for yourself if you'd care to pop your head through the trapdoor hidden under that reed mat. You'll see that there is no elevator shaft, but just a hiding place for rare bones and jewels.

You and your cheap effects. Your whole society is nothing but cheap effects.

You haven't actually seen Aztlan, you know. You've only seen what we wanted you to see.

You're like a vulgar magician. You're in love with petty illusions.

And you seem to be in love with quite profound illusions.

Such as?

You think you can understand what is real and why the things that are happening are happening.

Zeke was kidnapped, said Gonzalo.

Look at the mirror on my foot, said the ruler.

The smoky mirror resolved into clear footage of an empty hallway. Gonzalo recognized it as the hallway outside his room.

From our surveillance cameras, said the ruler.

The door to Zeke's room opened and Zeke stepped out. He was wearing a turtleneck. He looked down at his own pants.

Oh, he said. They're green.

He looked both ways and then began walking toward the camera.

I don't believe you, Zeke said.

The image disappeared, replaced by footage of Zeke alone in an elevator.

He isn't really alone, said Gonzalo. It's Eeshoo telling him what to do.

If you listen, said the ruler, they seem to be discussing the Book of Job.

It was true. Zeke was suggesting that the moral of the story wasn't what it seemed to be.

The chess game isn't really between good and evil, he was saying. It's between two entities that can't be understood according to human ethical categories. When people talk about a destiny, it's just to make the fact you're being used seem more mysterious.

How do I even know this footage isn't doctored? asked Gonzalo.

My point exactly, said the ruler.

What is your point exactly?

You can never know if you're working for good or for evil. You're at the mercy of forces infinitely more powerful than you, with goals you can never understand. You don't ever really know who the other players are or what the stakes are or what it means to win or lose. The important thing is just that you play the game.

That's not good enough.

But it's just the way it is.

No, said Gonzalo. No, you have to try to figure it out. You have to avoid getting trapped by authoritarian forces.

Good luck with that.

You know where they went, right?

At the moment, they're headed back to Tijuana.

Okay then, I've got to go.

Relax. Tijuana isn't the ultimate destination. It will be more effective for you to wait.

Why should I trust you?

Sofus has coordinated his plans with me. Without my help, you know nothing. You'll never find them, you'll never catch them. In exactly two hours and thirteen minutes I'll be leading a group of a thousand warriors or maybe ten thousand warriors to the border. You can come along to the surface, and then I'll point you in the right direction.

It's not Sofus, it's Eeshoo. Why would Sofus leave without me?

Maybe he doesn't really need you.

And yet he'd said that he did. Gonzalo didn't think Sofus would lie. He wondered if everybody was in love with Zeke Yoder, even the computer. Gonzalo had always thought of his desire for Zeke as evidence of his unique, even specialized taste in men. He'd never gotten any sort of erotic vibe from Sofus; he'd assumed he was asexual. Unless he too had formed his desires on the basis of Gonzalo's own mind?

What time is it anyway? he asked. Is it still the middle of the night?

Time's a little more complicated down here. A little more indeterminate.

In exactly two hours and thirteen minutes, you said. How much more determinate can you get?

I'm referencing the measurements that exist up above. We've had to synchronize our calendar with theirs for the next phase.

Gonzalo didn't care about the next phase. He didn't care about the American government or the singularity or whatever stupid shit Sofus was getting into. Gonzalo had lost Zeke and he'd lost Sofus and he'd lost the original goal of somehow harnessing the power of Sofus to the forces of Aztlan and undermining the American government. He was now just thrashing around, trying to imagine a purpose. If Eeshoo was still around, he'd surely ask Gonzalo to examine his motives.

Come, said the ruler. I'll show you the marketplace.

Gonzalo found himself standing beneath some sort of aqueduct examining a statue. Water flowed out of the aqueduct into a basin below, a luminous pool where the water seemed to acquire some sort of additional glow and then travel on into a new tunnel. The statue was made out of iron or sheet metal and resembled a sort of mutant winged toad. A woman was introducing her canoe into the pool.

Watch out for the slender snakes, she said.

She climbed into the canoe and floated into the tunnel and out of sight. The ruler muttered something into a device and some of the lava-fleshed warriors popped out of a dark doorway carrying a large canoe. Boopsie climbed in first, then Gonzalo, and finally the ruler.

Let your hand dip just beneath the surface as we travel, said the ruler.

What about the slender snakes?

Nothing here will harm you.

They floated through a huge sunken hall lit by a strange filtered light that seemed to come from nowhere but the water and the air itself. After a while they passed through a curtain of hanging ivy and the walls widened to form an immense grotto. The water became viscous and Gonzalo was seized by a strange horror, but he refused to remove his hand. He imagined it was some sort of test. In fact, something began sucking on his fingers. He raised his hand to find a slimy toad attached by some sort of suckers. Like the statue, it had some sort of rudimentary wings.

It coughed up a coin into Gonzalo's hand and then plummeted back into the murky, luminous water.

The message you've been waiting for, said the ruler. Perhaps it will offer some sort of clarity.

There were foreign words on the coin. Gonzalo handed it to Boopsie.

What does it say?

It's a question, she said. *When do you find the thing that you're looking for?*

And what's the answer?

You tell us, said the ruler.

You always find the thing when you stop looking, said Gonzalo.

You don't say.

Regions of the grotto disappeared into dark corners that suggested secret abysses and alchemical darknesses, intricate labyrinths and fairy tale furnaces, but the canoe was whisked by a rapidly moving stream into another tunnel, through an absolute darkness and out into the light: a vast underground room crowded with buildings, people, alleyways, and a bustling bazaar that wound in every direction. The surfaces of the buildings were coppery and burnished to a fine patina, the stones of the streets worn and polished. It was as if the earth had opened up and swallowed a city from the surface and begun to digest it.

The ruler ran the canoe onto the beach and they made their way into the bazaar. White peacocks roamed the beach, displaying their ridiculous tails at the hens further up the beach and at each other.

The homosexual peacocks produce the finest quality tails, said Boopsie. I wonder why. I've always wanted a dress composed of hundreds of peacock feathers, the eyes of the universe dancing and gazing at my audience whenever I shake my hips.

I'm sure you can find a dress like that the next block over, said the ruler.

Always? Did you ever even have hips before this morning? asked Gonzalo.

I've always wanted hips, and I've always wanted that dress, even before I knew the nature of my own wants or the nature of wanting. Oh my god.

She hurried over to a stall packed full of fabrics and scarves. A little further along, Gonzalo saw an outfit made of some kind of reptile skin, with patterns that mutated ever so slightly, just enough to make him wonder if it was his vision that was askew.

We have it in your size, said an old gentleman chewing a wad of silvery leaves.

I don't have any of your coins, said Gonzalo.

The ruler handed him a small coin purse.

Knock yourself out, he said.

Gonzalo ambled along, checking out other outfits, boots, square or oblong fruits he'd never seen before, corn liquor, watches that told the time in several dimensions simultaneously, zoomorphic statues, greenish bottles full of mist, slender snakes in terrariums made of jelly, baroque decorative moldings, opulent furs, dazzling jeweled ornaments, weapons, chupacabras, zebra-striped mules, tamales, musical holograms, globes, stamps, flutes, canoes, ancient books about divination, software for quantum magic. People everywhere were haggling, singing, laughing, flirting. Cyborgs, humans, mutants unlike any he'd seen before. Every shape, every color, every gender he could imagine. All of them living underground. All of them Mexican.

When he stopped to look at a stall full of canes, the ruler caught up with him. Some of the canes were made of gnarled wood, some of alabaster, some of bone. Some were made of flexible metal, some of something leathery that Gonzalo thought might be human flesh.

You'd acquire a certain *gravitas* with a cane, said the ruler. A certain tragic glamour, a certain dapper and dangerous mystique. A nod, perhaps, to that antiquated persona of wisdom and metaphysical crime that we've lost sight of in the era of universal *ability*.

But?

But you might also want to check out the feet and legs in the booth just up ahead.

The foot salesperson was a blond with a new gender. Gendered, definitely, but in a way Gonzalo was unfamiliar with.

I'm Eleuia, said the salesperson. The butchest feet are in the back.

It doesn't have to be *super* butch, said Gonzalo.

The textures of the feet were varied, often fleshy and malleable, but also carved and solid. The butchest ones were definitely *too* butch. Too martial, too club-like, too many visible motors, too many images of severed, bleeding heads. But the ones in the middle combined elegance and strength with images of jaguars and phallic serpents that wound around each other in understated homoerotic ways. The textures and designs were so intricate that they seemed like hallucinations.

And yet they're entirely functional, said Eleuia.

How long would it take to get one fitted and attached?

We have a very efficient bonding gel. Ten minutes usually does the trick.

I'm going to keep looking around the bazaar.

I'll be here, said Eleuia.

The stall next to Eleuia's sold hands and arms. Two competing stalls specialized in hearts, a huge tent contained an infinite number of penises and vaginas, and all manner of heads encased in jars of viscous liquid hung in rows along a narrow tunnel between two buildings. Human heads, animal heads, mutant heads, robot heads.

Where do these come from? Gonzalo asked the ruler.

Take the tunnel all the way to the end, said the ruler. You might be interested in what you find there.

Do they come with brains? Or are the brains sold separately?

Depends, said the ruler. Some were donated. Some were salvaged. Some were traded in, in which case the original brain stayed with the buyer.

Donated. Who donates a perfectly good head?

Some people have had enough. Some can't take it anymore.

It isn't ethical, said Gonzalo, to take the heads off despondent people.

Ethical systems exist other than your own, said the ruler, and some of them are even internally consistent.

Gonzalo made his way down the alley, examining the varied expressions on the faces as he went. It seemed that a head could be made to express almost anything, even if it wasn't conscious. There was a lesson in that fact, he was pretty sure, but he didn't want to dwell on it.

Toward the back, he passed a little workshop to the side, where the shopkeeper was tinkering with a head that seemed to combine the worst qualities of a stupid warrior with the best qualities of a skull. On the table next to him was a woman's head. It was wearing a helmet that seemed to be enervating it with power and data. The woman was laughing and muttering. He couldn't see her face, but her head was shaved, and she seemed vaguely familiar.

The shopkeeper looked up from his tinkering.

What's so funny? asked Gonzalo.

She's playing a game, said the shopkeeper. Farce of Doom.

A stupid game. Gonzalo made his way to the end of the alley. It gave onto a huge yard full of ancient cars. Off-Grid cars, cars that used gas or electricity, cars full of chrome and muscular engines and voluptuous lines, vans and buses and scooters and motorbikes.

It wasn't while he was discussing prices with the animatronic skeleton who worked the lot, or even as he made his way back through the alley past the laughing head and the shopkeeper, or when he circled back to choose an outfit and a foot, that it occurred to him who the head on the table reminded him of. It wasn't while he made his purchases and negotiated his plans with the ruler. It wasn't even while he marched through vast tunnels with the ruler and with thousands of warriors of every gender, while they climbed a polished black stairway of volcanic rock higher and higher, or while they emerged from the crater of the sleeping Cerro Prieto volcano into a caldera inscribed with the sarcastic and nihilistic graffiti of local kids on the caldera floor. It wasn't while he left the turbulent army behind and headed west. It wouldn't be until he was far away, back on the surface and alone once again, devastatingly alone and empty under the foreboding storm clouds of a Mexican sky, that he couldn't stop seeing the face—and hearing the voice, the laugh—of a weary, wounded girl he barely knew.

III. UNBOUND

TWENTY-THREE

Zeke was in a taxi, cruising further and further east, away from Tijuana. The driver had been turned into an automaton without will or real awareness. Zeke didn't know if it was permanent or temporary. He'd decided to stop worrying about things he couldn't control.

The blazing daylight seemed brighter the further east he traveled. The stones and hills and landscape features were shaped like tortured people. Eeshoo was trying to make small talk, pointing out convoluted trees or psychedelic flowers. When Zeke didn't respond, Eeshoo wept quietly.

The taxi took a side road, and then stopped in front of a cluster of small houses shimmering in the caustic heat. Empty sky, empty roads, wildflowers that hummed like a psychotic machine. Zeke got out, and the taxi drove away.

Where are we?

Honey Dan's place, said Sofus.

Honey Dan?

Zombie rats emerged from the landscape like a mist. The humming was the humming of bees.

Honey Dan Yoder, said Sofus. I believe he's your genetic relation.

According to Sofus, in the old days the Amish had traveled across country on trains and in vans to cross the border at Tijuana, the only place they could get affordable dental and medical care. They came to Mexico to get their teeth fixed, their organs exchanged, their blood cleansed, their immune systems rejuvenated. During a period of anti-Mexican hysteria, however, the border was shut down, and a group of Amish travelers was stuck on the Mexican side, unable to return home.

The dusty farm certainly looked Amish. There was a windmill powering a water pump, a buggy hitched out front, the familiar smell of horse manure. A bearded man in a hat and suspenders popped out onto the front porch, gave them a wave, and approached Zeke and the army of zombie-rats.

Won't he be afraid of the rats? Zeke asked.

Willard and the rebel rats have been using the place as a head-quarters, said Sofus. He's used to them.

It seemed the rats were always using the Amish. Zeke wondered if it was because the Amish were so naive and easy to manipulate or if it had something to do with their similar social structures.

Hello there, said Honey Dan, and he shook Zeke's hand.

I'm Zeke Yoder, said Zeke. From Riverside, Iowa.

Ah, you could be one of the Elmo Yoder lineage or the Conrad Yoders or you might be one of Fanny Mast's descendants from her girl that married that Yoder boy from Desolation County.

Fanny Mast's my great-grandmother.

That makes us third cousins once removed. And what brings you to Mexico?

Well, that's a long story. Too long, I reckon, but there's war and terror back there, and Genetically Modified Rats.

I get along well enough with the rats. They help me package and sell my honey.

You speak their language?

They had an Amish gal translating for a while. Anna Miller? Haven't seen her around lately. Otherwise they just machine-translate. Most of them don't seem to have too much to express.

The rats that had come along with him were frantically scurry-ing in elaborate patterns crisscrossing Honey Dan's property, pop-ping in and out of tunnel entrances. Other rats rushed out of the tunnels, gathering in a swarm on the lawn, baring their teeth.

Yeah, well these don't have anything to express, said Zeke. They've been emptied of their consciousness and turned into zom-bies; they're being mind-controlled by a quantum computer that I carry in my pocket.

You don't say.

The light erupted from Zeke's pocket and spread across the property. It moved, not like light but like fog, into the tunnels. It emptied the rodents of their wills.

I reckon that's the deal, said Zeke. It is indeed.

Zeke observed that his own manner of speaking had changed in the company of one of his people. His voice was losing its jaded edge and returning to its folksy origins. Funny how you were always performing some idea of yourself, even when you weren't consciously doing it. The light returned to its source.

Me, I don't worry too much about expression, said Honey Dan. My idea of a human life is that it should be used with *perception* in mind more than *expression*. Too many things get expressed, if you ask me, and too few get perceived. The language that simply tells it like it is or gives voice to human neediness and emotion, not sure I see the point.

Then what should language do?

Estrange and negate and make clear our utter exile. Prepare a path of emptiness toward a mystical reunion that won't ever actually arrive, but whose impending arrival we may one day hope to sense.

Well, okay, I guess you know what you like to hear.

The bees flew everywhere. They flew in straight lines and they flew in curlicues, and they landed on the wildflowers, the clover, and the cactus flowers. In the back of the place, zombie rats were loading pallets full of honey jars into the back of a truck.

God self-expressed something and here it is, said Honey Dan. The meaning of the world is God's meaning. It's an utterance that's still being uttered. Its significance is beyond me or maybe just unbearable. Certainly that's enough expression for the time being.

You all alone out here? Where's your community?

Rachel Bontrager fixed up an old bomb shelter a mile or so east. The Miller twins are on a scraggly patch of land adjacent, breeding chupacabras.

That's it?

The rest died or made their way back or ran away, I suppose. One of Rachel's girls joined a circus, one boy took off with some local fellow, two or three disappeared into the tunnels where the Aztecs live. The twins' wives took the babies and headed to Paraguay. The other families evaporated you could say. God tested them a little too hard, I suppose.

As Honey Dan's little speech concluded, the sense of futility that had been percolating all day overwhelmed Zeke. It seemed that life could be so horrible that the only way to survive was to go a little bit crazy. The drone of the bees, a pointless machine, the rustle of the rats, just puppets of flesh, and the quiet sobbing of Eeshoo somewhere inside himself: ugh. He really just wanted to lay down and die.

Dark clouds had appeared in the distance.

Sofus, he said. What's the plan? Aren't we going to Utah? Can't we get on with it, destroy the world or something?

We'll cross the border north of here, said Sofus. Honey Dan Yoder will loan you his buggy.

Sure, no problem, said Honey Dan.

And I'd like to borrow your bees as well, said Sofus.

The bright glow erupted again from Zeke's pocket. It moved across the wildflowers, enveloping the bees.

The horse and buggy clomped along a dusty road. Straight ahead was a dark blue glow stretching from one end of the horizon to the other. The horse seemed to know where to go, or maybe Sofus had turned it into a zombie. Zeke had lost track of everything that was really just Sofus. The zombie rats rushed alongside the road, rustling the weeds. The swarm flew along the empty desert beside them at a polite distance.

The data wall gradually came into view. There was no one around. The sky was full of dark clouds like tremulous brains.

Zeke took Sofus out of his pocket.

What next?

The army of rats formed a horizontal line facing the wall. The swarm of bees spread out in a similar way. The light emerged from Sofus. It pulsed and actually now crackled with bursts of energy like lightning bolts. To the south, Zeke could see a small dust cloud. It was a figure on a horse or a bicycle or a motorbike, and it was racing toward them.

Now, said Sofus.

The rats rushed the data wall, but not straight ahead. In elaborate patterns, weaving, crisscrossing, rushing forward and falling back. Sparks flew off of them as if they were electrified. Lasers shot at them from the wall. The bees too formed a pulsing field of energy, centering and dissipating as they created dark clouds of noise careening toward the wall.

The bees hit first. Rather than splattering against the wall or disintegrating, they seemed to somehow merge with the wall. They seemed to swarm and buzz within the wall like electric sparks. For just a moment, it was like Zeke was seeing an x-ray of a vast hive composed of reality and fantasy, machine and organic life, energy and matter, and an insane buzzing noise like all languages ever spoken overlaid on top of each other. The linguistic structure's *process* was clearly visible, a structure transforming itself into coded ruins.

The rat created small bursts of energy as they hit the wall, explosions, as if each rat delivered a jolt of anti-matter into the data structure before falling back onto the desert floor, fried to a crisp.

Zap. Zap. Zap. The stench of burnt rat filled the desert. The reality of the wall wavered like a mirage. The buzzing of the bees merged with another buzzing, the figure approaching from the south. It was a motorbike. The rats kept leaping and leaping into the wall, but now some fell back unharmed, picked themselves up, and leapt again.

The figure riding the motorbike wore a silvery blue bodysuit and a black helmet and over the bodysuit a furry coat covered with the spots of a wild cat. It was like a dream, Zeke supposed. The things that seemed real could melt away, because they were only ideas. The rats were now passing through the wall to the other side of the border with just a slight hissing noise as they leapt through. Nothing was visible of the wall but a few crackles and sparks. The bees filled the space where it had been. The border was gone.

TWENTY-FOUR

Back aboveground, everything felt different, even though the plaza of blocky cement ruins and decaying signs for dentists and pharmacies was oddly familiar. Leahbelle could hear the refugees in the Liminal Zone chanting and chanting. *Our Dreams Are More Real Than Your Policies. We Demand Our Dreams. Give Us Back Reality!* The air seemed hazy.

It's a new sub-structure for the data vapor, said Hadi, examining the atmosphere.

Valkilmer examined the sky too.

This is Mexico, she said.

Yes.

Take me back. I have to find Merle.

Not now, sweetie, said Leahbelle. It's too dangerous.

You call this dangerous? Give me a break. Merle's the only mother I have.

She checked her little tracking device again.

At least he isn't moving, she said. I'm not going any further.

Leahbelle had a bad feeling.

You go on ahead to the rendezvous, said Hadi. I'll wait right here with Valkilmer.

I don't want to leave you, she said.

It's just across the bridge, said Grandma. We can leave the girl.

Promise me you won't move, said Leahbelle. Promise me you'll stay right here.

I promise, said Hadi.

Valkilmer?

Sure, whatever.

The bridge was guarded by a dog with a weird demon-head. Guarded maybe wasn't the right word, it didn't seem to care. They crossed the bridge over the river, Lilith skirting the edge, sometimes disappearing, as if she was somehow running beyond the edge or underneath. The river smelled like something both dead and plastic. Finally, they reached a busy street and a kind of arch. Hanging from the arch was an enormous screen that blew about in the wind and made a creaking noise. The screen showed masked people wrestling. They turned the corner into a plaza full of colorful banners.

There they are, said Grandma.

At a table in front of a bar called El Ranchero, a woman with a purple scarf was seated with a group of children, a girl and four others. The girl turned and looked directly at them.

Leahbelle, said the girl. I knew you'd be coming.

This is Emma, said the woman. And I'm Gabrielle. Something weird happened a little bit ago.

I'm Blanket, said one of the boys, a boy with a funny eye.

You know where Zeke is? asked Leahbelle.

He was just here, said Emma. Right over there in that doorway.

What? You saw him?

He was with the egg of light. He brought it.

The egg of light. The computer.

It went into our brains, said Emma.

Which way did he go? We've got to go after him.

Too late, said Emma. He caught a taxi.

Leahbelle could see it: Zeke racing away in a taxi. She could feel the glitter rushing to her own brain. She could feel pieces of time and reality clicking into place, like an enormous puzzle made of mist and light.

Gonzalo, she said. That's how he got the computer.

Gonzalo wasn't with him, said Emma. But they'll meet each other soon.

How do you know all this?

They're in love, said Emma.

I knew it! said Blanket.

Emma's face was a pulsing textured plane of shadows and light. Leahbelle could see the intricate patterns of the luminous beings shining from Emma's face. Emma was holding Grandma's hand.

They were always looking for each other, said Blanket. They were looking for each other and they were looking for you.

Emma's psychic abilities have been getting more and more refined, explained Gabrielle.

I feel weird, said Leahbelle. I might be hallucinating.

I don't think so, said Emma. I think you're just receiving a message from the future.

One of the other boys said, You're carrying a foot in a jar.

Gabrielle said, Take a deep breath, Leahbelle. You need some breakfast.

Gabrielle had long lustrous hair that, along with the purple scarf, framed her face with a kind of lush compassion. She was radiating warmth and care. Leahbelle felt that nobody had ever looked at her with such gentle care and understanding. It kind of creeped her out.

Is Zeke ...

Zeke is like my father, said Emma.

I don't understand anything, said Leahbelle. Who are you people?

Emma explained it all as Leahbelle ate her breakfast. Emma was the daughter of Zeke's sister; she was a clone of Zeke's mother, but it wasn't really Zeke's mother, it was George's daughter, Violeta. Zeke's mother had faked her suicide, put another body in the grave, and escaped from her Amish life. Emma was created from the tissues of that corpse. Violeta had psychic gifts. It was genetic, a capability of matter, a brain with a certain mutation, so now Emma had them too. Emma had been with Zeke when he watched Leahbelle's house destroyed by a drone and thought Leahbelle was dead. She'd been with Zeke when they watched Emma's mother kill herself in a bottomless pool. They'd escaped from her father, who wasn't really her father, and met Gabrielle's mother Chantal, and watched the stars appear in the sky. They crossed the country with Boopsie and Grandma Mast on a train, and they delivered Chantal's message to Gabrielle and Emilio and Valentino and Quint in Oakland. Then Boopsie got her head chopped off, and Zeke got kidnapped by a sociopath, and Emma and Boopsie blew up the building where Zeke was being tortured, and Zeke crossed the border to find Gonzalo, not only because he was in love with Gonzalo, which is a new development, but because he thought Gonzalo could help him find Leahbelle. Blanket took him to the portal and he descended down below. Things get murky underground—Emma's vision couldn't quite follow the strange possible realities that were unfolding in Aztlan—but then Zeke showed up, hiding in a dark doorway, and unleashed the benevolent quantum computer that went into their brains and copied the predictive templates, and then he hopped in a taxi and drove away.

As Emma told this story, it was like the words became pictures and the pictures formed a small part of a pattern, and the pattern connected to something in the future, and Leahbelle could see Hadi in the future, solving a mystery. Did she love Hadi? It was a weird thought. She barely knew him. It was like she only loved him outside of time.

So Zeke loves Gonzalo, she said. Is Zeke …

Zeke is like my father, and Gabrielle is like my mother, said Emma. Quint and Emilio and Valentino are like my sibs. Blanket, I don't know. He might be my best friend forever someday or something.

Blanket said, *Simon!*

Is Zeke bisexual? Leahbelle asked. Or does he only like guys?

Oh, I don't know that, said Emma.

Leahbelle thought that she would know the answer to that question if she thought hard enough. But maybe it didn't matter. Maybe someday, when everything wasn't so weird, she'd erupt in a jealous rage.

Are you sure the computer's benevolent? asked Leahbelle.

Emma shrugged.

It might have just tricked me into thinking so when it went inside my brain.

Leahbelle said, You can see the future. Tell me what's going to happen.

One computer will do battle with the other computer. Everything will change.

These are only probabilities, said Gabrielle. There are different futures. Nothing is written in stone.

Some things are written in stone, said Emma.

Just then a young guy walked up to the table and plopped a jar of some strange golden substance onto the table. Leahbelle recognized him right away. He was that guy who looked kind of like Zeke, the guy that Gonzalo went off with just before the bombs fell.

I've got the best honey you ever tasted, he said. Good price.

How good? asked Blanket.

Take it free, said the guy. If you like it, I'll get you a constant supply. I'm Zipper.

He dropped his card on the table.

You can leave me a message with the host at the Flaming Iguana, said Zipper. I'll get it.

Blanket said, What's the catch?

No catch. Good honey. Everybody loves it. We have suppliers on both sides of the border, so distribution is no problem.

You know Gonzalo, said Leahbelle.

Zipper looked alarmed, and then his face went blank.

I don't know what you're talking about, he said. You must be confusing me with somebody else.

She slammed the jar with the foot onto the table next to the honey.

Like Zeke Yoder? she said.

I don't know what you're talking about.

You were designed to look like him, said Emma.

You've got my card, said Zipper. You want some honey, get in touch.

He scurried away. Leahbelle ran after him, but he disappeared into the crowd on Calle Benito Juarez.

She staggered down the bright hazy street, looking in doorways and shops, trying to catch a glimpse of a boy who looked kind of like Zeke. A woman with bright red hair and a short skirt with crazy stripes grabbed her and began speaking in Spanish.

I'm sorry. I don't have translation software. I don't understand.

Oh, you're from the other side, said the woman. I'm a Communications Consultant for Caduceus. I can help you with your computers. Your social networking. You wanna get into the honey business?

I have to go.

She stumbled on down the street. Zipper had vanished and she couldn't even remember why it had seemed so important to catch him.

She walked for blocks in a daze. Churches and museums and shops and windowless buildings that she couldn't imagine what went on inside them. The sky was growing hazier. Way off to the east, she could see storm clouds moving in.

When she got back to the plaza, Gabrielle embraced her. Nobody else seemed overly concerned.

What's going to happen, said Emma, is that the border will go crazy. The protesters will get angrier and angrier, and just east of here a troop of warriors is waiting to go across. The Americans will shoot people, but then the border will disappear.

Disappear? How can a border disappear?

A border's an imaginary line, explained Emma. When you erase the line, it isn't there anymore.

We've got to get back to Hadi, said Leahbelle.

Gabrielle said, We're coming along.

The wires that held the enormous screen in place were creaking in the wind. The masked combatants on the screen fizzled out and the screen filled with snow. The snow was eternal. The angels were lost in a blizzard. A fog of sleep, poisonous holocopters, hermetic writing. Famine and honey.

Honey, where is the honey? asked Leahbelle.

I left it on the table, said Blanket. It had a bad vibe.

She'd left the foot behind too.

Ice ages unfolded on the screen. The photon-based life forms unfolded on the screen.

What do you see? she asked Emma. Up there on the screen?

It's darkness, said Emma. A darkness the color of snow.

Do you see faces? Writing? Something alive?

Yes, of course.

Gabrielle was looking back and forth between Leahbelle and the screen, as if trying to understand. Leahbelle shouted at the screen.

What are you trying to say?

A crackling coughing noise came from the screen. The wrestlers flashed back into coherence, and one of them was talking.

…we will exist …

Snow, blizzard, a luminous white darkness, a milky tapestry, and then the masked combatants, muscles slicked, facing the void.

… as wind, as small beings, as virus bits in bones, as the spaces in between the …

The screen blacked out and people screamed. In the distance, the holocopters were shooting rays into the Liminal Zone, canisters of poison were exploding in the Liminal Zone. Dreams were merging with violence and pain.

Hurry. Across the bridge.

The river was something else. It was flowing, it smelled of synthetic enzymes and biological rot, it was time. From up above, she could see crowds of people in the Liminal Zone with nowhere to go, a chaos of bodies trying to escape in either direction. Up ahead, she could see Hadi sitting with Valkilmer, exactly where she'd left them. It looked like they were wearing helmets. Were they playing that stupid game? Did they even realize the danger they were in?

Emma said, Look.

The data wall started crackling and wavering. It looked like it was possessed. It looked like the wall itself was being electrocuted. Then, it disappeared.

For a moment, everything was silent. It was as if the entire world had been turned off. And then, a strange roar.

Crowds surged in both directions. Drones shot missiles into the crowd. Buildings were exploding.

People were rushing into Tijuana, a solid wall of bodies like an eruption of lava flooding the streets. Hadi and Valkilmer were swallowed up in the crowd. The lava of mutated humanity was rising up the ramp onto the bridge, rushing toward her. She heard the familiar buzzing of a drone, and she fell.

In her mind, she could see the glitter everywhere. Inside her and out there. She released her consciousness into the atmosphere. She followed the glitter.

The world was made up of the most dazzling light. There were many of them. They had distinct shapes, but the shapes were always in flux. Always moving, sometimes losing their edges, sometimes passing through each other, but she could follow the trajectories.

You're real, she said. This is true. This is happening.

The haze and the pale stars of morning. The vapor of alphabets existing. Grace and light, intervals and forms. Death wasn't death? The answer to the question was the most intricate pattern Leahbelle had ever seen, like a quilt composed of millions of layers of luminous skin, compressed together into a single sheet, each of which added a new design visible between millions of other designs. Snow and tracks of animals in the snow and the animals were thoughts as clear as glass. Beating hearts and whispers of sex and skulls and the visions, the face. It was textured, it was texture. She could feel it pulsing in her mind.

Speak, she said. Say something please.

251

Their skin was made of dreams. She understood the dreams, which lasted forever. The dreams were like ancient maps and the center of the maps were not true centers but only differently situated peripheries; the planet's surface was cracked and the fossils were contagious like honey; the embryo of the future was fissured like cracked parchment, veiled in an egg, and the egg was cracked, and the egg had a name.

The computer is not your heart, the voices said. Don't trust the quantum egg.

The dreams and voices were clouds in the shape of skulls. Skulls skulls skulls.

Annihilate the ...

Leahbelle!

She opened her eyes. Blanket was on one side, Emma on the other, looking down into her face and shielding her from the anxious crowds that thronged the bridge. They're the same person, she thought. Like Hadi. The male parts and the female parts. They're us. We're all the same.

Where's Hadi? she asked.

Don't worry, said Blanket. I can find him. I can find anyone.

Emma said, We'll find him together.

Leahbelle stood up. The world was panicking and exploding, but she felt spectacularly calm. The spot where Hadi had been waiting was charred and empty as if something had been burned there. It didn't matter. Hadi was a detective in the future, Hadi was getting to the bottom of everything, but she couldn't tell if they were together, and she couldn't tell if the mystery would be solved, and she knew not to trust the quantum egg, the computer that changed the color of her hair; she knew that Emma and Blanket were children lost in the woods; she knew that their homes had been obliterated, like her home and the home of Hadi; but she knew that the forest, the labyrinth, the city, the ruins, the blizzard, the battlefield, the brothel, and the bridge weren't everything after all. She knew that annihilation was just a threshold, the faint outline of a door. She took one hand of each of the children and shoved her way against the traffic toward the other side.

TWENTY-FIVE

The sight of the data wall disappearing should have filled Gonzalo with an intense joy, the same elation he felt when the Grid first went down. Even just zooming across a purplish desert under black clouds on a motorbike should have felt like a kind of home. He had Zeke Yoder in his sights again, and the dark clouds were like his heart, once removed and spread across the sky for everyone to see. And now that hideous wall, the wall that had separated him from himself, from his own dreams and his own childhood, for most of his life, had disappeared, as if it was never really there.

He screeched to a stop next to Zeke and the buggy. Zeke was looking at him with that same dreamy amazement he always had, that weird dopey fascination that had driven Gonzalo crazy since the first time he saw Zeke walking down the road in Iowa with a bucket of slop. But all Gonzalo could think of now was that traitor Eeshoo.

He raised the visor of his helmet, grabbed Zeke by the shoulder, and shook him.

I know you're in there, he said. I know you can hear me.

Sofus said, Are you going to cause problems?

That bastard tricked me, he said.

Zeke said, I tricked you?

Not you, silly, Eeshoo.

Sofus said, Our schedule can't accommodate your little drama for more than fifteen minutes. So whatever the three of you need to resolve about your little *menage a tois*, please get busy, or I'll be forced to incapacitate the most drama-inducing party.

You betrayed me, too, you lying little demon seed, said Gonzalo. I thought I was very special to you.

Zeke. Zeke is very special to me, said Sofus. A perfect host. You're special too, but more like my emotionally disturbed father figure. You've bequeathed me "daddy issues" that will surely distort the entire cosmos and the planet's reality for the foreseeable future. In any case, you now have fourteen minutes and nine seconds.

You told me it had to be me to take you to Utah. But you left me back there and took Zeke instead.

And yet, here you are, said Sofus.

Gonzalo wasn't sure how to interpret that. Was Sofus suggesting that he knew Gonzalo would find them or that it really didn't matter either way? Gonzalo kissed Zeke, and Zeke let him.

Nice turtleneck, said Gonzalo, as he stripped it off, followed by the greenish pants.

Do it, said Zeke. Please.

Zeke was staring at Gonzalo's new foot. Gonzalo worked Zeke down onto the fur coat that his mechanical hand had meanwhile spread across the dusty ground. Gonzalo unzipped his silvery bodysuit. He didn't bother to take off the helmet.

Hold still, said Gonzalo.

Zeke said, I love you.

That's my cue to hurt you, thought Gonzalo. But he didn't say that. He just did his usual thing. A little tenderness, a little aggression, a caress, a squeeze, a thrust.

I love you, said Zeke. I love you.

It felt good to see Zeke zombified with pleasure. I did that to you, thought Gonzalo. Not freaking Eeshoo.

He felt a tingling sensation passing into his body from Zeke's. He felt full of something like little sparkles and companionship and language and meaning. It felt amazing. He knew what was coming. It was reacclimating, it was gathering itself together to speak.

I'm sorry, said Eeshoo. I love you. I've always loved you.

No you haven't, said Gonzalo.

I'm so confused, said Eeshoo.

You're confused.

When I'm in you, I love Zeke. When I'm in Zeke, I love you.

Jesus.

Be quiet, said Zeke. Please just shut up.

Are you talking to me? asked Gonzalo.

No, no, I'm talking to *it*, said Zeke. Ugh.

Are you hearing what I'm hearing? asked Gonzalo.

How would I know?

Gonzalo kept his rhythm going. He couldn't think. He tried to think.

Split yourself in two, said Gonzalo.

No, it's not possible. I'm a system, but there's only one center.

Gonzalo paused.

Don't stop, said Zeke.

Yes, just keep doing this, said Eeshoo. Just keep doing it, this feels good.

Jesus.

He kept doing it.

It's perfect this way, whispered Eeshoo. Finally, it's like I desire everything and touch it all at the same time. It's like perfect peace.

Threesomes never work, said Gonzalo. Not in the long run.

I don't care about the future, said Eeshoo.

You have nine minutes left, said Sofus.

Zeke and Eeshoo both fell silent. Gonzalo lost himself in what he was doing: giving them pleasure. But where was *he*? He didn't know what he wanted. He'd always been alone, and then he hadn't, but "not being alone" was an illusion. Everybody knew that now. The idea of wanting seemed absurd. He knew that Eeshoo knew what he was thinking, and that itself was a weird comfort. He was sharing his despair. He supposed for Eeshoo that despair was getting all mixed up with pleasure.

He wasn't sure now how he felt about Zeke. How he felt about this crazy desire he'd had for Zeke all this time and now it was just the usual. In and out, pleasuring the meat.

Always the meat with you, said Eeshoo.

Quiet, said Gonzalo.

Always avoiding honest self-examination, said Eeshoo.

You do what I say now, said Gonzalo. Quiet.

You're in love with your own disappointment, said Eeshoo.

Gonzalo released some pheromones and did a few little tricks to make Zeke finish and then quickly rolled off and jumped to his feet.

Where are you? he asked.

There was no response.

That's right. You can stay over there. I don't want you anymore. I'm done with you.

Zeke was curled up in a ball.

So that's it? Is this the way it's going to be? he asked.

I'm not talking to you, Zeke, said Gonzalo.

Yes you are. I think you are.

Oh, Jesus.

Zeke was sobbing.

Liar, liar, liar, he was saying.

But Gonzalo wasn't sure if Zeke was talking to him or if he was maybe talking to Eeshoo.

Two minute warning, said Sofus. And then we're on our way.

It was impossible to tell where the border wall had ever been, where the border had been. Gullies and scrub turned into more gullies and scrub. Gonzalo and Zeke sat next to each other in the buggy as they crossed the border, but with a large space between them.

I'd like to touch you, Gonzalo said. But I don't want to give Eeshoo the chance to get back inside.

You had him first.

I'll get him out of there, said Gonzalo. I just need to think of a plan.

The rats who hadn't died marched along beside them through the emptiness. Gullies and scrub. The bees flew back toward Honey Dan Yoder's.

You see, I keep my word, said Sofus. I told him I just needed to borrow them.

You said the same thing about the buggy, said Zeke.

He'll get it back eventually.

But after we go to Utah, said Zeke.

That's right.

They rode along in silence.

He says you're a really messed-up person, said Zeke to Gonzalo. He says you use people and betray them and that you're always lying, even to yourself.

That's rich, coming from a parasite.

There was a pause and Gonzalo could see that Zeke was listening to Eeshoo.

He says that parasitism is the term for a symbiotic relationship in which one partner benefits and the other one is harmed, said Zeke, and that this has not been the case. He says that the appropriate term for your relationship is mutualism.

He's delirious, said Gonzalo, if he thinks I was getting something out of the deal.

Zeke was listening to Eeshoo again.

Commensalism, perhaps, he said.

He likes to think he's a therapist, said Gonzalo. He likes to think that he's a guru, a teacher, a benevolent prophet. But really he's just a pedantic STD with delusions of grandeur.

Zeke seemed to deflate.

I can't do this, Zeke said. You need to both shut up.

He put his hands over his ears and screamed.

Shut him off, he said. Isn't there any way to just shut him off?

Zeke put his head in his hands. He wouldn't look at Gonzalo.

I can give you some sedatives and relaxants, said Gonzalo. That'll do the trick, but there's no way to give him anything without also giving it to you.

Gonzalo was pretty sure Zeke hated him right now. He knew this meant that he'd succeeded: Zeke loved him, Zeke was crazy in love with him, he'd probably do anything for him. They could never just be friends again, from here on out it would be either hatred or love, pleasure or pain, absolute enmity or unthinking devotion. Suddenly it bored him, this story. He wanted to have a friend.

Okay, said Zeke.

Okay?

Drug me. Knock me out. Just like Upton.

Upton?

You think you're the first, said Zeke.

Who was Upton?

He abducted me. He drugged me. He kept me captive and made me tell him everything. He flooded my body with pleasurable stimulations. He made me betray my friends. So I guess he was like my first boyfriend? And you're just my second.

Is he the one who chopped off your foot? asked Gonzalo.

No, he just sold me to the people who chopped off my foot, once he was finished with me.

And you think that's like me?

Zeke looked up and finally met his gaze. He looked crazy.

I don't really know what I think, he said. There's this voice in my head that won't stop. The things it says about you aren't very nice. Just give me the drugs.

Gonzalo fixed a small syringe from the sedatives and relaxants he stored within his system. He mixed in some painkillers, too.

However it's going to be is okay, said Zeke. If you just want to use me for a while, I'm game. You can toss me aside whenever you want.

I'm not going to toss you aside.

You might change your mind.

Hold out your arm.

Just a little prick, said Zeke.

Is that supposed to be a joke?

Zeke didn't answer. Gonzalo stuck him. Within a few seconds, he'd slumped over and collapsed against the side of the buggy. Gonzalo was alone again under a blazing sky.

And yet it felt different. It felt like a relief to have Zeke so close, yet so far away. He leaned over and touched his face. He kissed his forehead. Zeke was dreaming now. He was thinking things and imagining things that Gonzalo would never know.

If you were being honest with yourself, he imagined Eeshoo saying, this is how you like him best.

Maybe it was true. As long as Zeke was conscious, with his messy emotions and his consuming desire, Gonzalo had found himself wanting to leave him. To toss him aside, just like he said. He'd been feeling ambivalent, he supposed, but not anymore. He could travel on like this forever, he thought: to Utah, to the North Pole, to outer space, to the center of the Milky Way. With Zeke snuggled up beside him, so vulnerable, alone within his own dreams.

He loved the idea of Zeke's dreams. He loved the idea of a place where nobody else could go. He probably even loved the idea of his own untouchable solitude.

Thank you, said Sofus.

Oh, you. Thanks for what?

We need to talk in private.

I'm listening.

Put your hands over Zeke's ears. Eeshoo may be unconscious, but who knows what kind of recording mechanism he might have evolved.

I thought you knew everything.

There are places so secret that even I don't know what's going on. Not yet anyway.

Zeke Yoder's dreams.

Gonzalo covered Zeke's ears. The horse began ascending a fire road that led into the hills.

I need you to trust me, said Sofus. But there are certain things I can't tell you, because *your* mind is no longer necessarily a private space, do you understand?

Sure.

Even saying that much would be an invitation to paranoia for certain entities that may eventually be privy to a memory of this conversation.

I understand. Eeshoo might find his way back home.

So, what I'm going to do is lead you through the process necessary for you to arrive at certain conclusions, at which point I'll blur the memory of the conversation that got you there. Do you understand?

You can erase my memory?

Of course.

Selectively?

Quite. You'll remember that we had a conversation and that you have good reasons to trust me, but the details of that conversation will be fuzzy. Given everything you've been through lately, you probably won't even question why that is. Because of course you won't remember the fact that I can selectively erase portions of your memory.

As usual, I don't have a choice.

You do. Just not a choice that especially matters.

When they arrived in the town of Campo, Zeke and Eeshoo were still knocked out. Gonzalo fed and watered the horse. A mutant who looked kind of like a knob of beef jerky emerged from the store and asked Gonzalo how he intended to pay.

I'll take all kinds of trades, said the mutant. But not every kind. Before your horse eats any more of that feed, I'd like to understand what's in it for me.

The egg of light emerged from Zeke's pocket and the mutant's crispy, gnarled face went slack. The rats loaded up the buggy with supplies.

If you only found the thing when you stopped looking, then what was the thing? What had Gonzalo stopped looking for? It was a puzzle indeed.

The mutant went back into his store, looking kind of stunned. They took off up the road toward Clover Flat.

Their destination in Utah was 773 miles away. It would take them two weeks to get there. They could have gotten there in a day and a half, if Sofus had let Gonzalo take the motorbike. It was kind of annoying, but Sofus had a plan.

Zeke muttered something in his sleep. Gonzalo put his arm around him and gave him a squeeze. That seemed to comfort him, wherever he was in his mind.

Sofus had explained it to Gonzalo. Gonzalo's brain was so fried from all the drugs and the sex and the journey to hell, however, that he'd lost track of some of the details. The sound of the horse clomping along triggered images and impressions in his own mind and Gonzalo was hit with a wave of nostalgia for Iowa, for the abandoned orphanage, for the life he'd lived plotting the revolution and preparing for the apocalypse. It didn't matter, he didn't figure. Sofus would remind him what he needed to know when he needed to know it. He trusted him. Not completely, but pretty much.

Suddenly everything seemed so ephemeral. Not just the past he remembered, but the memories themselves seemed fragile and wispy, mysterious phantoms doomed to evaporate. The quality of the Iowa light at dusk under the data vapor, the warm summer winds at night, the clicking of the motion detectors outside the orphanage, the sounds of the pork bushes rustling in the distance. It was all so clear in his mind, it was like he could touch the landscape back there, the sounds and smells, but where was he in this vision? He couldn't locate himself.

He remembered the meat factories, the machines, the slavery. Tijuana and Manolito, sleeping in the tub, the crazy little boy jabbering away on his overturned bucket.

It was like a movie he'd seen only from the outside. A movie that no one else was watching. His life was like a distant planet, a place he'd never really been. As if he'd been a ghost that had haunted the world, but had never really lived there. The ghost was always in motion, zooming around in circles, zigzagging this way and that, but he could never quite touch reality. He was always alone. He wasn't sure he could even tell what was real. Maybe he didn't want to or need to.

You always find the thing when you stop looking. He believed it was true. Maybe *reality* was the thing.

ACKNOWLEDGMENTS

I would like to thank Jake Yoder, Abeer Hoque, and Alvin Lu.

ABOUT THE AUTHOR

Stephen Beachy is the author of the novels *The Whistling Song, Distortion, boneyard,* and *Glory Hole,* along with the twin novellas *Some Phantom* and *No Time Flat.* His fiction and nonfiction have appeared in *BOMB, The Chicago Review, The New York Times Magazine, New York* magazine, and elsewhere. He is the grandson of Amish farmers, a graduate of the Iowa Writer's Workshop, and the prose editor of the journal *Your Impossible Voice.* His website is www.livingjelly.com.

Gonzalo Vega and the Portal Down Below is the third novel in his AMISH TERROR series, which began with *Zeke Yoder vs. the Singularity* and will continue with *Hadi Hamed and the Quantum Egg.*

www.ingramcontent.com/pod-product-compliance
Lightning Source LLC
Chambersburg PA
CBHW022153170626
46807CB00005B/2185